FIRSTBORN SON

Also by Jim H. Ainsworth

Story Collection
A River of Stories (It's Been Quite a Ride)

Novels
Rails to a River: A Long Awakening
Go Down Looking
Home Light Burning
Rivers Ebb
Rivers Crossing
In the Rivers Flow
Rivers Flow—2nd Edition

Business • Financial Planning • Financial Services
How to Become a Successful Financial Consultant
First Edition 1997 • Second Edition 2013

Memoir
Biscuits Across the Brazos

FIRSTBORN SON

A NOVEL

Jim H. Ainsworth

First Edition

This is a work of fiction. All the characters, names, incidents,
organizations, and dialogue in this novel are either the products of the
author's imagination or are used fictionally.

ISBN 978-0-9679483-9-3

Library of Congress Control Number: 2014910044

Design by Vivian Freeman, *Yellow Rose Typesetting*

Printed in the United States of America

Season of Harvest Publications
2403 CR 4208
Campbell, Texas 75422

For Jerald, a generous, loyal and true friend

and

the Cowhill Council,
with hope that some of you might read it.

What booklovers are saying about Jim Ainsworth's writing:

Jim Ainsworth has created some of the most endearing and interesting characters I have ever encountered in fiction.
—Author Suzanne Morris

Jim Ainsworth has a great writing style, and his use of the metaphor and simile is exceptional. His characters are truly realistic—no super heroes— just folks living their lives the best they can with all the ups and downs of humanity. Listen for the music; search for the flow.
—Ken Ryan

The characters' lives are so believable, so REAL... and so heart breaking.
—Sue Jackson

The story is poignant, well-told, and so real it hurts.
—George Aubrey

Texas novelist Jim Ainsworth provides stirring descriptions of hardscrabble life with characters that are complex, colorful and unforgettable.
—Alice Reese, entertainment writer
for GREENVILLE HERALD BANNER

Ainsworth is the real McCoy. A genuine, talented storyteller. His stories are full of richness and flowing charm.
—Dr. David Morris

Ainsworth weaves a story that transports readers to a different time and place... crisp prose and dialogue flow like a spring from a limestone bluff.
—THE PLAINVIEW DAILY HERALD

FIRSTBORN SON

1

TWELVE-YEAR-OLD BEN TOM LAWLESS TOSSED AND TURNED FOR
two hours before sensing someone was in the room with him and his two
brothers. When a shoe scuffed on one of the few remaining remnants of
cheap linoleum on the pine floor he slept on, he was sure. His brothers, Willy,
ten, and Trez, eight, asleep on matching army cots on both sides of Ben Tom,
did not stir. Their breathing remained rhythmic, safe in the knowledge their
older brother was a very light sleeper. And they knew he was armed.

Ben Tom had been more or less trapped all night between two quilts
that smelled of mildew and the sweat of working men who seldom bathed
before bedtime. Splinters grabbed the threadbare quilts each time he moved
during the night.

Careful to keep his head still, he opened one eye and tried to locate
the small billy club he laid beside his pallet. But the club had rolled out
of reach on the unlevel floor. He pulled his switchblade from the back
pocket of his Levi's and used the quilt to muffle the sound as he flicked
it open. Ben Tom heard the bedroom window open, the click of another
switchblade, and the sound of the window screen being ripped. A strip of
moonlight across the cobwebs and dust bunnies on the floor revealed a
pair of black Converse basketball shoes that looked familiar.

When he heard the clank of metal in the corner where he had left
his most prized possession, the gun his father had bought him, he risked
a move of his head enough to see the dark figure pick up his new .410
shotgun, Willy's .22 bolt action, and Trez's pellet gun—all gifts from their
father when he went away.

He closed the blade on the switchblade and returned it to his pocket, lay back and tried to figure what had happened. He removed the wooden cross he kept in his other front pocket, the cross he had made from a piece of scrap soft pine rubbed smooth with Tung oil. He didn't have the words to talk to God, so rubbing the cross was his way of praying, and Ben Tom felt compelled to pray a lot. The ritual usually put him to sleep, but not this night. He wondered why Uncle Clark had slit the screen in his own window and why he had taken their guns.

Over a breakfast of yesterday's sausage and cold biscuits, Ben Tom asked his uncle where their new guns were. Clark's eyes widened as he went into the bedroom where the boys had slept. The brothers looked at each other over cups filled with black coffee, the only thing hot about the meal. They heard their uncle's curses from the bedroom.

Eyes cold, Clark returned to the table. "You boys leave that window open last night?"

They shook their heads.

"It's open now. Screen's been cut, too. Damn thief got off with your guns. You boys ought to know better than to leave a window open in this neighborhood. "

Ben Tom stared at his uncle, disbelief in his eyes. Clark Mallory had been his hero. Next to his father, the man he looked up to most. Clark was athletic, tall and handsome with dark, thick hair. He had always seemed kind and generous. The man in their room last night could not have been Uncle Clark, but it was. Maybe he was just pulling a prank of some kind.

Clark erased all doubt as he returned Ben Tom's stare with a warning look like nothing Ben Tom had ever witnessed from his uncle. "You boys leaving that window unlocked...your own damn fault you lost your guns. Clean up them dishes before you go to school."

Ben Tom took a deep breath. He wanted the gun more than anything he had ever owned before. It was his only valuable possession. He stood and pushed back his chair as his uncle started to leave. "Why'd you cut your own screen?"

Clark paused at the kitchen door. He waved a hand dismissively toward the three boys as if erasing them. "You boys see this roof over your head; that grub on the table?"

Willy swelled with anger as he realized his uncle had taken their guns.

His face warmed and contorted. Small for his age, he had been angry most of his life. He could not wait to get big enough to fight back. He imagined sticking the fork he held in his hand into his uncle's eye. Trez just stared at the floor.

Clark saw the anger and returned to the table. "Didn't your mama or daddy ever tell you what I do for a living?"

Willy waited for Ben Tom to answer. When he didn't, he pointed his fork at Clark. "They said you was a damn thief, but they didn't tell us you was sorry enough to steal from your own family."

Clark chuckled. "Hell, boy, about half the orders I get for merchandise comes from my own family. I been known to steal from one relative to sell to the other. I had an order for them guns and I filled it. Simple as that. Man came by to get 'em last night and slapped a hundred dollar bill in my hand."

Ben Tom struggled to keep his voice from breaking. "I'd have given you a hundred."

Clark scooted his chair back. "Now where in hell you gonna get a hundred? You ain't got ten cents in your pocket and never have had."

"I'd have found a way. Anything to keep our guns."

Willy pointed the fork at Clark's eye. "Daddy's gonna kill you when he gets back. Hope he does."

"Your daddy knows what I do for a living. I filled plenty of orders for him, too. I ain't got no other skill, but I'm damn good at finding things people want and need."

He walked back to the door and turned again. "You boys need to get your heads screwed on right. Your daddy and mama split up, married other people. My sister, your mama, married a sorry bastard makes me look like a Sunday School teacher. You want to go live with him? He'll beat hell out of you every morning when he gets up and every night before he goes to bed. Just for the hell of it. He gets off on doing shit like that and she damn well knows it."

Trez ducked his head and started to sniffle.

"Well, boys. What's it gonna be. Here, your stepdaddy, or the orphan's home?"

The kitchen faucet's constant drip was the only sound for several seconds after Clark uttered his ultimatum. Ben Tom knew his uncle spoke the truth about Buck Blanton, his mother's new husband. He was meaner

3

than a junkyard dog. But that did not excuse Uncle Clark's theft. "How you gonna explain to Daddy how you stole the guns he bought for us?"

"First place, your daddy's long gone. When that bitch he married after your mama left him ran out on him too, he went off the deep end. Left you boys behind to go off chasing her and her new man. He should have left me money to pay for your keep instead of buying those guns. I just did what he should have done in the first place."

Ben Tom's chest swelled. "That ain't so. He's got a job traveling for a big oil company. Said he would send money, that he would come back for us and bring her with him."

"You believe that crap about working for an oil company as a mud-man? Even if he did have such a job, which I doubt, he's off looking for his woman. When he finds her, he's likely to kill her or her boyfriend or both."

All the boys' eyes filled with tears. Trez started to sob.

Clark pointed at Trez. "Let's say your daddy does bring that bitch back. Only one of you she ever wanted was Trez there. You ever wonder why she just wanted him?"

He nodded as if to affirm his own unfinished accusation. "I knew that woman before your daddy did. He don't even know she's got an unnatural attraction to little boys."

Clark bent and put large hands on the table. His hands looked more like a musician's than the sometimes violent thief they belonged to. He stared at his manicured fingernails and thought of the home safe he had cracked the night before. He might not have much education, but he was cunning, skilled at his craft, and knew it. "Look here, boys. I'm the only thing standing between you and Buckner Orphans' Home. Your daddy told you that. I heard him."

He straightened and filled his chest. "I'm just doing this for your mama out of the goodness of my heart. I ain't got no kids to take care of myself. Thought you boys would be grateful and maybe help out around here. Instead, you're giving me grief about the way I make a living."

The boys had heard threats about orphanages most of their lives. As their parents struggled with abject poverty, trouble with the law, and mar-ital infidelity, it had seemed the only resort on many occasions. The con-stant reminders had left them with an unnatural fear of such places.

Trez looked at Ben Tom. Willy looked into his uncle's eyes, still pointing the fork. Ben Tom stood and picked up the chipped plates and coffee cups. He scraped the remnants into an open garbage can by the kitchen sink. "We'll stay here."

Clark took a deep breath and nodded. "Well, that's settled then. Best get on to school."

The boys stared at each other. Ben Tom shrugged. "We don't know where the school is."

"Then you better get started a little early. I don't know anything about schools, but anybody on the street can probably tell you where one is. I think there's one about ten blocks south of here."

They ran hot water over Clark's toothbrush and shared it. They took turns in the illegal outhouse because the water in the bathroom did not work. There was no hot water heater, so Ben Tom hauled water heated on the stove to the bathtub. Willy refused to bathe, then Trez, so Ben Tom set an example.

When he finished, he forced Trez into the used water and ducked his head under it. When he tried to do the same with Willy, he was met with a steak knife Willy had taken from the kitchen. Ben Tom started to take it away, but thought better of it. "Go to school nasty, then. You'll embarrass me and Trez."

Willy waved the knife. "What's the use of bathing? We ain't got no clean clothes."

Ben Tom dropped their filthy underwear in the tub, thinking to leave them there to soak. But when he saw how full of holes they were, he dropped them all in the trash. They walked out in the street wearing the clothes they had slept in, without underwear.

Even in wrinkled and dirty clothes, the three boys walking in stair-step formation like soldiers going to war made quite a sight. They were all handsome, blessed with broad shoulders and narrow hips, olive unblemished skin, dark brown eyes protected by long eyelashes. Though Willy's was greasy and matted, each boy had thick, black hair with enough curl to make it look even better when it was windblown or mussed. It was as if God had given them the gift of good looks and good bodies to compensate for hard times.

But the boys were unaware of their good looks, only of their shabby clothes and lack of a real home. They knew what awaited them in another new school. Ben Tom had to restrain his two brothers from turning back twice. After six blocks, they spotted another group of children about their age walking with books and followed them.

Without an adult to enroll them, they spent most of the morning sitting in the principal's outer office. Ben Tom sneaked out as soon as they were left alone and ran to the phone booth he had spotted next to a nearby A&P grocery.

He dug the crumpled wad of paper with his mother's phone number out of his pocket, deposited a dime and dialed.

2

HIS MOTHER'S VOICE WAS THE SWEETEST SOUND BEN TOM HAD heard in weeks. Irene was a beautiful brown-eyed brunette who had retained her figure even after three boys. She could have had her pick of several men, but she chose Buck Blanton because he was her husband's worst enemy. She wanted to hurt Purcell Lawless as much as he had hurt her.

She knew Buck had been in trouble with the law and was a bully, but the burly redhead was a skilled carpenter and mechanic, a good provider, and she needed security more than anything else. Purcell had been a loving and kind husband, but could not be depended on to stay at one job more than a month. And he loved all women and made no attempt to hide it.

Buck had never hit her, but had no such reservations about her children. Six months after they were married, she found Trez facedown in Buck's gamecock pen, a fighting rooster pecking the back of his head. Buck had sent him in to clean up the pen and left him there. Buck made Willy cut Johnson grass in a large pasture with a steak knife and Ben Tom had been mauled when he was forced to feed and exercise Buck's vicious racing hounds.

Irene left Buck and moved away to Cleburne, but Buck followed. He brought her a '64 Black Ford, the first new car she had ever owned. The car and promises worked for less than two months. She caught Buck slamming Willy's head against a wall with Ben Tom running toward his stepfather with his billy club, trying to protect his little brother. When Buck backhanded him to the floor and took the club, Ben Tom pulled his switchblade.

Realizing all their lives were in danger, Irene took her sons to their father. Purcell seemed shocked, unprepared to accept responsibility for his sons, but pleased. He willingly ejected a woman who was living with him to make room for his sons, but hooked up with Donna less than a month later.

Irene's voice was sweet and kind to Ben Tom. "You mean your daddy didn't go to the school with you?"

"Daddy's gone off looking for Donna."

Ben Tom heard the expected intake of breath. He knew how his mother felt about Donna.

"You mean he just went off and left you?"

"Left us with Uncle Clark. We ain't got any clean clothes, underwear or toothbrushes. Daddy said he'd be back soon with lots of money. He's got a job as a mud-man with an oil company."

"Mud-man, my hind leg. Are you at that school a few blocks from Clark's house?"

She was there by noon, signed the papers to enroll them in their sixth school in as many years. They stood before her on the steps of the school as she prepared to leave. She kneeled and kissed each one on the cheek. She held their hands together as tears came into her eyes. "I can't believe my kids are gonna be Grove Rats."

Trez did not like being called a rat. "What are Grove Rats, Mama?"

"Never you mind, Trez." She didn't want to explain it was a term used to describe children, almost all disadvantaged, who grew up in the Pleasant Grove community in the shadow of downtown Dallas. She kissed them goodbye and was gone.

Underwear, toothbrushes and other essentials were there when they returned to Clark's house that afternoon with a note saying she loved them and would see them soon. Willy, closest to his mother, the one who would miss her most, took a pack of gopher matches from his pocket, struck one, and burned the note.

In the weeks and months that followed, the boys met at a 7-11 close to the school each day at noon. Ben Tom deposited a dime, let the phone ring twice, and hung up. The phone spit back his dime when the call was not completed. A few seconds later, their mother called the pay phone and they all talked. They visited Irene only when she could sneak away from Buck and meet them at a restaurant or pick them up from school. Their father sent one letter saying he had one more project to do for the oil company before he would be "furloughed" and come home. No mention of Donna.

All the boys had trouble making passing grades in school because they were absent so much. When one teacher found a poem Willy had written, Willy set fire to it in her hands as she tried to read it. She knew he was much brighter than his grades reflected, but was too angry to apply himself. And he skipped school at least one day a week. Willy wanted to be tough, not smart. He spent a lot of time in detention and bent over the principal's desk taking licks from a paddle.

Ben Tom had trouble with the three R's, but excelled in anything that fueled the creative fire stirring within him. When he was supposed to be reading or memorizing spelling words, he drew. When he was assigned a simple shoeshine box in shop class, he built a box with separate compartments for brown and black polish, polish cloths, saddle soap, and little hangers for brown and black brushes. Each compartment had a hinged door. The creation was hand lacquered to a warm glow. The teacher gave him a C for failing to follow instructions.

He designed and built a small metal sculpture to honor vets returning from Vietnam, complete with a metal American flag, a helmet, and intricately designed miniature weapons of the Vietnam soldier. He built it with a soldering iron, fusing wire hangers and other scrap metal. He was not given a grade because sculpting was not part of the curriculum.

Trez was also bright, but covered his pain and homesickness for his parents by becoming the class clown. He pretended to look at life as a circus and studiously developed an attention span limited to about fifteen minutes. At ten, he was already hustling for marijuana and beer. Outside the school, the brothers had trouble with bullies. Uncle Clark showed them all a little judo and they picked it up quickly. Bill Tom was big for his age and could take care of himself. He saw it as his duty to protect his little brothers and Trez called on him regularly. But Willy, not much bigger than Trez, wanted no help. His reputation for biting, kicking in vulnerable places, going for the Adam's apple, and sticking his thumbs in eyes protected him. If he lost a fight with his hands one day, he brought a knife or club the next day and exacted revenge. Even bigger boys soon feared him.

Ben Tom found work in a junkyard a few blocks from Clark's house and brought in enough money to buy the boys a few clothes and occasional snacks. The work kept him away from school more. Willy, too young and small to find work, put aside his grievance against his uncle when he discovered he needed his uncle for a partner. He kept his scheme a secret from Ben Tom.

But Willy never completely forgot a slight or insult and dreamed of ways to retaliate against his uncle for stealing his gun. He found a hammer in Clark's toolbox and drove nails into the side of the house, imagined the nails going into Clark's fingers. He swung a cracked baseball bat he found in an empty lot against tree trunks, visualized breaking both of his uncle's knees. And of course, at every meal, he imagined putting a fork into his eye. These visions fueled similar thoughts of vengeful acts against every schoolmate, teacher, or adult who had bullied him.

He pilfered Ben Tom's switchblade and carried it to school to use on a bully. He took a small slice out of the boy's arm during recess and ran from the school grounds. He hid in the back seat of an abandoned car until long after school had been dismissed, but two boys, brothers of the bully he had attacked, were waiting when he headed home. Willy used every judo move Clark had taught him, every dirty and fair fighting trick he knew, but the almost grown boys managed to take away the knife and pin him to the ground with the blade at his throat.

He heard the car door slam, but could not turn his head. He held his heavy breathing long enough to hear a familiar stealthy, slow walk down the plank boards used as a sidewalk. Clark's black Converse shoes stopped close to his ear.

He spoke to the boy with the knife at Willy's throat. "Well, boy, you gonna cut his throat or not?"

The boy held the blade against Willy's neck. "What business is it of yours?"

Clark took out his Zippo, shook out a Winston and lighted it. "Just curious why a boy nearly six-feet tall needs a blade to whip a pup this size."

When he heard the click of another switchblade, he turned to face the second boy. "Hell, not only does it take two big, tough guys, they gotta have knives, too."

Clark pointed the Winston at the boy who stood to his right. "What about you, Junior? You as tough as your partner here?"

He had barely finished the sentence when Willy felt the weight lift off his body. Clark had kicked away the boy as casually as he might swat a fly. The boy jumped to his feet, pushed back the greasy hair that had fallen into his face and pointed the knife at Clark.

Smoke from the cigarette flowed into Clark's eyes and made him squint. He dropped it and crushed it. "Well, you boys gonna use them stickers or you just gonna stand there grinning like a pair of shit-eatin' dogs?"

The boys looked at each other but did not answer. Clark's backhand lifted the closest one off his feet and dropped him flat on his back. Willy rushed to pick up his dropped blade and started for the other boy with it.

The boy slapped Willy to the ground and lunged at Clark with the blade. Clark feinted and struck a sharp blow to the boy's knee with his foot. He grabbed his wrist as the boy fell. By the time Willy got to his feet, the boy was on his back and Clark held his wrist with one hand while he extracted the knife with the other. "You wanna keep this arm, junior?"

The boy squeezed his eyes and tears rolled out from the pain in his knee and arm. He could feel the arm coming out of its socket. He nodded.

Clark turned him loose. "I see either one of you punks around here again, I'll rip that arm right out of your shoulder." He wasn't even short of breath.

Willy would never see his uncle through the same eyes again.

3

TREZ SKIPPED A LOT OF SCHOOL TO SMOKE DOPE; WILLY SKIPPED
it because he hated it; Ben Tom skipped school to work. Although Irene
sent money to her brother that she stole from Buck, Clark never told Ben
Tom and made it clear he expected him to help out with expenses. Ben
Tom feverishly bought and bartered for parts from the auto salvage yard
where he worked to build his own car. He also took a second part-time job
in a grocery store as a butcher's assistant. Ben Tom carved meat as skillfully as he carved wood or molded metal to his will.

Willy had his own ideas for making money. He found a hole in a chain
link fence that surrounded a metal scrap yard down the street and pro-
posed a scheme to Uncle Clark. Clark liked the idea. The next night,
Willy helped his uncle steal a pickup and a flatbed trailer. At midnight,
Clark parked the pickup and trailer next to the scrap metal yard. Willy
sneaked through the hole and threw aluminum scraps over the fence for
Clark to load. A day or two later, Clark sold the yard its own aluminum.
They repeated the operation a month later. Clark always abandoned the
truck and trailer after two trips and stole another. Willy's share of the
enterprise was soon bigger than what Ben Tom made at the salvage yard.

It took almost a year, but Ben Tom parked a splotched, dented '55 Ford
Victoria built from wreckage and scraps in his uncle's front yard. Just in
time for his driver's license. He expertly removed the dents with borrowed
tools and skillfully painted it cream and aquamarine with spray paint cans.
Although little about the car was original, it looked fit for any showroom.

Willy, in the meantime, had become a regular apprentice to his uncle.

In addition to his talent for filling orders, Clark was a skilled arsonist who took contracts to burn buildings. Sometimes it was for the insurance, other times it was to cover a crime or to settle a score for someone else. He had also been known to set fire to a residence to cover a theft. He also occasionally set fires as a distraction, a way to divert authorities from a house or business he intended to burglarize. But setting such fires was rare because it almost required him to be in two places at once and to set fires too close to the sites of his crimes. When Willy entered the picture, those fires became more frequent.

Willy came in handy for this duty because he could wander around neighborhoods without attracting as much attention as Clark. He could also squeeze into and out of tight places. Clark taught him how to burn things without leaving evidence of arson and how to delay ignition until he was safely away. He also taught him how to set fires to cause minimal damage. After all, Clark didn't want to intentionally burn a house or business down without getting paid for it.

Ben Tom complained to no avail as Clark kept Willy out later and later on school nights. A few months after their partnership began, Willy and his uncle came home an hour after midnight. Ben Tom feigned sleep as the smell of smoke wafted through the room. Willy seemed intent on making as much noise as possible as he came into the room carrying an armful of something that clinked. He loudly dropped his burden in the corner of the room. Ben Tom did not bite. He did not want to wake Trez. Willy snuggled into one of the three beds Clark had stolen and was soon breathing heavily.

Ben Tom lifted himself up on one elbow and examined the bounty by moonlight. Three guns. Hope filled his chest. He whispered loudly. "You found our guns?"

"Better than that. Them guns Daddy bought was cheap. Stevens and Savage models. Two of these are Winchesters. Got Trez a .22. He's too big for a damn pellet gun now. And your shotgun is a Remington. Sixteen gauge."

"My shotgun?"

"Damn right. Clark promised me a while back he would replace the guns."

"Stolen guns."

14

Willy rolled over and looked at his brother. "This old man had a safe full of guns. We just took three. He won't ever miss 'em. Doubt he ever opens that safe. They're brand new. Never been fired."

"Why do you smell like smoke?"

Willy rolled over on his stomach, signaling the conversation was over.

Ben Tom put his hands behind his head and leaned against a wadded blanket he used as a pillow. "Don't want no stolen gun. I want the gun Daddy gave me."

"What the hell you talkin' about? This gun is a lot better than the one you had."

Ben Tom rubbed the wooden cross under his pillow. "I won't have a stolen gun. I ain't no thief and I ain't ever gonna be one, either."

Clark nursed a warm Schlitz from a six pack he had forgotten to put in the fridge the night before as the boys walked into the kitchen the next morning. He used his fork to move around a plateful of scrambled eggs before pointing it at Trez and Ben Tom. "See them guns in the bedroom?"

Trez went back into the bedroom and returned wide-eyed and smiling with his small Winchester rifle.

Clark nodded toward Ben Tom. "What about your shotgun?"

Ben Tom walked to the stove and ladled out a serving of eggs for himself and each of his brothers. "That's not my shotgun."

Clark gestured toward Willy with the warm Schlitz. "Guess he's too good to accept a gift. And after all our hard work."

Ben Tom dropped Trez's eggs onto his plate. "Thieves don't work. They steal from people that do work."

Trez looked at the eggs and at his brother. "You sayin' I can't keep my new .22?"

Clark crushed the beer can. "Will that pile of junk you put together run?"

"It'll outrun anything you got."

"It ain't got a VIN number. How you gonna register it?"

Ben Tom had not thought of that.

"You need to start earning your keep. I got a job to do next week and we may need your car."

Ben Tom took a drink of the milk he had bought with his own money. "Not a chance."

"We're not stealing a thing. Just need you to give us a ride home after we do a favor for a friend. No danger to you or your precious car."

It was the moment Ben Tom had been dreading for two years.

Uncle Clark had a way of making things look and sound easy. Ben Tom only had to park his car on a side street in an industrial section near downtown. Clark had already taken care of the streetlight Ben Tom was to park under. All he had to do was sit there and wait for less than an hour until Clark and Willy strolled up and got in the car. Then drive on home nice and easy.

Clark told him he and Willy were not going to steal anything, just do a favor for a friend and make a cool hundred for easy, safe work. Spiva, Clark's buddy, was a night watchman at one of the industrial warehouses and needed to leave his post for a few hours to tend to a sick wife. The poor guy's car was in the shop and he needed to borrow Clark's pickup to make the trip home. Problem was, he had to clock in every two hours or risk getting fired. Clark was going to lift Willy over a chain link fence and Willy was going to punch a time clock to prove the watchman was on duty. That would allow the watchman four hours to care for his wife and get back to his post.

Ben Tom could not register the car he had built from scratch, so he fashioned a set of license plates from an old pair he found in the junkyard. Altering the plates to the current year was no problem for his skilled hands, but he could not resist making a slight alteration in the license plate number. He used a spray can to fill in the bottom circle of the number eight on the front plate and six on the back plate. He always put a personal touch on everything he made. No harm in that. After eliciting promises from both Clark and Willy he would not be breaking the law, the project began to have some allure for Ben Tom. Parking on a dark street, driving a fast car, doing something worthwhile for a needy fellow. It all appealed to him.

Ben Tom was told Clark and Willy had to arrive at midnight so Spiva, the night watchman, could let Willy into the building. The plan called for Spiva to drive Clark's truck to check on his wife and leave his car there to keep from arousing suspicion. All Willy had to do was wait two hours, punch the time clock, and walk out. But Spiva had to leave the gates and doors locked because leaving them unlocked would send a signal to a security firm and bring the cops. Willy was needed because he was the only one who could get in and out of the facility without setting off alarms. Clark would wait outside the fence in case something went wrong.

Ben Tom arrived at exactly two hours past midnight, parked in the appointed spot, and watched the windows and yard of the warehouse where his brother and uncle were to punch a clock of some sort. At ten after two, he saw two flashes through one of the windows and heard the delayed sound of muffled gunshots. The '55 Ford started on the first turn, purred like a kitten, twin pipes rumbling in the darkness. But Ben Tom did not know what to do. He rubbed the cross hanging from his rearview mirror. Fifteen minutes later, he felt more than heard the passenger door open. Willy crawled into the back seat and rolled to the floor. Clark slumped low in the passenger seat. "Turn around and head home. Don't speed." As they rolled away, the warehouse burst into flames.

Ben Tom fired frantic questions most of the way home, but got no answers. When he got home, Willy ran to their shared bedroom. Clark put a church key to a Schlitz. The refrigerator light revealed blood on the front of Clark's shirt. Ben Tom pointed at the blood. "You shot?"

Clark drank half the Schlitz in one gulp. "Nope. Stop asking questions. The less you know, the better."

Ben Tom, almost as tall as his uncle, was furious and afraid. "You lied to me. You were stealing or setting a fire in that warehouse. Somebody get killed?" Clark walked to his bedroom without answering.

Ben Tom found Willy hovering in the corner of the bedroom floor, his whole body shaking. "They killed him, Ben Tom. I watched Spiva die in Clark's arms." He had stopped calling him Uncle after their first theft.

Ben Tom had seen Spiva a few times. He was a short, pudgy man, one of many petty thieves who hung around Clark and looked up to him as their mentor. "Who shot him?"

Willy's voice had reverted to his pre-puberty level. "Spiva really was the night watchman. The owners told him to find somebody to burn the building for insurance. But it was a setup. Clark said they wanted Spiva to burn with it so there would be no witnesses. When he saw what was up and ran, they shot him when he was going out the window I left open for him."

"So where was Uncle Clark while all this was happening?"

"Waiting just outside the yard. He tried to help Spiva, but he was

17

bleeding like a stuck hog when he came out of there. Clark caught him as he fell. I saw his eyes roll back and lock open."

"So, if Spiva set the fire, why did Clark need my car and where is his pickup?"

"It's over at Spiva's. He thinks the pickup is gettin' pretty hot. Seen near and around too many fires and burglaries. We rode with Spiva."

"Why the hell were you even there?"

"I sneaked in through a hole he made for me in the fence and I showed him how to set a fire that would give him time to get away. Spiva don't know anything about that stuff."

"So where is Spiva's body?"

"We hid and watched two guys drag him back into the building so he could burn up."

Ben Tom choked with rage. "We have to get out of here before he gets us all killed."

4

BEN TOM STOOD IN THE YARD WITH HIS HANDS ON HIS HIPS, fought back tears he felt too old to shed. His car was gone. Only the few wispy strands of dying grass and weeds that had survived oil, anti-freeze and spray paint identified where his '55 Ford Victoria had been. The weeds and grass mocked him. He futilely looked up and down the street and to the side of the house, but knew his most prized possession had once again been taken from him.

Anger came unbidden as he reached for the switchblade in his back pocket. He wished for the shotgun he had turned away, but Clark had already sold it. Blood rushed to his face as he clinched and unclenched his fists and paced around the faint outline in the dirt and grass where his car had been. His mind filled with vengeance as he imagined someone driving it away.

These were unfamiliar and unwanted feelings for Ben Tom Lawless. He was known for his patience and tranquility in the face of danger or violence. He remained calm when others around him reacted with anger or panic. He seemed to have an innate ability to fix not only things, but people. He had sutured cuts, knew where to press and apply tourniquets to stop bleeding and had even put bones back in place and splinted compound fractures while waiting for ambulances. Willy, of course, was his most frequent patient.

Without any formal training other than what his father and uncles had taught him, he seemed to possess an uncanny ability to see into the inner workings of not only machines, but the human body. Yet Ben Tom did not seem to recognize these abilities, did not understand his desire to create. He also had an enormous capacity for mental and physical punishment before he fought back. He was quick, too quick his father said, to forgive serious transgressions against him. He sincerely believed everyone meant well.

Of course, he had a capacity for violence, but only in the defense of his family. He had fended off plenty of physical attacks in the schoolyards and vacant lots of the many slums he had lived in. Because he and his brothers were perpetual new kids, fresh meat in various schools, they were constantly belittled for their often dirty and usually worn out clothes and lack of money for the basic essentials. But Ben Tom mostly overlooked the ridicule and tried to make friends with his tormentors.

Trez also made friends by being a clown, but not Willy. He never asked for help, but Ben Tom regularly rescued him from difficult, often life-threatening situations. He had also waded into conflicts with his much larger stepfather when Buck Blanton was cruel to Willy or Trez. But the theft of his car was more than he could bear. The Ford had been as much a part of him as his appendages. It was as if a thief had taken his arms and was holding them hostage. He was too deep in his thoughts to notice both brothers were beside him.

Willy's voice had become guttural. "Figured he would do it sooner or later."

Ben Tom turned to him and knew without asking who he meant. Why had it not been obvious from the start? He felt hope swell in his chest. Clark had taken his car. That meant he might return it. Worst case, he could tell Ben Tom where he sold it. He was so relieved, he walked with his brothers to a hole-in-the-wall barbecue joint more than two miles from the house and bought them each a sandwich and fried pie.

Clark was less than a mile from his house when he saw the bubble lights rotating in the side mirror of Ben Tom's custom built Ford. He groaned, pulled over and stepped out to greet the policeman courteously. He smiled and turned on the charm as he met the cop halfway between their cars. "What's the problem, officer?"

The officer did not return the smile. "No problem. Just noticed something about your rear license plate."

Clark tried to remain calm when he noticed the bottom circle on the eight had been painted in. He kept his peace while the cop walked to the front to see if the damage was repeated up there. The circle on the six was painted on the front plate. "You aware that defacing license plates is against the law?"

"Sorry, officer. Never noticed it. Kids in the neighborhood, I guess. Lucky they didn't run a key down the whole side. I'll scrape it clean as soon as I get home."

The officer sauntered rather than walked back to Clark, stopped to press his hands against the side windows. "What's that in the back seat?"

Clark kept his cool. "Just some junk from my sister's house. I'm helping her move."

The officer pulled his weapon and pointed it at Clark. "Put your hands behind your back and lean over the trunk."

Ben Tom expected to see the car in the yard when he returned. But it wasn't. And it wasn't there the next morning. It was not unusual for Clark to stay out all night, but Ben Tom's spirits sank as he put cereal, milk, glasses and bowls on the stolen Formica table the next morning. He skipped school and took an extra shift at the junkyard so he could slip away a couple of times during the day to check the yard for his car. But there was no sign of it. Not all day, and not when he went to bed that night. Clark was seldom gone for two consecutive nights.

Ben Tom and his brothers were listening to a Joe Frazier boxing match on Clark's radio the third night when they heard a car door slam and a car speed away. Clark entered the room and turned off the radio as Joe landed a knockdown punch. "Which one of you little bastards took a can of spray paint to them license plates?"

Ben Tom stood. "Where's my car?"

"It's been impounded, you stupid little shit."

"Where?"

"Where the hell you think? In the auto pound close to downtown. Cops stopped me because you took to the license plates with a can of spray paint."

"They arrested you for that?"

"Cop found some loot in the back seat when he stopped me."

Willy's eyes widened at the word loot. "What kinda loot?"

"Somebody called in a description of a few things I found in somebody's yard. Police station radioed it out and these cops had a list. Then they figured the car was stolen because the plates don't match any damn vehicle on the road."

Ben Tom looked out the window as if his car might magically appear. "Yard, my ass. You pulled a burglary using my car because yours is too hot. Now my car is the same as a convicted criminal. I'll never get it back."

———◆•◆•◆———

Ben Tom and Willy threaded their fingers and toes into the links, climbed six feet up the eight-foot fence, and searched the cars inside the Dallas car pound. It was easy to find the Ford. It stood out like a sore thumb, gleaming beside its less impressive, dingy counterparts. The guard lights made it seem to sparkle, almost bringing tears to Ben Tom's eyes. They climbed back down and leaned against the fence.

Willy felt sorry for his brother. "Only way you ever gonna get that car back is to steal it."

"Wonder what the fine is? Maybe I could come up with it."

"You're dreaming. You heard Clark. You'll have to show a title and your driver's license. Soon as you identify yourself with the car, they're probably gonna arrest you for stealin' it. They already know the plates are fake."

"I can tell the truth... that I built it from parts. Maybe they'll let me register it."

Willy worked on the padlock at the side gate. "Might have before it got in the pound, but these assholes in there ain't about to turn it loose. They make a lot of money auctioning off cars like yours. These people take payoffs to see that people with money get the car they want at the right price."

Ben Tom paced the street, expecting the police at any minute. "Stop with the lock, Willy. I ain't taking the chance."

Willy looked up at his brother. The guard lights shadowed his expression, but Willy knew Ben Tom was desperate. "It's your car. I can open this gate; you can hotwire the car and drive right through. They probably won't know it's even gone for a couple of days."

"Don't need to hotwire it. I got another set of keys."

"Well, then, what are we waiting for?"

Ben Tom walked in the general direction of Pleasant Grove. Willy followed. "You ain't planning on walking all the way back, are you? Must be more than a hundred blocks through rough territory."

"That's how we got here. How else we gonna get back?"

"That was in daylight. Now that it's dark, we could steal a car. Or call Clark to come and get us since he caused all this, anyway."

Ben Tom kept walking. "You know as well as I do he's out stealing something else. How did he get out of jail, anyway?"

"He keeps a shyster handy. But I think he's in real trouble this time. He's just out on bail. Has to stand trial unless his low-life lawyer can cut a deal."

Ben Tom felt a twinge of guilt. "Just because I took a can of spray paint to the car tags?"

"No, but he'll blame you for it. He had stolen goods right in the back seat. The stuff was so hot it was burning a hole in the upholstery. He hadn't had the loot for an hour when he got stopped. Bad luck."

Ben Tom imagined a burned hole in the new upholstery he had put in the Ford as a cab slowly pulled alongside them. The cabbie, a dark-skinned man whose face was all angles and bones, hung an elbow out the window. "Where you boys headed?"

Willy stepped back and put his hand on the switchblade he had recently stolen. "What's it to you?"

The man's mouth smiled, but his eyes seemed sad. "Thought I might offer a ride."

Ben Tom was grateful and as usual, trusting. "No thanks, mister. Flat broke and we live over in Pleasant Grove. Long way from here."

"I'm going that way. Hop in. It's on my way home, so I won't charge you."

Willy shook his head and stepped back. "You live in the Grove?"

Ben Tom looked in the direction of home. "You serious? You'll take us home for nothing?"

"Only if you get in the car."

Ben Tom felt a strange connection to this cabbie. He reminded him of someone, possibly his grandfather. He opened the back door and motioned for Willy to get in. Willy pulled him aside. "I ain't getting in there. He's probably a pervert. Cabbies don't give free rides."

"Both of us are carrying switchblades and I probably outweigh this guy. What's he gonna do to us?" Ben Tom sat beside the cabbie and Willy sat in back.

The cabbie reached to turn the lever on the meter, smiled and pulled his hand away. "Old habits are hard to break. You boys got business at the car pound? Lose a car?"

Ben Tom noticed the cab was as immaculately clean inside as it was outside. "1955 Ford Victoria. Cream and turquoise. I was saving up for lake pipes, maybe a continental kit."

"Well, you may have to use that money to bail her out. Then you can save up again for the custom stuff. That the car sits in the yard over on Gould Street?"

Ben Tom's eyes widened. Willy's suspicion grew as he leaned over the front seat back and studied the pins and licenses on the dash and sun visors. He pointed to an AA button. "You an alcoholic?"

Ben Tom turned to push his little brother back into his seat. "Sorry, mister. That's none of our business. So you've seen my car?"

"I live in the neighborhood. A few blocks over and down. That's one fine car. What's it gonna take to get her out of hock?"

"Afraid to ask." Ben Tom told him the whole story.

Ben Tom's candor and trust always astounded Willy. He pointed to another button on the visor. What's the NA stand for?"

The cabbie smiled. "Narcotics Anonymous."

Willy laughed. "Man, sounds like you like to attend a lot of meetings. You must be really messed up."

The cabbie kept his eyes on the road, smiled and nodded. "I've been up the street and around the block a few times. Seen things and done things I hope you boys never experience."

Ben Tom really studied the man for the first time. Thick gray hair cut very short, heavy, black eyebrows, black eyes, deep dimples and other lines in his face made him look like he had been carved from hardwood and etched. Ben Tom imagined every line could tell a story. He wasn't smoking, which was unusual for a cabbie and for an alcoholic. All his uncles and his father drank and smoked heavily. When one of his uncles quit drinking, he smoked even more as if the cigarettes made up for the alcohol abstinence.

"So how long you been quit? The drugs and alcohol, I mean."

"Nine years today, as a matter of fact. An old Mexican cab driver picked me up right where I picked up you boys. My car was in the pound, too. I was trying to figure out a way to steal it. I come back here every year at this time to remind myself who I was back in those days."

The story was starting to scare Willy a little bit. He couldn't decide if the cabbie was crazy or had something up his sleeve. With wide, interested eyes, Ben Tom urged the cabbie to continue. The cabbie worked his fingers on the wheel. "The old man started preaching to me when he got me in his cab. Made me sit in the front seat just like you are."

Ben Tom felt a strange serenity come over him as he met the cabbie's gaze. Willy interrupted it. "So what did this old man look like?" Ben Tom turned and gave him a look that said to shut up.

The cabbie raised one finger on his steering wheel hand. "He was darker than a lot of Mexicans, like he spent a lot of time in the sun. Deep lines in his face. Gray bushy hair. Had a near white handlebar mustache. I remember he had to move a big sombrero out of the front seat so I could sit."

Ben Tom was intrigued. "Sounds like somebody out of a picture show I saw once."

Willy was skeptical. "Or somebody you made up."

The cabbie ignored Willy and spoke to Ben Tom. "That's what I thought at the time. But the old man started preaching to me. He knew a lot of the really bad things I had done and chastised me for them. Rattled off a long list of my bad deeds."

The cabbie chuckled. "Made me really mad before he got through. I considered stickin' him with my knife and leavin' him beside the road, but he kept talkin' and preachin'."

This got Willy's attention. He leaned over the seat. "What kind of bad things?"

"You mean besides being a drunk and dealing in drugs? I was hauled in several times for beating my wife. Broke her nose once and both arms. A shoulder. Beat my kids, too. Nearly killed a man for just looking at my wife. I stole to support my habits, rolled other drunks. But just before this old man picked me up, I had started pimping my fifteen-year-old daughter. I had hit bottom."

Willy took a deep breath and blew it out strongly enough to whistle. "You one bad-ass, mister."

"That's only a short summation of what I've done, son."

Ben Tom's calmness was gone. "What about the old man? What was he saying, exactly?"

"To tell the truth, I didn't understand a lot of it at first. Nothing made

25

me madder in those days than a holy-roller preacher. So I asked him, 'Where is this God you keep talking about? He sure as hell never done nothin' for me. He ain't found time to come to my house.'"

The cabbie's voice lowered as he seemed to struggle to recall. "Well, that old man just kept driving. Didn't answer me. I figured I had him dead to rights. So I decided to press him a little more, really show him I wasn't as stupid as some those rubes who buy into that religion talk."

Ben Tom was getting anxious. "So what did you do?"

"I pointed up to some birds sitting on a high wire and asked the old man, 'You see God sitting on that high wire? All I see is birds.' I pointed to a house with a chimney. 'Is he standing on the roof of that house over there, ready to take gifts down the chimney like Santa Claus?' I laughed a little at how clever I was."

"So what did he say?"

The back of the cabbie's fist struck Ben Tom in the chest hard enough to steal his breath. "He hit me harder than I just hit you and said, 'Fool. God is everywhere, but mostly he is there.' Then he slapped me on the back of the head and said, 'And there'."

"So what did he mean?"

"The old man was telling me God is in our hearts, our minds and our souls. Something that had never occurred to me before. We pulled over to the side of the road and the old man gave me a good raking over the coals again for all the terrible things I had done and was doing. That night in my bed, God started talking to me. Now, I get down on my knees every night and talk right back to him."

The cabbie went on to tell the boys how the old Mexican carried him to his first AA meeting and his first NA meeting. "He came by my house in the cab to pick me up and was there to take me home after the meeting. We became good friends. Then one day, he just disappeared."

"So what happened after God started talking to you?"

"I decided to devote the rest of my life atoning for my sins. I asked forgiveness from my children and my wife. I'll spend the rest of my life making it up to them. Now I have a good job and this fine cab. And I try to do the same thing for other people that the old man did for me."

"That why you picked us up?"

"That's right. I've picked up an unbelievable number of folks who have strayed right there in the same spot where I found you. In nine years of coming there on this day, I have not missed a day in picking up somebody who needs help, even if it's just a ride. But I had the feeling you boys were thinking of breaking into that yard. Were you?"

5

CLARK PACED THE YARD WHEN THE CAB PULLED UP AND BOTH boys stepped out. He tried to see the face of the driver when the cab pulled away, but could not. He turned to the boys. "You boys in the chips now? Got the money to hire a cab? Where the hell you been?"

Ben Tom tried to walk past him, but Clark grabbed his arm. Ben Tom pulled his arm away and faced his usually calm uncle. A couple inches more and he would stand eye-to-eye to him. "We were down at the car pound looking through a chain link fence at my car that you stole and got impounded."

Clark's eyes fluttered and widened as if he had been struck or was about to be. "You get on inside and look after Trez. You left him here by himself."

"Trez has been big enough to stay by himself for a long time. He likes being alone so he can smoke maryjane. Besides, it was safer here than taking him with us. He can't keep his mouth shut longer than five minutes, especially when he's high."

Clark touched Willy's shoulder, led him to a '63-and-a-half Ford Galaxy parked in the street. They were gone before Ben Tom could ask where they were going. An hour later, they stopped in front of a trailer house in the deep woods south and east of Dallas, near Terrell. The trailer's insides had been gutted and looted of every appliance and stripped of copper.

Clark pulled back a piece of worn, filthy carpet, revealing a rotting plywood floor. He took a hay hook from a kitchen drawer and put the end into a hole in the plywood that seemed to have been sized for the hook. He pulled the sheet of plywood loose and slid it across the floor to reveal a stairway. Willy peered into the dark hole as Clark pointed a flashlight down the stairs. "A basement in a trailer house?" How's that possible?"

Clark tested the first step on the ladder. "It's an old storm cellar. I just pulled this piece-of-shit trailer house over it and installed an old attic ladder to reach down. Had to shore up the walls so water couldn't get in. Follow me."

Willy stepped back as Clark's head disappeared down the hole. "I ain't going down there. You know I'm afraid of snakes."

"Hell's bells, you won't even have to step off the ladder. Come on. I need to show you this stuff."

Willy eased down but kept both feet on the ladder.

Clark opened a hinged door to a cedar chest big enough to hold two bodies and Willy fully expected to see them when he looked inside. The inside of the box looked even more like a coffin. It was lined with something that could have been purple velour.

"This box is fully insulated and cushioned. I don't even think water can get inside it when it's properly closed. Temperature won't vary all that much, either, even down in this hole. And not much humidity."

Willy was fascinated. "What's that you got covered up?"

Clark was impatient. "Stop asking questions and listen. You're the only one I can trust. What I'm about to tell you is important. A buddy of mine works at the Amon Carter Museum over in Fort Worth and told me how they store works of art. I ordered this box, then did some custom work on it so I could leave it down here."

"What are those little pills, moth balls?"

"No, they're supposed to control humidity."

Clark pulled away a sheet of material that looked like thick silk to Willy, revealing a western painting. He pulled away another and revealed two bronze sculptures of mounted cowboys. The flashlight made them all seem to come alive. He half expected the cowboys to talk. "What is all that?" He couldn't help but notice Clark's usually calm exterior had given way to trembling hands.

"These are original works of art by famous artists."

"Where'd you get 'em?"

"I stole them from another thief. He probably took them out of a museum of a rich fat cat somewhere."

Willy took a deep breath. "This thief—does he know you're the one what stole his stuff?"

"Not yet. If he finds out, your life and mine won't be worth a plug nickel. He's well connected."

"My life? Why me?"

"Everybody knows you're my apprentice. They'll come after both of us."

"I don't want no part of any big time art shit."

"Well, you're part of this now whether you want to be or not."

They stepped out of hole in the floor and Clark pulled the cover and carpet back into place. "Now listen, Willy. I may be going away for a while. If I do, I may call or send you a message one day to come and get one or two of these pieces and deliver it someplace."

Clark grabbed Willy's shirt collar and pulled him close enough to smell his breath and the fear oozing out of his glands. "You understand that?"

Willy nodded. "Where you going?"

"If I can sell one of these pieces and get a fake passport, I'm headed to South America. If not, I may go to jail for the stuff they found in Ben Tom's car. Hell, that piss-ant haul they found wouldn't pay for the price of this box alone."

"When you gonna find out?"

"I'm waiting on my lawyer. If he can get me a passport before I have to go to trial, I'm gone. If not, I may have to cop to a few burglaries and spend some time in jail."

"How long you had this stuff?"

"Never mind that. Long enough."

"You never hang on to stolen stuff. Why this?"

"I told you. This is original art. You can't just sell it at a flea market. It's worth tens, if not hundreds of thousands. But it's too hot to fence. Can't get anybody to touch it yet."

Willy whistled under his breath. "You're a rich man."

"Can't spend money you don't have."

"So, all I have to do is wait till I hear from you if you leave? Don't I need to get Ben Tom to drive me out here once in a while to check on it?"

Clark jabbed a finger hard into Willy's chest. "You can't ever tell Ben Tom. He'd turn it in to the cops or give it away. I'm gonna leave you the keys to my old pickup. I'll take you to get your driver's license tomorrow and you can drive out here once every month or so. Don't come more often. People will notice and be suspicious."

31

Willy already saw himself driving the pickup. "I can do that."

Clark showed him his hiding place for a key behind some underpinning by the front steps. "I'll leave the second key in the ashtray of the pickup."

"If it was me, I'd padlock both doors."

Clark laughed. "You ought to know by now that would just attract thieves. They can take the roof or sides off this dump in a matter of minutes. Two padlocks would just make 'em curious. I'm betting they won't ever notice that loose sheet of plywood if they do break in. Thieves around here already know everything worth having in here has already been stolen."

Willy laughed. "Except for hundreds of thousands in artwork."

Clark did not have to wait long to learn his fate. When his lawyer told him the detective working burglaries had witnesses who placed him at or near the scenes of other crimes, he knew he was not going to make it to South America. The detective and the assistant DA wanted to mark the other burglaries as solved. If he admitted to them, they would agree to a five-year stretch, possible parole in two.

———

The boys sat in uncomfortable silence with their uncle as they waited for the lawyer to come for Clark and deliver him to authorities to begin serving his sentence. Ben Tom jerked a little when they heard a car door slam. Then a second door. They looked out the living room window to see their mother and father walking side by side up the sidewalk.

A sense of foreboding had haunted Trez since the day he learned Clark was going to prison. He concealed his dread behind a stream of chatter and antics meant to make his brothers and uncle laugh. It did not work. When he saw his parents together for the first time in years, he locked his hands on the back of his neck and unwanted tears streamed down his face.

Willy thought of all the robberies he had helped his uncle commit. Getting caught had never really entered his mind. Clark planned meticulously and never suggested the possibility either of them might go to jail. Willy knew as long as they carried out Clark's plans, there was no possibility of getting caught. He now had to face the possibility he might follow his uncle to jail or at least, reform school. When he saw his parents walking up the sidewalk together, he resolved to never steal again.

Ben Tom and Willy tried to subdue their joy out of respect for their uncle's predicament, but they could not erase their smiles anymore than they could banish the joy that filled their hearts at the sight of their parents coming into the house together. Irene took each boy's face in her hands and kissed him. Purcell was all smiles as he squeezed each of their shoulders hard enough to hurt. When they sat on opposite sides of the room, Ben Tom felt the sense of elation leave him as quickly as it had arrived. He knew they were there at the same time, but not together.

Irene hugged her brother and broke into sobs as the lawyer walked in to deliver him to the police station. The lawyer had good news. Clark would be housed at the minimum security prison in Seagoville, not too far from where she and Buck lived. But Irene would not be consoled. She knew her brother was a professional thief—she had come to accept stealing as a sort of profession for her brother—and he was at the top of that profession. He had been doing it for so long it seemed inconceivable he could be caught as a result of something as simple as a defaced license plate.

Clark consoled her. "Hell, Sis, I can do five standing on my head." He pulled her arms from his and led his lawyer back to the car. Irene stood in the yard and watched as they drove away.

Inside, Purcell broke the news to the boys. He was there to take Trez home to live with him and Donna. He had not found his runaway wife in Tennessee, but at the Dallas bus station when she called and asked to come home. Purcell felt redeemed when she called. He made her beg a little and make some promises. But the one bedroom walkup where they lived could only accommodate one boy.

Ben Tom and Willy really wanted to live with their mother, but the prospect of living with Buck Blanton frightened them. They begged to stay in Clark's house until he got out of prison. They had been pretty much making it on their own, anyway. But Irene was adamant. The long talk she had with Buck would yield results; he was a changed man, she said.

Ben Tom stared at the portable storage building in the backyard. "At least let me stay here long enough to find a place for my stuff."

Irene looked at the storage building. "What kind of stuff?"

Ben Tom's face warmed. "My antiques." He had been collecting junk from the scrap yard, garage sales and dumpsters since he moved in with Clark. He saw a carving in every piece of scrap wood, a sculpture in every

33

piece of iron, a story in every antique. Most of his collection had been given to him, or had been thrown away by others, but he had had to pay for a few items that were too good to pass up.

"Honey, you know Buck will throw a fit if you show up with more junk. Our whole place is covered in junk as it is."

"Don't aim to take it over there. I just need to find somebody to hold it till I can come for it."

"Sorry, honey, but we have to go now. I want you boys settled in by the time Buck gets home."

Willy was waiting in Clark's pickup when they walked out into the yard, but Irene told him it would not be a good idea to take the truck. "Wait till we all get used to the new arrangements."

They arrived in Seagoville less than an hour after Clark entered prison only a few miles away.

6

BUCK WAS CHANGED. HE WAS DOWNRIGHT SUBSERVIENT TO THE
boys as long as Irene was around. But he made fun of them and slapped
them in places where they would not bruise when she wasn't. The backs of
their heads were a favorite target. But the boys could handle ridicule and
the occasional slap. Ben Tom was big enough to control the dogs now and
Buck eased up on his treatment of Willy when he recognized Willy was
fully capable of sticking him with a knife while he slept.

Spending time with their mother seemed worth it to the boys until
Buck purchased a new, fully loaded Chevrolet pickup. He kept it only a few
weeks before he began to hate it. The first payment notice sent him into a
rage, as if the credit union had a personal vendetta against him. When the
radiator boiled over the next week, he took it to the dealership to get his
money back. They fixed the problem and sent him on his way, but then the
electrical system shut down, leaving him stranded. The dealership had to
call the police when he returned. But Buck still did not get his money back.

Ben Tom and Willy were surprised when Buck pulled them out of bed
and invited them for a late night ride in his new truck while Irene slept.
They had been salivating over it since he brought it home, but had never
been allowed to touch it, much less ride in it. They were not even disappointed when Buck banished them to the truck's bed for the ride. As they
entered a shaded, dark, deserted street near a wooded creek right after
midnight, Buck accelerated the truck enough to squeal the tires and soon
reached eighty on the long street. When he suddenly turned the wheel,
the boys had to drop to the floor of the bed to keep from being thrown

out. Even then, they worried Buck was going to turn the truck over as it fishtailed and the back tires slid into a ditch.

Buck quickly jumped out, brandishing a screwdriver and hammer. He told both boys to get out of the bed and handed the tools to Willy. "You got sense enough to find the gas tank on this pickup?"

Willy nodded.

"Then crawl under there and punch a hole in it. Just enough to drip."

"Why?"

"Don't ask why, boy. Just do like you're told. I want this to look like the wreck caused the tank to rip open and the truck to catch on fire."

Willy did not understand. "You're gonna burn your brand new truck?"

"Damn straight. It's a lemon and the dealer won't make it good. I'll show those sonsabitches. Figure to collect the insurance and buy a sure nuff good one."

Ben Tom filled his chest with air. "Burn the truck yourself, Buck. Come on, Willy. We're going home."

Buck reached inside the bib of his overalls and pulled out the sawed-off shotgun he carried there in a pocket Irene had sewn for him. He pointed it at Ben Tom first, then Willy. "You want to burn it, or you want to burn in it? Makes me no difference. I can get rid of three problems at once."

Ben Tom understood. Buck wanted Willy to do it because it would keep them from telling what he had done. "I'll do it. No use getting Willy involved."

Buck curled his lip. "Oh, how sweet of the big brother. Why you think I brought Willy along? He's the only one can crawl under there and punch a hole far enough underneath to make it look good. Besides, he's a firebug. This ought to be right down his alley. He gets his grins doing this kinda stuff."

Willy was already underneath the truck before Ben Tom could reply. The smell of gasoline soon overpowered the smell of nearby honeysuckle. Willy stayed underneath the truck until Ben Tom yelled for him to get away. Willy kicked his legs, signaling he was almost done. "Just building a little nest of leaves and weeds."

Buck struck a match on his thumbnail as Willy stood. Willy blew it out. "Not now. You want to set us all on fire, leave evidence? Let's go." Willy started running in the direction of home. Ben Tom fell in behind.

Buck yelled after them. "Where the hell you think you're going?"

The boys broke into a run and Buck gave chase, but had no chance of catching them. They were completely out of sight of the truck when they heard the explosion and turned to see flames reach over the treetops. Buck looked back and smiled.

The boys were gone when Buck got home. The burned truck was one more reason to leave their mother and Buck behind and move back into Clark's house. Ben Tom had already been planning a trip to recover his property from Clark's storage building, anyway. And Clark's truck sitting idle was more than Willy could bear. And he needed to check on Clark's stash of stolen artwork.

Meager belongings in duffels their mother had fashioned out of scrap denim strapped over their shoulders, they walked along the highway, miles from Pleasant Grove. Traffic was meager during the wee hours and the boys gave up hope of thumbing a ride. They had decided to camp in the woods when they saw a yellow car parked on the side of the road ahead of them. The driver lightly tapped the horn.

Willy eyed the vehicle suspiciously. "Damn, that's a cab. Looks like the same one that took us home the other night. He's following us around. Told you he was a pervert."

Ben Tom was filled with a sense of relief. "He ain't no pervert. Just can't figure what he's doing way out here in the middle of the night. Maybe somebody held him up and he's hurt." He trotted to the car and stuck his head through the open passenger window. "You hurt?"

Moonlight revealed a smile. "Doing just fine. Just had a feeling you boys might be needing a ride again."

Willy shook his head. "And you just happened to come along way out here in the middle of the night."

"One of my AA buddies fell off the wagon. Had to get him home. I was at the end of my shift and ready to head home when I saw that pickup go up in smoke and Buck running after you boys."

Ben Tom looked back down the road they had traveled at the mention of Buck. He had not considered Buck might give chase in his mother's car. "You know Buck?"

"As it happens, I do. Everybody within a hundred miles knows it's healthy to know who Buck Blanton is. Fella could get himself hurt not knowing who to stay away from."

"You going back to Pleasant Grove?"

"I am. Hop in."

Clark's house was dark and there was a foreclosure sign in the front yard when they parked out front. The cabbie pointed at the sign. "I tried to rent this house when Clark went away on his little vacation, but the bank just wants to unload it. And I can't swing buying it right now."

Ben Tom thought of his antique collection in the building out back. "We know where the spare key is. We can camp out here tonight and figure something tomorrow."

The cabbie shook his head. "Not a good idea. Bank will call the cops sure as the devil. Besides, I know the lights and water are off. I know somewhere you can spend the night."

But Willy was already out of the cab. Ben Tom stepped out and leaned back through the window. "I have some things to check on here. We'll sleep a little and figure something tomorrow. We're much obliged to you for helping us again. You seem to show up just when we need you."

The cabbie nodded and smiled, waited until Ben Tom opened the door to the house, cranked the cab and drove away. They tried the light switch and water faucets to no avail. The house had been ransacked, and most of Clark's belongings taken. Ben Tom found Clark's burglary flashlight in its usual hiding place taped underneath the commode tank, walked to the backyard, and opened the padlock on the little storage building. His spirits sank when the light revealed the building was empty. Years of collecting gone.

The boys walked to their father's rented duplex the next morning. Purcell seemed rather pleased they had run away from Buck, but he still had no room. He tried to get the utilities turned back on at Clark's house, but only the bank could do that, and they were unwilling.

Willy remembered the trailer house near Terrell where Clark had stashed his art treasures. A little work might make it livable. No reason for Ben Tom to ever know about the cellar or what was in it. Ben Tom had to do a little carburetor work, but Clark's old pickup finally hummed. They threw their meager belongings inside and drove toward Terrell.

Ben Tom took a long look inside the gutted trailer, bounced on the unsteady floor. "How come Clark showed you this place and not me?"

"I came out here with him sometimes when he used it to stash loot until he could fence it. He knew you might turn him in."

"I might be able to fix this place up, but we both need jobs and we don't know anybody to work for out here. Dad said he might get us on a construction crew if we can manage to get ourselves back and forth to work."

They headed back to Clark's house to camp another night. A few blocks away from Clark's, Ben Tom leaned out the window and told Willy to stop. The cab sat in the driveway in front of a lighted garage converted to some type of shop. Next to the garage-shop, a car covered with a tarp occupied a single-car carport.

The door was up and the lights were on in the shop. Sparks flew as a man hammered a piece of iron on an anvil. The light and warmth from the fire made his skin appear the same red color as the iron he hammered. Sparks and smoke danced as the man pumped his forge.

Ben Tom hung his head out the window in the crisp air and inhaled the smell of hot metal and coals. Ambrosia. "That's the cabbie."

As the man worked bellows and made his fire hotter, Ben Tom opened the car door and slammed it harder than necessary. He tried to make himself seen as he approached the open door to the shop to keep from startling the blacksmith. He needn't have.

The cabbie smiled and looked up as if he had been expecting him. "Appreciate your dropping by, Ben Tom. Expected you a little sooner. That Willy in the driver's seat?"

Ben Tom nodded and motioned for Willy to join them. He wandered around the building, examined the tables and walls full of tongs, trivets, meat hooks, candle holders, triangular dinner bells, and ornamental fences. "You make all this?"

The cabbie put down his hammer. "Most of it. Some of it was made by students."

"Students?"

"I have a few folks want to learn how to work with hot iron."

"You teach people how to become smithies?"

"Sometimes. You interested?"

Ben Tom stared at the red coals illuminating the cabbie's face. "Would be if I could afford to pay, but I can't."

"Won't be a problem. I keep what you make and sell it. We split the profits. Deal?"

JIM H. AINSWORTH

Willy had looked over the collection of forged metal and was bored. "Say, what's your name, anyway?"

The cabbie smiled. "Deacon. Deacon Slater."

"Deacon, huh? That some kinda church title or your real name?

"It's my real name."

"Why would you teach my brother how to be a blacksmith?"

"Because I like him and I have a feeling he might be good at it. You boys find a place to stay yet?"

Ben Tom shook his head. He did not want to admit the desperation he was beginning to feel. "We're working on it, though."

Deacon pointed a pair of tongs toward a door in the back of the shop. "Take a look in that room back there. See if it suits you."

The room had bunk beds, a worn couch, and a maple dining room suite with three chairs. The finish was worn off the table and chairs. Where most would see worn-out furniture, Ben Tom saw collectibles and started thinking of buying the pieces. There was a hot plate, a refrigerator, a sink hung from the wall with a leaky faucet and a bathroom in one corner. A window looked out on the backyard.

Willy was again wary when they walked back into the shop. "What is that place? Looks like a hideout or something. You in trouble with the law?"

"I lived in there a few months while I remodeled the old house I live in now. Some of my AA buddies use it as a place to dry out once in a while. Everything still works, but it could use a paint job and a little maintenance. I got the paint. You boys take care of that and I'll let you stay rent free for a couple of months."

Ben Tom did not hesitate. "We'll pay as soon as we can get back on to jobs somewhere. That your car you got covered in the carport?"

Deacon reached into his pocket and withdrew something as he walked toward the car. He opened his palm to reveal Ben Tom's cross.

Ben Tom sucked in an audible breath. "That was hanging from the rearview mirror in my car."

Deacon pulled back enough of the tarp for Ben Tom to see a fender. He felt lightheaded when he recognized his handiwork. "How did you get it?"

"Four one-hundred-dollar bills at the pound auction. Highway rob-

40

bery, but I was still lucky to catch it." Deacon stared at Ben Tom for several seconds, tried to judge his reaction. Ben Tom was speechless.

Deacon chuckled. "Fellow down the street already offered me five for it. I don't like him much, though. He doesn't take care of his vehicles. If you think you can come up with the four I paid, I'll hold it for you. Man builds a car from scratch, he deserves to keep it."

Ben Tom did not hesitate. His world outlook had changed in a matter of minutes, and his voice was filled with determination. "I'll come up with the money."

"I've got to finish one piece before the forge gives out. You boys go collect your things and I'll be done by the time you get back."

He took Ben Tom's hand and pressed the wooden cross into his palm. "Hang onto this a little better from now on. Never know when you'll be needing it."

7

WHEN THEY RETURNED FROM CLARK'S HOUSE WITH THEIR things, Deacon was not in the shop, though the lights were still on. They dropped their duffels on the floor of their new living quarters. Deacon had rolled in a small chifferobe while they were gone. Ben Tom ran his hands lovingly over the scarred oak piece. "This is my piece."

Willy's eyes widened. "You sure?"

"Course I'm sure. I found it in a garage sale a few months ago. Lady gave it to me for hauling off a few of her other things."

"So that means old Deacon, the church man, is a damn thief."

They looked out the back window and saw light coming from a small building in the yard. The building sat on wooden skids and looked like it had been used as a construction office. They were waiting in the yard when Deacon came out of the building. Deacon laughed when Ben Tom looked inside. "Recognize any of that junk?"

"That's my stuff from Uncle Clark's building. How did you get it?"

"Bank put it all out for the trash man a few days after Clark left. I loaded it up and brought it home. I thought I recognized a few things that might be worth something. Decided to just keep it all. Figured you were collecting it."

Ben Tom was skeptical. "How did you know I collect old stuff?"

Deacon smiled. "This stuff has got your name written all over it. You like metal, wood, anything old and primitive. The more rustic and worn the better. Am I right?"

"Yeah, but how did you know?"

"I'm an observant man, Ben Tom. Aren't you?"

"How much do I have to come up with to get this stuff back?"

"About ten bucks a month for storage. You can work it out doing blacksmith work as soon as I teach you."

With a new place to live, the boys returned to their old school. Deacon made school attendance a requirement for living in his shop. Willy took Ben Tom's job at the salvage yard when Purcell got Ben Tom an apprenticeship with the construction firm he worked for. Deacon registered the Ford and allowed Ben Tom to drive it back and forth to work and on the few dates he had time for.

Ben Tom had less than a year left of school and Willy had three. Both struggled to catch up on missed days and had trouble making passing grades. Ben Tom wanted Deacon to teach him how to work with metal, but his time was limited to an occasional hour at night and on Sundays in the blacksmith shop. Willy surprised everyone when he held his temper long enough to keep his job at the salvage yard. Ben Tom hoped his brother's days as a thief were over.

Ben Tom was a construction gofer at first, but was soon allowed to help hang sheetrock. He tried the stilts as a stunt at first, but Purcell recognized he was a natural. The walkers seemed like mere extensions of his legs as he moved easily and quickly around construction sites. When he was allowed to hang a few sheets, Purcell and his boss stared in wonder as Ben Tom deftly maneuvered both eight and twelve-foot sheets into place and screwed them down with speed and dexterity.

Purcell soon pitted his son against more experienced drywall men and made wagers. He shared his gambling winnings with Ben Tom. Money from bets and his construction pay enabled Ben Tom to buy nicer clothes and school supplies for himself and Willy. He even had enough money to begin dating Penny, a girl he had met while he was working at the grocery store her parents owned.

Penny was shy and petite with thick curly hair she had trouble keeping under control. Her brown eyes seemed to sparkle on the rare occasions when Ben Tom could coax a few words out of her. She reminded him of pictures he had seen of his mother at that age. He planned to ask her to marry him as soon as they graduated and he could afford a place for them to live.

The pieces he constructed in the blacksmith shop sold for enough to pay his rent. He began taking custom orders. He made a complete set of poker chips out of bois d'arc. He made spurs and designed his own unique pieces with metal bent into the shape of horses, boots, cowboy hats, cowboys, and farm and ranch scenes complete with houses, barns, livestock, even ponds, flowers and trees.

Late on a Sunday night, Deacon picked up a pastoral scene Ben Tom had created. A tiny metal fence surrounded a miniature barn and house carved out of scrap wood. A chiseled farm couple stood in a yard painted green. "You understand what's happening, don't you, Ben?'

Ben Tom did not stop his wood chisel. "What do you mean?"

"You're expressing your innermost desires with these creations. These are the places where you want to live. The wife and family you want. The life you want."

"Never really thought of it that way. I just make what comes into my mind."

"Like me, you seem to have a deep desire to cleanse your past life and start a completely different one. Don't wait as long as I did."

"I been wondering. Where are your wife and kids?"

"Kids are grown. Remember when I told you I devoted my life to making it up to them?"

"I remember."

"Well, love and trust are sort of like bank accounts. I made a lot of withdrawals, and it's taking me a few years to fix the overdrafts."

"What does that mean, exactly? Where is she?"

"She lives with one of our children in San Antonio. Keeps house and babysits my grandkids. They let me come and visit, but I can't stay in the house with them."

"After all this time?"

"It takes a long time to regain trust once you lose it, but I try to make a deposit, do something to prove myself, every time I visit. My family has forgiven me, but they still don't trust me. Take that as a lesson the first time you think about doing something stupid. You may be paying the price for the rest of your life."

Ben Tom didn't have the words. "I'm sorry."

"I'm just grateful I'm a free man. I belong in jail."

45

Within a few months, Ben Tom had saved enough to buy his car from Deacon. By the time of his graduation from school, he had a union card and Purcell organized larger contests and took bets on his son's proficiency and speed with both stilts and screw guns. Ben Tom took on all comers and beat them. The crew called him Spiderman because he seemed to go up walls with sheetrock like the comic book character. He carried his screw gun in a holster like a gunfighter.

Blacksmith and wood carving creations were a tidy source for pocket money, but construction was where the real money was. And escaping poverty was job one for Ben Tom. Working fulltime after graduating, he quickly advanced to foreman and began taking smaller jobs to be done on weekends and after work. He was as adept at taping and bedding, painting, laying carpet and tile, driving nails, framing, and other construction jobs as he was at hanging sheetrock.

When he was promoted to superintendent of construction for a small strip shopping center, he bought a small rent house, intending to move out of Deacon's shop as soon as he could fill his new purchase with antique furniture. Willy's volatility had made their single room too small for both brothers.

He planned to ask for Penny's hand in marriage as soon as the house was ready. He felt an urgent need to get married and start a family. He knew Penny was the right one for him, but he was also on a mission to prove he could hold a family together, be faithful to his wife, and provide their children with all the things he never had. He just was not sure Penny felt the same way. He also feared her devout parents would never give their permission.

But the family living in the rent house he purchased pleaded with him not to make them move. Even though they failed to pay rent for several months, Ben Tom did not have the heart to evict them, so he postponed his proposal to Penny. But moving became more urgent when he opened the door to the small room he and his brother shared in the back of Deacon's shop and found Willy in bed with a thirteen-year-old girl.

The young girl stood defiantly before him in a flat bra and cotton panties in the room he shared with Willy. The sight filled Ben Tom with horror and a rage toward his younger brother he had never before experienced. Willy recognized the rage but was defiant. "It ain't what you think. I'm just protecting her from two older brothers who been foolin' with her."

The explanation did little to quell Ben Tom's anger as the enormity of the possible consequences of such a damning act overwhelmed him. Hell could rain down on him and Willy and on Deacon. Willy was going to hell and all of them could go to prison. "Dammit, Willy, you were in bed with her. What the hell are you thinking?" He turned to the girl. "What's your name, how old are you, and where do you live?"

She glanced at Willy. When he nodded his assent, she spit it out like something vile on her tongue. Her name was Colleen, she said she was sixteen but Ben Tom knew she was lying, and she lived about twenty blocks west. Ben Tom knew the neighborhood. When she was dressed, he took her hand and led her to his car. Willy followed, shouted warnings. When Ben Tom did not stop, he drew back his fist and buried it into Ben Tom's kidney from behind. Not even his brother would be allowed to insult him by taking his woman.

There was a fight, the fiercest and bloodiest the brothers had ever had. Ben Tom finally managed to tie his brother to a post in Deacon's shop so he could take the young girl home. She scratched and fought like a wildcat to keep him from taking her away from Willy. He had to hold her wrist with one hand and drive with the other to keep her from jumping out of the car.

Sunset neared as he maneuvered the Ford through a neighborhood worse than the ones he had grown up in. He stopped in front of a small hovel with peeling paint and a porch turning loose from the main house. The yard was occupied by a '41 Ford and a '53 Chevy, both up on blocks. A woman seemed to be standing vigil behind the screen door. She brought a flat hand above her eyes to shade them from the setting sun and stared at Ben Tom's shiny Ford.

Ben Tom pulled a reluctant Colleen up the dirt trail that led to the porch. "This your daughter?"

The woman's eyes were gun metal gray and cold, as if evil memories lurked behind them. "What's she doing with you? You been pestering her?"

"No, ma'am. Just bringing her home."

The woman opened the screen door and Ben Tom pushed the girl inside. The woman hit her on the back of the head. Ben Tom turned to walk away, but turned back. "That girl gonna be safe here? I heard she's got brothers that bother her."

Dark approached, and the woman nodded toward two figures emerging from the shadows created by large shrubs in the side yard. "You mean them boys?"

They were on him before Ben Tom could react. One had a blackjack and Ben Tom managed to get it from him after one lick had split the skin above one eyebrow. Blood flowed through his eyebrow and onto his lashes. He blinked it away as he took one of the brothers to his knees with a club across his knee. He swung the club for protection as he backed to his car.

As he sped away, Ben Tom was upset, but still not angry. *The brothers were probably just defending their sister.* He tried to chase away the thought they might really be molesting her. Back at Deacon's shop, he wiped away blood from the steering wheel and door handle of his car before washing his face.

Ben Tom could not get the girl or the incident out of his mind. The entire episode made him feel a desperate need to cleanse himself, to erase not only the sordid memory, but his entire past and everything associated with it. That night, he braided a necklace with tiny strips of leather for his wooden cross and began wearing it around his neck to ward off evil. Deacon had shown him the short prayer of Jabez in the Bible. He recited the prayer each night and several times during the day.

> *Oh, that You would bless me indeed,*
> *And enlarge my territory,*
> *That Your hand would be with me,*
> *And that You would keep me from evil*
> *That I may not cause pain*

Penny and her family seemed to be the answer to his prayers. The exemplary life her family led and her own innocence filled him with the need to be part of her family and to protect her. The desperate need gave him the fortitude to visit his renters. The eye that had been hit was partially closed. The blood around his pupil, the scratches and scabbed knuckles from the fight with Willy and Colleen's brothers frightened his renters and convinced them to move.

In less than a month, Ben Tom pulled enough furniture from his various stashes to make the house livable and suitable for showing to Penny.

Deacon helped him load the last of his clothes and toiletries into his car. "Hate to see you go, Ben Tom. Don't know if I can control Willy. I won't stand for him bringing girls in here, especially ones barely off the nipple."

"Think he plans to move in with our daddy. In fact, I'll make sure that happens. Daddy and Trez got a new house that's big enough."

"What about Purcell's wife?"

"Daddy ran her off when he caught her making a move on Trez. Uncle Clark always said she would, sooner or later."

"You still gonna come by the shop to build your stuff?"

"If you'll let me."

"You're always welcome at my fire."

Ben Tom had not completely healed from the beating when he knocked on Penny's door. Her parents refused to let her leave until he explained the scratches and scabs. Ben Tom would not tell them a lie, so Penny made up a story about his being attacked by thieves on his way home from work. It worked.

After a nice meal at El Fenix, Ben Tom took her to his new home. He left the door open and made sure all the lights were on as he showed her each antique piece of furniture, each wall hanging.

8

BEN TOM AND PENNY WERE MARRIED LESS THAN SIX MONTHS later. It was a small affair in the family's church. The wedding seemed more like a baptism to Ben Tom. He felt liberated, cleansed, as he began his new life with Penny in their new home filled with old things.

After a weekend honeymoon at the Statler-Hilton in downtown Dallas, Ben Tom was anxious to carry Penny over the threshold of their new home. As he left on Monday morning, the world seemed washed and clean and he was anxious to get started providing for his new wife as a man of the world. Deacon wanted him to follow his creative spirit, but Purcell told him he could build an empire in construction. Ben Tom didn't understand what Deacon meant, but he thought he understood the construction business and was pretty confident he was good at it.

His only weakness in construction was his inability to delegate. Purcell recognized the weakness, but Ben Tom refused to acknowledge it. He tried to do almost all of the jobs himself because few could equal his skills. He was a perfectionist and refused to accept anything less—even for work hidden behind walls or covered in concrete. Both brothers and his father were soon working under his supervision.

He fired Trez and Willy more than once for being late or absent, or for showing up on the job site drunk or stoned. Both were excellent and talented workers, however, and he always hired them back. They were always in need of funds and Ben Tom was an easy mark.

Purcell, however, still had many things to teach his son about the business. Ben Tom soaked up his father's skills and experience and improved on each trick of the trade his father passed on.

In two years, he and Penny had two children, a boy and a girl. He celebrated each birth by buying the child a rent house, deducing the child would receive rental income for a lifetime. Each of them had a detached garage, shop or apartment Ben Tom did not rent. He used them to store his growing collection of antiques.

Ben Tom now had the family life he had been denied as a child—a near perfect family and a home, not just a house. But something was missing. All his houses were in his old neighborhood. He felt the urge to live somewhere else, but could not seem to venture away from the familiar—his physical surroundings or his family.

Construction and being a husband and father kept him away from Deacon's blacksmith shop and he had to satisfy his creative urges by taking on more and bigger construction projects and doing the most difficult jobs himself. With a positive persona Ben Tom scarcely realized he possessed and skill he was just discovering, he soon had a network of building managers who worked in some of the largest and most prestigious commercial buildings in and around Dallas. With these contacts, he brought millions of construction dollars to the firms he worked for.

Ben Tom made a good living for himself and his little family and still made small loans to his brothers. He helped them buy cars of their own. The Lawless family, father and three sons, began taking on small repairs and remodels on weekends. They called their little firm Lawless and Sons.

Still, it wasn't enough to satisfy some inner craving he could not identify. He needed to build his own buildings, not just remodel or repair a building someone else had built. And the buildings he dreamed of were different than any he had ever seen.

When Scott, one of his building manager contacts, told him he and his wife were going to build a custom home, Ben Tom volunteered to design the home of their dreams free of charge. The couple was thrilled with his ideas and almost begged him to build the home himself. Ben Tom agreed, provided he and his family could do most of the work at night and on weekends.

They used few subcontractors, electing to do all of the carpentry work, most of the plumbing and electrical, the flooring, painting and wallpapering, even the roof. He had friends who "loaned" him their appropriate licenses for permits as needed. The house was almost complete when a check he wrote for carpet bounced. Scott had not transferred a draw he had requested weeks ago into his account. He went to the building Scott managed and was told he had been fired. He called Scott's wife. She told him Scott had been fired for drinking on the job and she had filed for divorce.

Ben Tom, Purcell, Willy and Trez stood in the street facing the home that looked complete from the outside. Purcell shook his head. "All she needs is carpet, a little paint touch-up, wallpaper in one room, and land-scaping."

Ben Tom remained committed to finishing the job. "Still have to do the flatwork. Shouldn't take more than a week."

Purcell lit a cigarette and blew a plume of smoke toward the house. "What the hell you talking about? You don't seriously plan on finishing it, do you?"

"I finish what I start. We can't get the reputation for leaving a construction job before it's finished."

"What are you gonna do with it then? The savings and loan will tie it up in court till hell freezes over."

"Old Scott will come through. He's a good guy."

Purcell stood in front of his eldest son as if he did not have his full attention. "What's wrong with you? Don't you see what's happened? Good guy Scott has screwed you over big time. He ain't even had the decency to call you."

Ben Tom did not waiver. "He will."

Purcell looked at Willy and Trez, incredulity all over his face. They shook their heads. "How come you didn't check to see if the draw hit the bank before you started writing checks? How much of your own money you got tied up in this thing?"

"Haven't added it up, but I expect about twenty thousand. Don't you think the bank will make it good? Scott had an approved interim construction loan."

Purcell looked at his son as he dropped the cigarette to the ground and crushed it. "When you gonna get it through your head this guy is out of the picture? And the bank damn sure ain't gonna pay you what you're owed."

Willy made a growling sound in his throat and spat in the yard. "Let's go find the bastard. I'll make him pay."

Purcell's face still showed disbelief as he stared at Ben Tom. "When are you gonna learn that people will cheat you? You have to look out for number one."

Trez stood with his hands in his pockets, wished for a cold one. "Yeah, big brother, when you gonna learn?"

They were about to walk away when Willy's pickup horn honked. Ben Tom turned to look. "Who's in your pickup?"

His question was answered when Colleen, not quite sixteen, stepped out of the pickup on the passenger side. She was pregnant, about four or five months along. Willy put his arm around her when she stopped by them. "Boys, I want you to meet my new wife."

9

WILLY'S FINGERS DRUMMED AGAINST THE STEERING WHEEL AS he drove away with his new bride. He had been married for two months before he told his father and brothers. They had only stared at his new bride. Nobody said anything. But that was the least of Willy's worries. The night before he and Colleen were married in a courthouse clerk's office, he had bought himself a baby-blue '60 Ford to drive to their one-night honeymoon motel. He had also splurged on a few furnishings to spruce up the drab rent house they were to occupy.

With his cash stash depleted, he borrowed from a local loan shark, planning to repay him with his share of the profits from the custom house Ben Tom was building. Though it had never been discussed or promised, he considered himself a partner in the venture. Now—there would be no profits. He silently vowed to exact revenge on Ben Tom's friend.

Desperate for funds, he tapped Ben Tom for a hundred, but Colleen's doctor visits and needy quirks quickly ate the hundred. The thousand he had borrowed from the loan shark was now due. The shack he lived in was not fit for his new bride and wasn't safe. He needed money for a deposit on a rent house or apartment. He also needed money to support Colleen and the child soon to be born.

When he stopped in front of the shack they called home and looked out the car window, he noticed the porch was one day closer to falling in. What if it fell on his new bride? He waited impatiently for Colleen to get out and go inside. She kept her seat until he reached across her and opened the door. "I got some things to do. Go on inside."

She shook her head like a small child having a temper tantrum. "Where you going?"

"That ain't none of your damn business. Now get out." He pushed her toward the open door.

He left her standing in the yard with her hands on her hips as he left rubber on the street and headed for Terrell. Inside the trailer house, his hands shook and he knocked the skin off his knuckles attempting to pull back the cover Clark had made look easy.

Trying to get his mind off of snakes, Willy quickly skimmed the stash with the light from his flashlight. He had not noticed the careful and organized placement of the pieces when Clark had brought him here. In fact, he was almost certain there had been some haphazardness to them then. Now, they were organized, protected with Styrofoam peanuts used in packing fragile objects for shipping. When he picked up the piece easiest to reach—a simple bronze of a cowboy holding a rifle, he saw slits in the floor of the box. A *false floor*.

He clicked open his switchblade and ran the blade down one of the cracks. The small door about the size of a legal document opened easily. A maroon velour sack with a drawstring lay inside. He picked up the sack, loosened the drawstring, and peered inside. Even the sparse light from the flashlight was enough to make the diamonds and other precious stones in the jewelry sparkle as if alive, waiting to be found and anxious to be brought back into the light.

But Willy closed the drawstring quickly, as if he had found a poisonous snake inside it. Clark had not shown him nor had he mentioned any jewelry. Willy knew he had seen something he was not supposed to see. His hands shook as he set the bronze cowboy on the floor of the trailer, replaced the plywood cover, locked the door and drove back toward Dallas, the bronze on the seat beside him.

Willy headed for Oak Cliff, figuring nobody would know him or Clark there. He was still shaking when he took the bronze out of a paper sack in front of the first pawnbroker he found. His fright turned to anger when the broker offered him a hundred for it. He was boiling mad by the time two others made no offer at all. They examined the piece, shook their heads ominously, and pointed toward the door. The fourth broker sent him to a real fence, who questioned him about the piece's history and where he got it. He stared at Willy long enough to make him ball his fists, peeled out four hundreds and laid them on the counter.

Willy shook his head. "This thing is worth ten times that and you know it."

The man stared at Willy and at the hundreds on the counter. "Not to me. That piece is too hot to even pick up."

Willy squirmed as he realized the artwork might be better known on the streets than he feared. He became contrite. "Come on man, I got to have a thousand."

The fence picked up the piece again, held it up to the light as if he were examining a diamond. Willy looked toward the front window to see if anyone was watching. "Hey, man, keep that thing down on the table."

The man peeled off three more hundreds to add to the four. "You got about ten seconds to take the money or your piece and get the hell out of here."

Willy wanted to take a swing at the much bigger man, but he kept his eyes on the seven hundred. He swept it up awkwardly, stuffed it into his jeans.

The man wrapped the bronze in a piece of soft cloth. "Don't ever come back in here again. Understood?"

Willy gave the man a threatening stare he knew was pure bravado, then walked out. He drove directly to the loan shark and handed over the seven hundred. The shark looked at the crumbled bills. "You forget how to count?"

Willy tried to calm his temper, tried to control his desire to stick a screwdriver up the man's nose to his brain. "Cut me some slack. Some dude shorted me on a construction draw. Take me a week or two to figure it out. You'll get the other three hundred."

"Three hundred? You forget the juice? Don't you mean four hundred?"

"I owed you a grand. I'm short three hundred."

The shark smiled. "You're short four and it'll be five tomorrow. Juice keeps running on the whole loan till you pay it all off."

Willy hustled away before his temper drove him to do something stupid.

The looks on the faces of the brokers who turned him down and the one who paid him now haunted Willy's dreams. He had slept little since the night he sold the piece and vowed to reclaim it and return it to Clark's stash as soon as he could borrow the money from Ben Tom.

He approached his brother for twelve hundred a week later. But Ben Tom was tapped out. The house had taken all his cash and left him with a debt much larger than Willy's. Willy couldn't believe it. His brother had always been good for a few hundred. He had never turned him down. Better, he had never asked for repayment.

At home that evening, Colleen complained like a whining schoolgirl as Willy nursed a six pack of Schlitz. She had not fixed supper, a requirement that seemed reasonable to Willy. After all, she had nothing else to do all day. She cowered when he threatened her, but cajoled him into taking her out to eat. Willy placed a can of beer between his legs and peeled rubber as he drove from the house. That usually gave Colleen a thrill.

As they left the drive-in with fried chicken takeout, a motorcycle passed them on Colleen's side of the car. She gasped and pointed at the rider. "That guy winked and waved at me."

Willy ignored her at first, but she persisted. "Did you hear me?"

"I heard you, Colleen. What do you want me to do, run over him for winking and waving?"

"He made a nasty gesture, like he was grabbing his crotch."

It was not the first time Colleen had accused a complete stranger of accosting her who was only flirting. Willy had already beaten a young man to near death in the parking lot of a bar when she accused him of pinching her. Willy and Colleen had fled the scene when they heard sirens, Colleen giddy all the way home.

Willy looked at the motorcycle and at his wife's petulant expression. She pursed her lips like a child who had been denied a sucker. He knew she was probably lying, but still saw her less as a wife than a child who desperately needed his protection. He could not take the chance that she was telling the truth, could not lose face.

Willy showered down on the accelerator and quickly caught the motorcycle. He honked, but the rider, dressed in the new leather garb of a man just getting used to motorcycle riding, ignored him. Willy honked again as he came alongside the rider. When the rider turned to look, Willy flipped him the bird and shouted for him to pull over. The rider grimaced, took one hand off a handlebar, and returned the gesture. Willy gunned his baby-blue Ford, swerved into the rider's lane, and ran the motorcycle into a bridge banister.

Colleen was excited as she turned to see sparks fly as the motorcycle collided with and careened off the banister. But her face showed petulance again as the cycle slid along the pavement, the rider only a few feet behind. "Guess that'll teach him to flirt with me." As the driver flailed on the pavement, her expression changed. "Willy, you coulda killed that guy. What got into you? You crazy?"

What did she want me to do? Willy felt a twinge of panic, but subdued it as he slowed the Ford and looked in the rearview mirror. "Nah. He's wearing those leathers for a reason. Doubt if he got more than a scratch. Look, his head is already moving."

"Probably 'cause his neck's broke. You better stop."

"I can't stop. I been drinking and still got four beers in here."

10

WILLY HAD PUT THE INCIDENT WITH THE MOTORCYCLE OUT of his mind by the next morning as he concentrated on how he was going to keep his legs from being broken by a loan shark. But he had picked the wrong motorcycle to run over. The new Harley belonged to a lawyer—a shyster whose clients occupied the lowest rung of society—a lawyer with a broken leg and arm caused by a collision with a bridge banister. And a witness had taken down the plate number of Willy's Ford.

When Willy walked out his door two days later to head for work, two cops were examining the scratches and black paint on his baby blue Ford. His temper flared. "Stay away from my damn car."

The officers put their hands on their weapons and turned to face Willy. When they saw he was unarmed and of non-threatening size, they smiled as if they looked forward to his resisting.

The biggest cop stuck out his hand like he was directing traffic. "Stop where you are, sir. Where did this black paint and those scratches come from?"

"Clumsy guy scraped it with a forklift on a construction site where I'm working." Willy's answer was quick, but his mouth dropped open when a burly, menacing man rolled a wheelchair from the other side of the Ford. The man in the wheelchair had a cast on one leg and the opposite arm. He pointed at Willy with his good arm. "That's the bastard ran over me."

The smaller cop stepped forward. "You'll have to come with us down to the station."

Willy turned to flee and the smaller man threw his baton and tripped

61

him. The bigger one was on his back in an instant. "Go ahead, bad boy. Make it tougher on yourself."

Ben Tom called in all his chits and favors to gather together bail money for Willy. But he could not come up with the upfront money required for a lawyer. The loss on Scott's house had tapped him out. Willy settled for a public defender whose heart was not in the case, especially after Willy repeatedly threatened him. He was sentenced to a year in the county jail and a five-hundred-dollar fine.

Willy was paranoid about leaving Colleen alone, fearing not so much for her safety as for her fidelity. His first call after receiving his sentence was to Ben Tom, asking him to keep an eye on Colleen. With no money for rent, she asked to return to her mother's house, but her mother had already rented her old room and turned her away. Ben Tom and Penny took her in.

Willy's paranoia about Colleen grew with each day he spent in jail. His imagination about suitors pursuing his new and pregnant wife took flight and rage began to build, exacerbated when Colleen refused to visit him. She said she could not bear the thought of taking the baby in her belly into a dangerous and filthy jail. Penny even expressed sympathy for her position.

So Willy was reduced to speaking with her only by phone. And as the new inmate, he was last in line. On his third Sunday, he paced as he waited for a large black inmate to finish using the phone. The inmate covered the receiver with a ham hock hand and spoke to the pacing Willy. "Sit your white ass down over there, honky. I can't concentrate on what I got to say to my lady."

Willy thought his head might explode as he explored the somewhat dark hall for a weapon of some sort. Nothing. When the inmate began to work into Willy's allotted phone time, he panicked and tapped him on the shoulder. He tried to keep his voice firm and not to say what was racing through his mind. "Time's up. Hang up, or I won't have any time to make my call."

The inmate turned to him and sneered, then chuckled. "Guess you gon' just have to wait till next week."

Willy bit his lip and tapped him again. "Look, man. My wife is pregnant. I can't wait till next week."

The inmate turned, smiled and held out the receiver. "Well, I be sorry about that. Here you go."

When Willy reached for the phone, the black man drew back the receiver and rapped it hard against the side of Willy's head, pulled it out of the base and began to hit him across the face. Two guards heard the commotion and pulled Willy's tormentor off him.

Willy rose to his knees and spit out a tooth. The guard chuckled. "That second tap you put on Junior was just too much for the big man. You got a lot to learn, kid."

Junior, without realizing it, had done Willy a favor. He had given him something to think about and plan for every day. And he had taken his mind off Colleen and her possible infidelity. Willy carried his tooth in his pocket and rubbed it regularly while he plotted. But even with this new project, he still spent hours alone in a six-by-nine cell. And he began to pay more attention to details of his cell and the other parts of the jail facility. He asked Ben Tom to send over some framed family pictures to make him feel a connection to home.

He had other motives for asking for pencil and paper, but as he stared at the Big Chief tablet and the pencil Ben Tom brought him, he began to think. He began to recount his years as a child, the hard times. But during those times when he was bullied in school or bullied by Buck, Willy always felt he was in control. He knew he could fight back, knew he would eventually get even. The thoughts of revenge and the knowledge he would pick the time and place to exact it had always consoled him. Taking revenge on Junior, however, was out of his control. He could not pick the time and place. The guards made sure their time to make phone calls did not coincide. He began to worry Junior might be released before he got his chance.

He picked up the pencil and tablet and began to write each night. After several erasures, fits and starts and frustrating wadding of paper, he composed the first poem of his life.

I'm No Criminal
With a girl in my arms
And a beer in my hand
In my drunken stage
I could barely stand

With the beer that I spilt
On these clothes I wear
And this drunken story
I'm fixing to share
I shouldn't have been driving
I should have been walking
But then she said he got nasty
He shouldn't have been gawking
I remind myself every morning
I wake up in this cell
"I'm no criminal"
I shouldn't be here in this jail

The writing of poems and letters brought him a serenity he had never experienced. But he was not serene enough to forget about Junior and the tooth he had taken from him. He remembered it each time he rubbed the tooth or ran his tongue through the hole where it used to be. He had some work duties, but not many, so Willy began to volunteer for more. He was given a broom, a mop bucket and mop and told to clean the halls outside the cells. He told the guards the sweeping and mopping cleared his mind, took his mind off his troubles. He asked for more chances to clean in other parts of the jail. After a month of thorough cleaning by Willy, his presence became accepted, almost as if he were invisible. Being small helped. The guards allowed him to come and go inside the broom closet as he gathered his cleaning tools every other day.

When Willy finally cleaned the hall outside Junior's cell, he expected a few slurs and taunts. But Junior did not taunt him—he ignored him. Willy stopped and stared at him. Junior did not notice him for several seconds. "Whatchu lookin' at? Get away from here, fool."

Willy leaned on his mop and stared as if he was a visitor to the zoo and Junior was a caged animal. It gave him a rush, a sense of power. But Junior seemed to have no recollection of the incident with the phone and Willy's lost tooth. He did not even seem to recognize the man leaning on the mop. Willy could have handled taunting, but he could not handle being forgotten, being insignificant.

As the guards gave him more and more freedom to reward his good work, Willy began to schedule which halls to clean, began to observe Junior's schedule. He had a plan, but it was not complete until a guard dropped by one night when Willy was storing his cleaning tools. The guard leaned in the dark closet and dropped a thick pipe over the handle to Willy's broom. It had been painted to match the broom's wood handle and fit it perfectly. He placed a cotter key into a hole in the top of the handle to keep the pipe from slipping. The guard had an ugly gash over his right eye.

"Junior was up to his old tricks with the phone again two nights ago. Got this gash pulling him off of another prisoner."

Willy trusted nobody, especially a man in police uniform. He stared at the gash. "He hit you with the phone?"

"He was about to kill the other guy. I got this on one of his backswings. Pulled the whole phone off the wall this time."

They stared in silence for a few minutes until the guard looked both ways down the hall. "He lost his phone privileges this week, but I think he may be making a call on Saturday week. About two o'clock."

Willy kept his head down, tending to his mopping, when Junior walked into the hall where the phones were, but he needn't have bothered. Junior had his mind on talking to his lady. He had barely said hello to her when the mop caught him in the jaw. Willy had painstakingly bent the metal holder that held the mop strands together to fashion a claw. The hooks dug into the soft flesh of Junior's face and Willy jerked the handle at the right moment to rip his cheek as he yanked his head back. Great quantities of blood flowed from Junior's cheek as he dropped the phone to pull out the claw.

His eyes were wide and menacing when the pipe that looked like a broom handle broke one of Junior's knees. The second blow across his cheek knocked him on his back and stopped his screaming. Willy removed the pencil he had concealed in his thick hair, considered Junior's eye, but probed around his gums instead. He wanted to extract the same tooth he had lost and was disappointed the pipe had not broken any teeth. The guard who had supplied the pipe appeared and pulled him off. Willy struggled at first, then stopped and stared at Junior, then the guard. The guard removed the cotter key, pulled the pipe from the broom handle, and placed it out of sight behind a radiator. He dropped the cotter key into his pocket and motioned with his head for Willy to leave.

Willy walked out of the room, carrying his mop, bucket and broom. Feeling redeemed. Tomorrow, everybody in the jail would know about the guy who slammed down a man a hundred pounds heavier. No need for them to know about the pipe. He would be somebody. Everyone would know who Willy Lawless was. A man not to be messed with.

11

PENNY CAUGHT BEN TOM IN THE YARD AS HE RETURNED FROM visiting Willy in jail. "We have to talk."

Ben Tom had been expecting it. "Okay, babe. Colleen?"

"You have to do something about her."

"What's she done now?"

"That's part of the problem—she doesn't do anything except lie around and complain. And you can't believe the kind of words our kids are picking up from her. Not to mention she walks around half naked."

Ben Tom's heart was soft and his innate tendency to protect his brother and his family was strong, but Penny's happiness trumped everything else. "You think we can talk to her, or does she have to go?"

"I've talked till I'm blue in the face. The woman doesn't listen. Besides, her old furniture makes it too crowded in there to walk."

Ben Tom's only vacant rent house contained a lot of his treasures, but he moved Colleen into it the next day. He moved and rearranged his possessions to allow Colleen enough space to live. He told Willy when he visited on Sunday. Willy jumped to his feet, turning over the table where they were sitting. That almost brought their visit to an abrupt end when a guard came running. Ben Tom took the blame and told him his belt had hung on the table and he had accidentally toppled it over. Willy was not grateful. "You telling me my own brother turned my wife out onto the street?"

"She's not on the street. She's in a rent house almost as nice as the house we live in."

"Yeah, well. What's she gonna eat? Who's gonna protect her?"

"I bought her a bill of groceries to start with and I drop by with take-out almost every night. I think she likes being alone there. It's not a bad neighborhood."

Ben Tom kept delivering food to Colleen, even staying long enough to visit and listen to a litany of Colleen's needs and complaints every day. He did this even when it became obvious she had been gradually hocking or selling off some of his antiques. Willy was as happy as possible in his new role as the mad jailhouse rat too crazy to mess with.

Ben Tom paid his five-hundred-dollar fine and picked up Willy on the last day of his sentence. He told him on the way to the rent house that he and Penny were moving, that they wanted their kids to grow up in a small town and go to school there.

This was beyond Willy's comprehension. "Where the hell you goin'? You can't leave everything and everybody you grew up with. How you gonna survive? You got contacts, jobs here."

"I can commute until I make new connections out there. We're moving to Riverby, Texas. Found us a little place there on the banks of the Red River."

"Never heard of it."

"Not much there. Small town, small school. It's by the river. You know, river by?"

Willy cleared his throat. He had smoked heavier than ever during his year in jail and his voice had a new raspy sound to it. "I get it. Stupid name. I give you a month or two. Then you'll come crawling back."

"Don't count on it. I ain't ever coming back." Ben Tom stopped in front of the house where Colleen lived.

"What about your rent houses?"

"I can collect rent by mail and I can look after them when I come up here. Dad said he would look in on my renters."

"How long before you throw me out of this one?"

"When you get back to work, you can pay me $150 a month. That about covers the mortgage. Get the utilities transferred over to you as soon as you can swing it."

"Back to work? Who's gonna hire an ex-con now that you're buggin' out on me?"

"Dad can find you work. You know damn well a lot of ex-cons work construction."

Ben Tom had made up his mind. He had mentally closed the door on Dallas and opened it on Riverby. He had located a historical home near Riverby badly in need of repair. He planned to restore it. It sat on a hill overlooking the Red. The family would live in half of the huge house while he restored the other half.

Willy's time in jail was a disguised blessing for Trez. It scared him, made him realize it could have been him cooling his heels in the lockup. Though he never thought he would go through with it, Ben Tom's discussions about moving away made Trez feel more vulnerable. He had always felt safer around Ben Tom than either of his parents. He had never had a home where he felt secure and he desperately wanted one now.

So he could save for a place of his own, he used his slim good looks and gift of gab to persuade an attractive woman in the middle of a divorce to let him live with her rent free. He moved into her house and into her bed. At work, he cajoled Ben Tom into looking for a house he might afford. Ben Tom agreed, under the proviso that Trez would show up every day for work sober and stay sober all day. He would also be expected to work overtime when Ben Tom needed him to, something Trez had almost always refused to do. Trez agreed not only to work overtime when requested, but to volunteer for it. Like Ben Tom, he was a natural on the walkers and an exceptional drywall man. He knuckled down and worked steadily the entire year Willy was incarcerated. After eleven months, Trez showed his brother a wad of hundreds he kept hidden in a jelly jar. "Enough for a down payment. Now you need to find me a house."

Ben Tom soon found a repossessed home that was a good buy. Built in the 1920s, the previous owner had underestimated the cost of restoring it to its former glory. Ben Tom saw that as a challenge, not an obstacle, something to keep Trez busy. He helped his brother complete his bid paperwork and cosigned a mortgage. When it was time to move in, Trez immediately dropped his girlfriend and went back to his old habits. He laid off work most days, luxuriating in the best home he had ever inhabited.

When he got low on cash, he showed up at one of his brother's jobs after enjoying a few joints. After two lunchtime beers, Trez challenged his older brother to a race. Ben Tom scoffed at the challenge, but Trez found two identical walls and chided him for being afraid to face his younger brother and lose his undefeated status. Both walls had to be done, so Ben Tom stepped into his walkers and started one. Without a race being declared, Trez began on the opposite wall. As usual, Ben Tom did not let the quality of his work suffer because of speed. He was both fast and good.

A half hour later, only three sheets of rock sat on his scaffold to be installed. But only two remained on Trez's. Ben Tom had ignored his brother until then, but looked over his shoulder as Trez engaged in catcalls and laughter. "Better pick it up, brother. You're one behind."

Ben Tom tried to slow his pace to allow his brother to win, but could not keep from showing his almost inhuman speed with rock and a screw gun. He installed his three sheets before Trez could finish two. When they both stepped down, Ben Tom snickered when he saw Trez's wall. "Just like I figured. You got in a hurry to beat me and did shoddy work. You'll have to do that wall over."

Trez looked at his brother's wall with panels so flush and straight they could almost be painted without taping and bedding. His own wall could only be described as irregular. "There's something wrong with a man who takes that many pains with something that's gonna be covered up anyway."

Ben Tom shook his head. "The hell you say. Do it over. They'll have to put a bucket full of mud in some of those cracks you left. "

"That's what taping and bedding is for. Won't be able to tell yours from mine when it's done."

"I'll be able to tell. Somebody tries to drive a nail to hang a picture and gets in the mud, they'll blame me. This is my job and you do the wall over."

Never one to take anything seriously, Trez got on his walkers and started unscrewing and adjusting. "I expect to collect overtime for this."

Ben Tom left him to finish. He had told his mother and father and Willy, even Buck, that he was moving his family. Trez had heard him discuss the possibility but never took it seriously. Ben Tom did not want to tell him at work, so he parked by White Rock Lake and waited for Trez to pass, then followed him down the middle class street. When Ben Tom pulled in the driveway, Trez was already sitting on the porch of his new home.

Trez alternately sipped a beer and drew on a joint. The house still needed the repairs Trez had vowed to make as soon as the mortgage was approved.

Ben Tom leaned on a porch post and pointed up. "What happened to replacing those fascia boards and repairing these eaves?"

Trez smiled through a haze of smoke. "Don't worry, big brother. I'll get around to it."

"Cops are gonna come by here one day and arrest you for smokin' dope. You ever gonna get around to coming back to work on a regular basis?"

"Funny you mention that. I was planning on showing up again in the morning. Where do you want me?"

"I don't want you anywhere. I'm done with that job. I just stopped by to tell you I'm moving."

Trez dropped the remnants of the joint into the empty can of beer. "The hell, you say."

Ben Tom told him the details and Trez seemed more disturbed than Willy had been when he heard about the move. He cracked another beer and feigned indifference. "Well, I give you six months in Podunk. Hell, you a city boy. Ain't cut out for country life."

12

BEN TOM HAD MOVED MOST OF HIS POSSESSIONS AND RENTED the house he had been living in to a nice elderly couple. All that remained was to say goodbye to Deacon Slater. On the night before his final departure, he found Deacon at his customary place by his forge.

Deacon, like always, sensed his presence before Ben Tom announced himself. "Long time, no see."

"Yeah. Sorry I've been missing in action. I miss the smithing. Been busy. Just wanted to come by and let you know I'm moving my family to Riverby."

Deacon paused in pumping fire to the forge long enough to give Ben Tom one of his piercing looks. "Think I've been there. Little town about an hour and a half from here?"

"That's it. Right on the banks of the Red." The Red River, like all rivers, held some sort of fascination for Ben Tom he was unable to define or explain.

"I figured as much after I saw all those little art objects of farms and ranches you used to make. Most of them had a river or stream. Guess that's a destiny you're meant to fulfill. Hope you're planning on making maximum use of your talents."

"I may do some river fishing, but I plan on building me a shop so I can do some of the same stuff I did here with you. Course, I'll have to keep my hands in construction till I get on my feet. I'll be in and out of Dallas until I can scare up work down there."

"Not many high-rises in Riverby, I expect."

"Expect not. Figure I might do some residential stuff in the other small towns around. If I can't find it there, I'll commute. I got a house that will take a year or two to restore, so that'll keep me busy."

"Restoring your own house is a worthy occupation, but it won't put food on the table."

Ben Tom had expected only unbridled optimism and encouragement from Deacon. It was all he had ever expressed in the past. Deacon recognized the look of disappointment on his face.

"Course, a man of your talents can make a living in a ditch if you give him a few tools."

Ben Tom looked down at his boots and smiled. "Well, I got to be going. We still have a few things to load in my truck. Come down to see me sometime."

"I might do that. You drop in when you're up this way."

Ben Tom turned to walk away, then turned back. "Hey, Deacon, I'm taking the Ford with me."

"I wouldn't have expected anything else. Man builds a car from scratch, he expects to keep it."

Ben Tom had the door open to his pickup when Deacon put a hand on his shoulder, slapped his chest with the other hand, then the back of his head. "Trust in the Lord to help you realize your dreams. Don't forget God is in there. He is with you, just be sure you are with Him."

Ben Tom had plenty to think about on his way to his new home. He mentally checked off his list to see if he had missed anything. He had borrowed money from a loan shark to cover his losses and bad checks for the house he had built for Scott and his wife. When the shark came calling for his money, Ben Tom sold one rent house and two rooms of antique furniture to pay him. It still pained him to think of losing those assets.

When he reached the outskirts of Riverby, he stopped to take in the sight of the old house on a hill by the river. Weather-beaten and abandoned for years, it had a ghostly quality that seemed to speak to him the first time he laid eyes on it. The gingerbread trim and porch posts were in a sad state of disrepair and the old white paint with maroon trim had faded and chipped. Ben Tom relished the idea of lovingly dismantling it and restoring it to its former beauty. Check that—he intended to make it better than it had ever been.

Ben Tom was gregarious and loved his fellow man, but living in Riverby was like moving to another planet. He had to become another person, had to clean up the construction language that had become as natural as breathing to him. It felt good, cleansing, to reinvent himself. He placed his new rural neighbors and friends on a pedestal. Some deserved the pedestal; others did not.

Penny was painfully shy, so the couple seldom socialized together during their first years in Riverby, sparking much speculation about the young pair who had purchased the old home built by the town's founder. Ben Tom and Penny watched from their porch as curious passersby slowed to examine their progress on the house that had once seemed lost to history. There was little to see, because Ben Tom concentrated on refurbishing the inside while he dreamed of the showplace the outside would be.

When their children started to school, the couple was forced to interact with other parents, teachers, and school administrators. The neatly and expensively dressed Lawless children intensified curiosity about the family. Ben Tom loved doing things for his wife and children his father had never done for him. Yet, he didn't blame Purcell Lawless for his shortcomings as a father and husband. He had long ago determined Purcell and Irene had done the best they could with what they had. The forgiving nature he had earnestly cultivated on the road to forgiveness shaped all of Ben Tom's relationships.

He enjoyed interacting with the homespun folks he encountered, but was self-conscious and not comfortable discussing his past. Penny's shyness made her more than willing to let her husband assume virtually all of the social obligations that came with living in a small community. Ben Tom shouldered the mantle eagerly, almost appearing too anxious to please his new neighbors and to impress upon them the model family his little brood represented. Because of his jack-of-all-trades superb skills, he soon became the go-to man in Riverby, causing a new friend to warn, "Better be careful. Folks around here will stick a needle in your arm and start drawing blood till there ain't none left."

Ben Tom still had to spend many days in Dallas tending to his rental properties or supervising construction jobs before returning to Riverby to work on community projects. Volunteer work soon superseded the restoration of their historic home. But Ben Tom was not worried. He had limitless energy and was happier than he had ever been. Helping his neighbors and his community filled a hole that had long been empty.

But doing volunteer work does not pay material rewards, and Ben Tom soon found himself short of cash again. And his family was confined to only about a quarter of the living space in the old house while he renovated the rest. It was not unusual for Ben Tom to work all day on volunteer projects, then most of the night on his home. Penny soon became impatient with the cramped quarters and the sound of saws, drills and hammers in the middle of the night. But she really became frustrated and embarrassed when a check she had written to the grocery store bounced.

The call from Dallas could not have come at a better time. It was a call he wanted to answer. He had played a pivotal role working for one of the subcontractors who built the downtown high-rise known as the LTV Tower. He even had a nodding acquaintance with the big man himself, Jimmy Ling (the L in LTV), an internationally known titan of industry, and his second in command, Paul Thayer. Ling knew Ben Tom only for his craftsmanship but Thayer actually knew his name.

Ben Tom was thrilled when Ling requested the handsome young man with thick dark hair who had helped design and build his offices to work on a new conference room. Ling's private offices occupied the entire thirty-fourth floor. He also wanted the nameless young man whose work he had admired to make some modifications to the Lancers Club on the top floor. Ben Tom started leaving Riverby hours before daylight and returning well after dark. He was eager when he left and tired when he returned, but creating something he was proud of filled another void. Work on refurbishing his residence ground to a halt.

Ling was a daily visitor to both the conference room and the Lancers Club. The internationally known Merger King had a presence about him Ben Tom could sense when he came down the hall. Full of energy and self-confidence, Ling had a way of making everyone want to please him, and nobody wanted to please him more than Ben Tom. And he seemed to be succeeding. Ling learned his name and nodded his approval of his work with each visit.

But on Ben Tom's long awaited and eagerly anticipated final presentation day to Jimmy Ling of his finished product, Ling seemed distracted. He and Thayer were involved in deep conversation when he entered the conference room. As Ben Tom put the finishing flourishes on the bar inside the conference room, making sure no nails, screws or scratches were visible, he could not help but overhear their conversation.

Thayer was wide-eyed. "He just came in through the upstairs window when you were home?"

Ling's usual positive energy seemed to exert a negative aura as he shook his head. "Hell, no. Police say he walked right in the first floor hall, opened a window, then used that ornamental lamp we have on the wall outside to swing himself up to the second floor balcony."

"You're kidding. Where were you?"

"Had to be watching television a few feet from where he sneaked in. In and out in less than fifteen minutes, but he took about twenty grand in jewels with him. The wife says she feels like she's been raped. I do, too."

"Think it was the King of Diamonds again?"

"Who else would have the nerve to come in the front door and swing himself to the second floor? And they found those waffle type shoe prints that are his trademark."

"Guess it's no consolation, but he's hit about half the wealthy homes in your part of Dallas."

"And still not a clue about who he is."

The two men must have felt Ben Tom's stare boring into them. He was glad his Uncle Clark was still in jail. Or was he?

13

BEN TOM WAS FLUSH WITH MONEY AGAIN AFTER THE LING project. But cash had always burned a hole in his pocket and he was already thinking of ways to spend it, give it away, or invest it. Holding on to it seemed wasteful. He traveled with a guilty conscience for being so well off as he cruised the streets of his old haunts. He could not locate Purcell, so he drove to Trez's house and found Willy there. He was relieved he would not have to deal with Colleen in order to see Willy. His brothers had skipped work, were drinking beer, but not drunk. Both complained because Ben Tom had not called them in to work on the LTV job.

"You both know that was high-level finish work. I did almost all of what the big man wanted myself. He didn't want anybody else to do it."

Trez held up his middle and index fingers snug against each other. "Yeah, you and the big man just like that."

Ben Tom changed the subject. "Either one of you ever go out to see Uncle Clark at Seagoville?"

Willy's eyes flickered a little as he looked down. "Nope."

Trez shook his head. "I imagine Mama visits him." Trez snapped his fingers. "Ain't it time for him to be out? How long did he get?"

Willy shook his head. "Ain't been five years, has it?"

Trez stood, excited all at once. "You know, it may have been that long."

Ben Tom shook his head. "I think he was supposed to be eligible for parole in two." The thought made Ben Tom feel anxious to get on the road. He saw his father occasionally on construction sites, but had not visited his mother in several months. By way of an apology not due, he gave his brothers two hundred-dollar bills each and headed toward Seagoville to see Irene and, if he was unlucky, Buck.

Irene was thrilled to see her eldest and favorite son. Buck was not expected until after dark, so she took her time quizzing him thoroughly about his life in Riverby and about her grandchildren until Ben Tom finally got around to the question. "You ever go by to see Uncle Clark in prison?"

Irene put her fingers over her mouth. "Sure did, almost every month."

"I got to counting up. He should already be out."

Irene nodded. "He got some extra time tacked on."

"What for?"

"Something about peddling stuff from the inside to the outside or vice-versa. You know how Clark has always got to have some business working. And I heard something about a fight."

"So when does he get out now?"

"I went by there last week to arrange to pick him up when he was due to be released. They told me he had been moved to another prison. I can't believe he would just let them move him and not tell us. He'll get a piece of my mind when he shows up."

The possibility Clark was on the street again sent Willy into a tailspin. He headed for Terrell at speeds faster than the law allowed. He had not checked on the trailer house loot in almost a year. Little beads of sweat broke out on his forehead when he arrived at the site where the trailer had been parked. Nothing but burned metal, blackened commode and sink, and ashes greeted him. Willy stumbled through the debris until he found where he thought the trap door had been. He used a charred two-by-four to push away the rubble until he found it. But the plywood door was gone and the hole, if it was a hole anymore, was filled with wreckage. He dug as far as he could until he cut both hands and was covered in soot. Nothing. Clark, if he was out, was probably going to kill him. But at least any evidence of his theft of one little cowboy sculpture had been destroyed. His hands shook on the steering wheel all the way home.

Willy was up at dawn after not sleeping all night, his greed stronger than the fear he had felt the night before. He hadn't looked hard enough with the right tools. He gathered the tools needed and headed back to the trailer house to see if his nighttime thoughts had been right. It took him most of the day because he had to stop each time a car slowed and curious drivers peered at the wreckage. He finally uncovered the box, charred and scratched, but not destroyed. The small sculptures inside seemed to look at him smugly from their cozy, safe positions.

Willy chuckled as he cradled one in his hands. He silently congratulated himself for coming prepared with clean pillow cases, rags, cardboard boxes to hold packing peanuts, and Styrofoam coolers to hold some of the loot. It was past midnight when he put the last cooler in the trunk. The back seat was also full.

He returned to the crypt for what he hoped would be one final treasure. The door in the floor of the box opened easily and he withdrew the little velour sack, squeezed it slightly to make sure it still held jewelry, opened two buttons on his shirt and slipped it next to his belly.

Willy sat behind the wheel of his car, breathing in the exhilaration that had been building since he salvaged the first sculpture. He was surrounded by riches, more than many men accumulated in a lifetime. Heck, the little bag snug against his belly was probably worth more than most men would ever see. Sure, it belonged to his uncle, but he owned it now. Technically, of course, it belonged to the people Clark had stolen it from. But hadn't he rescued it from a fiery grave? Who was to say it had not melted? He cranked the engine to head home, then thought better of it. He retrieved his shovel and tools from the trunk and laid them beside the open wound in the earth, found a yellowed catalogue and newspaper from the long abandoned outhouse in the backyard. He gathered kindling and pieces of lumber that had survived the fire and filled the storage box. He stood back from the underground vault and threw his shoulders back. Standing tall in the moonlight, Willy imagined himself a powerful creature of the night, a vampire with a flowing black cape. He felt as if he could fly as the cool air embraced him.

He knelt, spun the steel roller of his Zippo with his thumb, and set the paper on fire. The sudden burst of light when the kindling blazed up made him feel vulnerable as the firelight highlighted him. He squeezed as much lighter fluid as possible from his lighter to hasten the burn and to make sure the box was completely destroyed, then trotted to the car. Willy drove back feeling like king of the road. But his feeling of wealth lasted only until he stopped in front of his home. Colleen and his daughter and son slept safely inside the small shack Willy had great plans for when he bought it. He had thought of Kleberg and Seagoville as high class suburbs of Dallas, the dividing line between urban crime and rural tranquility.

But he soon accepted both small towns still had crime-ridden neighborhoods and the house he bought because he liked the big lot sat in the middle of one of the worst. Dwarfed by the giant oaks and pines that had attracted him, his unpainted small house looked like a neglected weekend cabin, a piece of trash offending the regal oaks. The entire lot was covered in a lush layer of pine needles, pine cones, acorns, oak leaves…and trash. And he had discovered the rural-like area also attracted people who wanted to be ignored by the law. He learned his neighbor across the street was a coyote who illegally transported aliens from Mexico into the country for a fee. And the illegals seemed reluctant to go out into the world. His own lot became a picking-up-and-dropping-off location for the coyote who smuggled them in. His neighbor even had a bold sign in his yard proclaiming his stock in trade—Rent-A-Mexican.

Mexicans loitered under the shade of his old trees day and night. Willy's anger grew into hatred for them. More than once, he had fired a shotgun at their feet and over their heads. But each new batch of illegals had to be retrained not to set foot on his private property, causing Willy's head to feel as if it were about to explode.

A group was there when he pulled up with his car full of treasure. He had intended to stash his loot close to home where he could watch it day and night, but the Mexicans' presence made him realize he could not unload the cache into the storage building and shop on the back of his property. He couldn't even bury it, so he drove to the only other place he could think of.

Willy sat by the shore of White Rock Lake close enough to watch Trez's house without being seen. There were no lights on he could see, but that did not mean Trez was not there. He tried to plot a strategy that would not come as he watched for signs that would tell him whether Trez was home.

His car was not there, so Willy knocked loudly on the door. Trez did not answer, but he still could not be sure. Trez had a habit of ignoring his doorbell or loud knocks, especially when he had a woman upstairs or suspected the doorknocker might be a bill collector. Willy pushed open the dog door Trez had cut for the pit-bull puppy that had lasted a few weeks before a car ended his short life.

Trez was known to go out drinking with friends and regularly leave his keys locked inside the house, so he had installed a magnet inside the dog door for a magnetic key holder. Willy found it easily, opened the door and walked quietly inside. He shouted Trez's name. No answer. He walked up the stairs and into both bedrooms before being satisfied Trez was not home.

He backed his car up the steep driveway and stopped in front of the antique garage. The garage door was barely wide enough to accommodate today's cars, so Willy knew Trez had never used it. He found the key to the side door at the back on a nail beside the door. But it wasn't needed. There was nothing but junk in the garage, so Trez never locked it. He had even joked he wished someone would steal everything in it.

The stacks of boxes filled with used clothing and appliances that no longer worked were exactly what Willy needed. He could hide his boxes of treasure in plain sight with the other boxes. He stashed some in a refrigerator and more in an old washing machine. Neither Trez nor any visitor would even notice the added boxes of junk. He would, however, have to lock the door and take the key. He kept the jewels next to his belly. He could not bear to part with them. He drove two blocks in the dark before hitting his car lights.

Willy stopped his car and watched a Mexican urinate on one of his majestic oaks and others meander around his lot as if they owned it. He walked to his pickup, pulled his .410 from the gun rack, and fired a warning shot. They scattered, flinging Spanish curses in his direction. Colleen was on him like a hawk on a field mouse when he walked in the door. Both kids were screaming their lungs out before she finally stopped her tirade. Willy usually fought back with more vigor than Colleen could muster, but he sat quietly, fingering the sack against his belly while she screamed. When she and the kids finally went to bed, he started his second poem.

> With my eyes still burning from the fire and smoke
> With my wife screaming till her I could choke
> How loving a woman could be such a curse
> And having two children making things worse

Willy stashed his sack of jewels in a pair of boots he never wore, turned out the lights, and went to bed.

14

WHEN THEIR CHILDREN WERE OLD ENOUGH TO PARTICIPATE IN sports, Ben Tom happily agreed to coach their teams in sports he had never played. He even paid for uniforms for the whole team and equipment for the children who could not afford it. Even though Ben Tom was deeply involved in work for the small town he called home, he still felt like a stranger. The couple's social involvement was limited and much of his volunteer work was done after hours and often alone. He spent most workdays in Dallas, trying to meet the increasing demands on his cash flow caused by his almost nonstop acquisition of real estate and old things of all types.

Ben Tom's cash flow problems seemed to be solved when he met Mark Conley, president of Main Street Bank. Mark solicited his business, offered a line of credit that allowed Ben Tom to buy and sell real estate with abandon. Mark's bank financed Ben Tom's acquisition of more than half of the buildings around the square. Most of his purchases were vacant and badly in need of repair, but repairs were no obstacle to a man with Ben Tom's talents. And Ben Tom knew value when he saw it. Used to Dallas prices, all real estate in and around Riverby seemed dirt cheap to him. And the downtown buildings provided a perfect place for storage of his most valuable possessions, including his '55 Ford Victoria.

But the board of directors of Main Street Bank was a little more cautious than Mark Conley. When the first note came due, Mark called Ben Tom in for a chat. "It's not me, you understand, Ben, but one of my board members is asking for a little more documentation before we renew this first loan."

Ben Tom shifted in his chair. Used to borrowing from credit agencies or loan sharks in the past, he was still not comfortable in a real bank president's office. "What kinda documentation?"

"We usually get balance sheets, income statements, tax returns, that sort of thing."

"Always before, I got money based on a real estate appraisal. Figured you were loaning the same way. You and I both know I'm buying this stuff for pennies on the dollar. It's already worth a lot more than I paid for it."

Mark held up both hands. "Hey, I agree. My opinion, we got more than enough collateral." He laughed heartily. "Hell, I sorta want to foreclose. Bank would make a lot of money." Mark leaned back and locked his fingers behind his head. "It's just that a line of credit is different. We've more or less agreed to loan you money to use pretty fast and loose. Not necessarily tied to real estate. A line of credit is usually for working capital, so that's how the paperwork is filled out."

Ben Tom's nervous laughter showed how helpless he felt. The pause that followed made them both uncomfortable. Ben Tom wanted nothing more than to please his new friend. "Well, guess it's like you said; if the board wants more information, then I'll try to provide it. But it's all new to me. Never done any real financial statements before."

"Don't you do stuff like that when you do your taxes?"

"I got this really sharp ex-IRS agent who does my taxes. I take in a big box full of checks and receipts every year and he sorts it all out."

"Where's he live?"

"Office is out by Fair Park in Dallas."

Mark opened a drawer and withdrew a set of forms. "You think he can help you out with these?"

Ben Tom stood and took the forms. 'I'll run it by him next time I'm in Dallas. How soon you need 'em back?"

"See, that's the thing. Your note will be due in less than a week. I can extend it a few days, but we need the paperwork as soon as possible." The concern on Mark's face worried Ben Tom.

The expression on Ben Tom's face drew sympathy from Mark. "Tell you what, there's a fairly new fellow right here on the square not more than fifty yards from where we sit right now. You know Tee Jessup?"

Ben Tom had seen the CPA's sign, but was embarrassed to admit he did not know him. "Don't guess I do."

"Got his CPA and everything. The last building you bought is two doors down from his office."

Ben Tom held the forms like they were a nest of poisonous snakes as he walked across the street. He was surprised when the old woman who served as a receptionist ushered him in to see Tee Jessup unannounced. The CPA sat behind an old oak desk Ben Tom admired. He was conversing with a very tall, thin, cowboy in a big hat and jeans tucked into boots with tall, red tops.

When Tee Jessup came around the desk to shake his hand, Ben Tom was surprised and pleased to see he was also dressed like a cowboy, though not as flashy as his tall visitor. Tee Jessup looked to be about his own age, maybe a few years older. "Tee Jessup."

Ben Tom shook his hand. "Ben Tom Lawless."

Tee nodded toward the black hat. "Meet Joe Henry Leathers, my next door neighbor and landlord."

Joe Henry towered over both of them as he stood and shook Ben Tom's hand. "You're the fella who's bought up most of downtown. Been hearing about you."

Ben Tom was both pleased and wary he already had a reputation. He wondered why he had not met these two men before. "Surprised I haven't run into you two before now. Mark Conley over at the bank sent me. Seems I got to fill out some forms."

Tee returned to his desk as Joe Henry tipped his hat to Tee. "Be seeing you." He turned toward Ben Tom. "I'm outta here. It's painful to watch this bean counter swing into action."

Ben Tom jerked his thumb at the departing Joe Henry. "What's he do, run a ranch around here?"

Tee glanced at the forms. "He's a lawyer, believe it or not. That's his office next door."

Sudden recognition showed on Ben Tom's face. "That the one with the chairs made out of cow horns and hide? Thought it was a ranch office or something."

"It is, among other things."

"Never seen a cowboy lawyer."

"Joe Henry is as good as they come at cowboying and lawyering."

Nervous, Ben Tom examined his surroundings as Tee Jessup shuffled through the forms. The sound of paper crinkling was interrupted with a sort of beeping noise, sounds of static, and intermittent, muted, human voices. His eyes traveled up the walls to the ceilings, quickly measuring eighteen feet. They were covered with tin squares stamped with an ornate design he did not recognize, and he knew almost every tin ceiling design. The tin tiles' white paint was losing the battle to time and rust and some squares had turned loose, revealing pine beams in various stages of rot from leaks. Ben Tom lusted to bring in scaffolding and repair the tin and the beams.

The perimeter walls were made with bricks so old they were beginning to crumble and drop particles on the floor. Ben Tom could see the remnants of sheet rock and silently approved that the rock had been mostly removed. The inside walls had been covered with cheap plywood. He could barely resist the urge to go over and run his hands along the walls in preparation for restoration.

He jerked when a noise came from the back of the room and a waft of strong ladies' cologne mixed with something pungent and sour drifted in like a stray cat. An attractive woman with big hair seemed to bounce into a side hall at the back of the office.

"Hello, Tee honey."

Tee waved without looking back. "Hello, Verda." He saw the look of confusion on Ben Tom's face. "That's Verda Lemon. She runs the beauty shop in the back of this building."

Ben Tom's expression begged for more information. "Pleased to meet you." Verda stepped into the ladies' room.

"Beauty shop is called The Four Forces. You've probably seen the sign. Entrance is on Texas Street. We share a restroom, unfortunately."

"What's that beeping sound and static?"

"She's got a police scanner. Keeps her up on what's going on around here."

The interruption brought back Ben Tom's sense of uneasiness, even embarrassment. "You take the sheetrock off these brick walls?" He longed to return to turf he understood.

"Had a client help me with it. I hope I can redo the whole office after tax season next year."

"Mark said you were new to town. How long?"

Tee chuckled. "I think I'll still be new when I'm an old man. I've been here about three years."

Tee bounced the papers back together. He looked down beside the chair Ben Tom occupied and saw what he expected to see—nothing. He was getting used to folks coming in with blank forms and no data to fill them out. "I can fill these out, but I'm gonna need something to work with, less you got a damn good memory. Have you ever done financial statements or loan applications before?"

"Done plenty of mortgage applications, but they was mostly about the property I was buying. No financial statements like this. What do I need to get for you?"

"We could start with the last three years of tax returns."

"I can have them up here in about an hour. Just have to go home and dig 'em out."

"I have to pick my boy up at school, but I'll probably beat you back."

Ben Tom returned in an hour with three years of tax returns along with three years of assorted checks, receipts, and bank statements.

Tee used to inwardly groan when he saw this much paperwork to muddle through, but he was getting used to it. And he was getting better at going through it, making sense of a mess. He picked up the most recent tax return and peered over it. After three years and about five hundred returns, he could read one like a novel. He stopped on Schedule E. "Hmmm. You only got one piece of rent property? Did you buy all these buildings on the square this year?"

Ben Tom shook his head. "One? Heck, no. I got about twenty pieces of rent property."

Tee turned the return around so Ben Tom could read it and put his finger on the penciled-in line that said simply "buildings." Ben Tom looked at the number in the first column. "Oh, yeah. That must be the total of all my real estate. I sure don't own one that cost so much."

Tee shook his head. "We're gonna need a list of what makes up that number. Each piece of property is supposed to be listed separately."

"Wonder why my guy didn't do that?"

"I wonder, too, but I've seen just about everything in the last three years of tax seasons. Did you ever have to report any sales of property?"

"Year before last. I sold some rent property in Dallas. Didn't want to, but I had to."

"So how did your tax guy figure out how much it cost, what the accumulated depreciation was, and what the gain was?"

Ben Tom was perplexed. "Beats me. So you need a list of everything I own?"

"Yep. And I need to know when you bought it, what you paid, and a short description and address for each holding. I notice rental income is all in one number, too. I'll need the rental income for each property. We'll also need to know what you owe on each and who you owe it to."

Ben Tom stood. "All that just to renew a note."

Tee stood and extended his hand. "That will get us started. Look at the bright side. It will make doing your taxes a lot easier next year. And, if and when you sell a piece of property, we can quickly know the gain or loss for your tax return."

Ben Tom stood and shook the hand. He liked this guy. "I won't be selling any property. But I will get the list back to you quick." Tee was impressed, but doubtful. He figured he had just assigned an almost insurmountable task to Ben Tom.

Tee was wrong. Ben Tom was back in two days with the detailed list of his real estate holdings. Coming up with a list of his collectibles and junk, however would have to wait. Ben Tom estimated the value of all his holdings. Tee knew if he could come up with sales and an ending inventory by the time the next tax return was due, he could get by without a detailed list for a while. Ben Tom made several more trips back and forth to his buildings and to his home. At the end of the week, Tee had enough to do financial statements. He had learned not to expect perfection. Mark, the banker, came over and offered to buy Tee a beer after Ben Tom delivered the documents.

15

AS THE NUMBER OF WHAT HAD BECOME KNOWN AS SEE-THROUGH
buildings grew to glut proportions in the Metroplex, Ben Tom's construction
work there ground to a halt. He was almost relieved because he now considered himself as making a living in Riverby through buying and selling collectibles, old cars and real estate. He chose to ignore that the Dallas construction
business had always provided the bulk of the funds to finance his acquisitions.

Ben Tom's optimism for his own future did not rub off on his father
and brothers. He stood in the middle of a desolate downtown street in
what had once been Mesa, Texas, about twenty miles from Riverby, when
a dented and scraped Chevy Luv pickup stopped in the desolate street. Ben
Tom heard George Jones crooning through the open windows before the
driver killed the engine. The door creaked when Purcell Lawless opened
it and faced his son. The wind was blowing hard out of the southeast and
a tumbleweed almost as big as the little pickup stopped against the back
bumper as if it were announcing a change in Ben Tom's life.

Ben Tom already knew what this meant. He smiled. "Pop."

"Son."

"How did you find me way out here?"

"Wasn't hard. I just asked for directions to buildings ready to fall down
that were full of old junk." Purcell lit a cigarette and nodded toward an
abandoned building. "You already fill these up with crap?"

"You're one to talk." Ben Tom knew his father was almost as addicted
to junk as he was, and his quality of junk was much lower. "What are you
doing here?"

"Penny told me where you might be. I'm just looking around. Ain't no jobs in Dallas, figured I would kill some time around here a few days. I hear you got more work than you can possibly ever do."

Ben pointed to the building Purcell had alluded to. "Take a look inside that old building you scoffed at."

"What did it used to be?"

Ben Tom pointed at words engraved in stone under the roof—*Merchants and Planters State Bank.*

Purcell pushed open the massive door and walked in ahead of his son. Signs of a long ago fire not evident from the outside showed inside. The roof had partially caved in and bent bars from a teller cage lay on the floor along with the leavings and dens of raccoons. "Suppose you paid good money for this wreck."

Ben Tom pointed to a massive iron door leaned against one outside wall. The iron handle shaped like a ship wheel identified it as the door to a vault. "That thing alone is worth more than I paid for the whole building."

Purcell smirked. "If it ain't old, heavy or worn out, you wouldn't own it. My back still kills me from helping you haul all the heavy junk you bought over the years."

Ben Tom was wary of his father's arrival, but secretly relieved. Purcell was the only person he could trust to do work almost as well as he could do it himself. And if he didn't do it right, Ben Tom could make him do it over. Their roles had reversed years earlier. He had worried Purcell might be broke and he looked as if he was.

Within a week, Purcell and Ben Tom had dragged up an old used trailer house and parked it at the end of the main drag in deserted Mesa. Purcell became the only resident of the ghost town. Mayor by acclamation, he said. But he had been right about buildings full of junk. Six buildings with roofs were left in Mesa, and Ben Tom owned five of them and one without a roof. The missing-roof building had been part of a package deal. Although he worried his father would open up old wounds, maybe tell his new friends in Riverby about the lifestyle he had left behind in Dallas, taking care of Purcell filled another hole gnawing at Ben Tom since he left his family behind in Dallas. He had an itch to nurture others and he wanted it scratched. Besides, Purcell's needs were minimal and his skills were good and sorely needed.

Purcell was second only to Penny when it came to influencing the hard-wired brain of Ben Tom Lawless. Penny's wish was his command, but Purcell could sometimes curse, argue, and shame him away from foolish decisions and spur him to make good ones. Within a year, over Ben Tom's illogical objections, Purcell had readied two buildings and rented them. But each time a building was emptied, remodeled and rented, Ben Tom had to purchase another to hold the junk the rented one had held. His purchases now included property in most small towns within a fifty mile radius of Riverby. Main Street Bank's portfolio of Lawless real estate loans was growing.

Ben Tom had also become a recognized community leader in Riverby. He helped to revitalize the small downtown square, helped in renovating historic buildings that belonged to the city or other people while his own buildings sat vacant. He even led the team that removed and restored historic brick streets. He was named Citizen of the Year at the Chamber of Commerce banquet. Appointed to fill the unexpired term of a city council member who died, Ben Tom was urged to run for a permanent position on the council. But attending the meetings and poring over documents was not for him. Such things reminded him of his days of struggle in schools. He elected not to subject himself to possible ridicule and did not run in the next election.

Though he was gradually building a small empire of real estate holdings, antiques and collectibles, cash was almost always short. Only the joint efforts of his new friend and accountant Tee Jessup and banker Mark Conley kept him out of serious trouble. Jessup kept the bank happy with financial data, and Conley kept loaning money.

Ben Tom continued to keep almost everything he acquired, selling only when forced to meet a payment he did not have cash for. But he grieved over the departure of any of his holdings like the death of a close relative.

The '55 Ford he built from scratch now kept company with ten more antique autos, construction surplus materials, even scraps of lumber in his growing number of houses and buildings. When the buildings were all filled, he stored his less valuable treasures outside and left them to the elements rather than sell them. The constant shortage and lack of everything in his youth drove him to accumulate more and more. The only wealth he recognized was something he could touch, feel and visualize using some vague date in the future in some obscure dreamscape. The only meaning cash had for him was to invest in more tangible assets he could admire, hold, renovate and restore.

Ben Tom had a dream. That dream included living in the restored-to-its-former-dignity house on the hill. In his dream, the surrounding acreage was filled with houses for each of his children and grandchildren, and now, his father and brothers. He was well on his way to achieving his dream of such a family empire when the local real estate market and housing mimicked the collapse of commercial real estate in Dallas. But Ben Tom paid little attention to the swings of markets and accelerated his acquisition of rental properties as prices began to nosedive. When his real estate suffered a higher and higher vacancy rate, he framed it as a blessing that provided more storage for antiques. But dwindling rental income punished his cash flow, forcing him to borrow more from a banker more than eager to lend to such a talented entrepreneur and community leader.

16

TREZ STOPPED THE ALMOST NEW '85 BUICK RIVIERA MAROON convertible on his sloping driveway, leaned back and breathed in the night air. He could scarcely make out the stars due to city lights, but he liked to pretend he could. He could see the full moon. It was a perfect fall night for driving around in a convertible or sitting in one in your driveway. He was sober for a change and could not believe he felt as good as he did. He attributed it to the night air and the convertible and wondered why he had not bought himself one before. It had been easy as pie to come into this fine car.

A buddy had owned the car and could not make the payments. Trez's credit was a little shaky, so he took his buddy's payment book and the duplicate title showing GMAC as the lien holder and began making payments. As soon as he paid it off, it would be his. GMAC would never realize they had loaned money to a man with a poor credit history.

Sleepily, he thought of his brothers—Ben Tom with his two kids, working night and day to keep his head above water and to please his wife and a whole community of rednecks. And Willy, almost destitute from trying to support two wild kids who seemed destined for prison and a wife who was a sure bet for the nuthouse. Not to mention the high crime area where Willy and his family lived and the wetbacks who populated his yard. And then there was him, Trez, sitting pretty in the driveway of his middle class home in an almost new convertible without a care in the world. He had a stash of weed in his pantry and plenty of beer in the fridge. Where had his brothers gone wrong?

He had enjoyed the car a week before it rained. Of course, downpour would be a more accurate description of the five inches of rain that fell in two hours. Trez slept peacefully through it. The next morning, he opened the door to the convertible and water spilled out, ran down the driveway and into the street. Trez stood, hands on hips, watching the water run. It looked like enough to fill a small swimming pool. The upholstery and carpet, of course, were soaked and permanently damaged. Trez could handle a little fading, but he sniffed the seat to see if mildew had already set in. The sky was still cloudy and the air moist. He could have raised the top, but what was the point of having a convertible if you kept the rag top up? And it looked so cool sitting in the driveway, like the weather gods would never defy Trez Lawless or his Riviera. And his buddy had told him the top sometimes malfunctioned. He had not wanted to find out how bad the problem was.

Now, the exposed and soaked Buick didn't seem so cool. He looked at the antique garage he had never used. Using it seemed better than putting up the top. A tape measure confirmed the convertible could squeeze inside. There would be no room to open any door, but he could easily climb over the seat and trunk to exit. Another practical benefit of owning a convertible. He opened all the doors to the car, left it in the driveway to dry out, found the key to the old garage and opened the side door. He pushed aside and climbed over junk to reach the big front doors. They creaked and protested, but he finally dragged them back.

An hour later, he had two piles of junk on the sidewalk and a "free" sign painted. Someone had already picked up the old washing machine he had pushed down the driveway and several boxes of used clothing and linens. As he pulled an old dryer out of its cobwebbed hole, he felt something move inside. He opened it and found a bronze sculpture, one of the treasures Willy had hidden there without telling him. He ran to the driveway and rummaged through the boxes that had not been picked up. Nothing but old clothes. He looked down the street and wondered what might have been in the washing machine that had already left. His hands shook as he gradually found the rest of Willy's stash.

It was mid-afternoon as he stepped out of the convertible, his pants and shirt wet from the soaked seats. He shivered a little from the cool, wet ride as he waded through the Mexicans still puddled outside Willy's house. Colleen answered the knock on Willy's door.

"What do you want?" She put a little emphasis on *you* to let Trez know he was not welcome. Colleen had been listening more than once when Trez had brought up the issue of her sanity to Willy.

Trez detested dealing with his sister-in-law, thought she belonged in a mental institution. "Willy here?"

The words were barely out before Willy lightly shoved Colleen aside and looked at his brother though the screen door.

Trez pointed his thumb in the general direction of the Mexicans peering into his convertible. "We need to talk."

Willy grimaced when he looked at the people who continuously populated his lot without his permission. "Let me run them wetbacks off and we can drag up some chairs and talk out here."

He started for his pickup and the shotgun he kept in the gun rack.

Trez held up both hands. "Don't stir 'em up. They likely to take it out on my car. Where can we get a beer around here?"

Willy noted the trembling in his brother's hands. "There's a little joint called Fat Boy's a few blocks over. Cold beer and barbecue."

Trez refused to leave his convertible there, sure his treasure would be halfway to Mexico before he returned. So they sat on wet seats for the ten minutes it took to get to the bar. They stepped out in the parking lot, their backs and seats soaked.

Fat Boy's, like Willy's house, was a small unpainted shack that bordered Highway 175, a main thoroughfare. It was dark and smoky from cigarettes and the cooking pit. All six tables were occupied, so Willy and Trez sat on a long plank bench that bellied up to a splintered pine bar. Neither had an appetite, so they ordered beers Trez paid for.

Trez downed two before his hands stopped trembling. Willy was losing his patience. "What the hell's wrong with you?"

"When we lived with Uncle Clark, I used to sneak into his room when nobody was there and take a look at what he stole the night before. Most of the time, it was just boring stuff I wondered why he had bothered to take. But a couple of times, I saw some really shiny shit that impressed me."

Willy took a deep breath. "Okay, so you saw some really shiny stuff. You were a little kid with less of a brain than a newborn piss ant. What of it?"

JIM H. AINSWORTH

"Bullshit. I may not have understood art work that looked like it was made out of gold, but some of the jewelry I saw had to be expensive."

Willy signaled for another beer. "So what? Where's this going? I got better things to do than to listen to your baby memories."

Trez turned to face his brother. "Well, okay smartass, I found some of that stuff in my garage today."

Willy should have been prepared with an explanation for the treasure Trez found in his garage, but he wasn't. He never expected Trez to open the old door. It looked too much like work, something Trez studiously avoided. "How can you be sure it's the same stuff?"

"Can't be sure about all of it, but I'm damn certain about a few pieces."

"You find any jewelry or diamonds?"

"No, but a hell of a lot of bronzes. I ain't no art expert, but they look like high dollar stuff. Good enough to be museum pieces. You ever hear of Russell or Remington?"

"How you figure the stuff got there? Maybe the guy you bought the house from was a thief."

"Hell, no. The house had been foreclosed. You think he wouldn't have sold some of it to save his house or at least take the loot with him?"

"Maybe he died or went to prison."

"Nope. Neighbor said he still visits him."

"Well, there you go. He drops by the neighbor's to keep an eye on his loot. Neighbor probably watches your garage night and day. You ought to charge the bastard storage."

Trez leaned back and looked into his brother's eyes. "You seem pretty desperate to explain this away. You don't believe I know this is Clark's stuff, but I do."

Willy felt exposed, as if nothing he owned was safe and all his secrets had been revealed without his permission. He thought of the sack full of jewelry and chided himself for carelessly leaving it in the closet he shared with Colleen inside an old boot for weeks with nothing but old socks to conceal it. But he congratulated himself for finally moving the sack full of jewels, boots and all, to his workshop last week.

He had tried to imagine where Clark would hide it, and then pried up two boards in the shop floor. The jewels seemed safe under the floor, but there was still the matter of the wetbacks growing each day in numbers

98

and boldness. He had hidden it at night, but had one been hiding in his shop or had one watched him go in with the boots filled with diamonds and come out without them?

He had found a Mexican sleeping in his shop a few months back and never knew how he got in. Willy managed to break a rib or two with an axe handle before the Mexican could get out and run.

Trez was still staring. "Are you hearing me? Looks like your brain is a thousand miles away." He leaned forward and poked a finger in Willy's chest. "I'll tell you one damn thing. I ain't going to prison for stealing stuff I didn't even know I had. I've got a good mind to find me a fence and invite him over to bid on the whole damn thing."

Willy slammed his beer bottle on the counter. "Don't even think about it. Clark said..."

"Clark said what? You know about this shit in my garage, don't you? I can tell by looking you know something you're not telling."

Trez felt and saw the air leaving Willy like a deflating balloon. "Maybe I ought to call the police and tell 'em the truth."

The bar and the benches bellied up to it were in the shape of a U. Trying not to meet his brother's stare, Willy's gaze traveled its length, trying to fake intense focus on the other patrons who had arrived since he and Trez had started drinking. His eyes stopped and widened as he made the turn of the U.

He didn't believe his eyes at first. Must be a dream, no, a nightmare. It could not be him. But it was. Clark's face was expressionless as he picked up his can of Schlitz and started toward his nephews.

17

CLARK SET HIS CAN OF SCHLITZ BETWEEN WILLY'S LONE STAR and Trez's Budweiser. They had to move down a little as he sat between them. "Boys. Fancy meeting you here."

Trez gaped at his uncle, speechless. Willy stared at Trez, feeling he had been set up. Clark took a swig of his beer. "Ain't you boys glad to see your old uncle a free man?"

Willy stayed frozen; Trez nodded. "How long you been out?"

Clark ignored Trez and focused his attention on Willy. "I gave you a little easy job to do before I left. You take care of it?"

Fear mixed with anger and resentment until Willy could feel his heart throbbing in his eyeballs. His old desire to stab his uncle rekindled. "I expect you already know there was a fire. What could I do about that?"

"I know about the fire. I had somebody set it. The fellow who was making the payments on that trailer house for me got sent to the big house and I didn't know it. Left my money with his wife and she run off with it when he went to prison."

"Why didn't you let me know? You coulda got me the money and I would have made the payments."

Clark stared at Willy as if he were trying to determine if anything worked behind his eyes. "Loan company was about to re-pop the trailer house and a fire was the only way to keep a bunch of goons from messing around in there."

Willy's shock showed. "You mean you burned the whole thing just to keep 'em from dragging it away? Hell, they probably wouldn't ever have seen your loot."

Clark could not believe he was related to such a simpleton. "They would have to go beneath the trailer to unhook the utilities before they drug it off, dumbass."

Willy looked warily at his intensely curious brother before replying to his uncle. "So, you burned the shit up on purpose?"

Clark shook his head as disgust clouded his features. "Fire was not likely to ever reach my stuff. Did you forget it was underground, way underground?"

Trez inched forward to hear better as Willy nervously replied. He had to be careful. "So it's still there?"

Clark drained his Schlitz and tapped the can on the bar to call for another. He looked into Willy's eyes with a cold stare until it arrived.

The silence that followed made Willy more nervous. "Look, Clark, I got two kids now and a wife that's a little off. I couldn't afford the gas to run out there every whipstitch to check on things. Besides, I was locked up a year myself."

"So you didn't know about the fire?"

"How would I know? Maybe the firebug took your stuff."

"I couldn't trust the firebug, so I didn't tell him."

"Don't mean he didn't find it."

Trez was out of patience and he was starting to get the picture. "Mind telling me what stuff you're talking about?"

Clark turned to Trez. "You let go a washing machine today by any chance?"

Trez looked at Willy, then turned to Clark. "What's going on? How do you know about that washing machine? Look, Clark, I ain't no kid anymore. You can't just drop back in here and act like ain't nothing changed. Can't speak for Willy, but I don't answer to you anymore."

Clark stood and downed the other beer. "You little bastards got no idea what kinda tiger you got by the tail. If my neck wasn't in the noose with you, I'd let you stew in your own juice."

He looked around the bar and nodded at a few familiar faces. Willy wondered how he knew anyone there. This was not his part of Dallas. Or was it?

Trez stood and faced his uncle, now tall enough to stand eye to eye. "How about you tell us about this tiger."

Clark swept the room again. "Can't do it here. I can tell from your wet asses and backs you two dumbasses came in the pimp car. Willy, you ride with me and Trez, you follow."

Willy reluctantly sat in the black Chevrolet Impala and stared straight ahead as Clark pulled away. Clark headed south and let Willy sweat for ten minutes before he spoke. "You want to tell me what happened or do you want me to tell you?"

"Tell you about what?"

Clark drummed his fingers on the steering wheel. "Look, I know you carried off the stuff and I know you burned the box to cover your tracks. I know you hid it in Trez's garage. What you don't know is that your life, your kids' lives and your idiot wife's life are in danger."

Willy squirmed. "I was just holding your loot for you. Couldn't very well leave it out there in the middle of a burned trailer carcass."

"Yeah, I know you were only looking out for my best interests. That what you were doing when you hocked the one piece?"

Willy wondered if his uncle knew every pawn shop and fence in Dallas. "Look, I was about to get my legs broke by a loan shark. I was gonna replace it with my part of this house me and Ben Tom built. Then that deal blew up."

"You really had a lot of hard luck since I went off on my little vacation, ain't you?"

Willy felt his face grow warm. He had to tolerate this as a kid, but didn't have to anymore. "So what's this bullshit about our lives being in danger?"

They pulled into Trez's driveway and Trez pulled in behind them. Clark put it in park and opened the door. "Might as well let Trez hear this story, too, since you got him involved in it."

They pulled the tabs on three more beers and each lit a cigarette inside Trez's living room. Clark looked around the room. "Nice place you got here. How you gonna feel when somebody burns it down around your ears?"

The beers gave Trez courage to face his uncle. "What the hell you talking about?"

"You two little bastards got no idea who you're fooling with. Your death sentences and mine are out there in that garage."

Willy stood. "If this is some kinda game you're playing, get to it. Spit it out."

Clark pointed a long slender, manicured finger at him. "I told you this stuff was extra hot when I showed it to you, didn't I? Told you to do exactly like I said or both of us could get killed."

He walked to the window next to the driveway, pulled back the see-through frilled curtain, and pointed at the garage. "That stuff out there don't belong to me."

Trez chuckled under his breath. "No shit. You stole it."

"I didn't get it from a rich man's house or a museum. I took it from the thief who stole it himself—a well-connected thief."

Willy's skin was starting to feel prickly. "What's that mean, well-connected?"

"The less you know, the better, but let's just say he was hired to steal this stuff by the Dixie Mafia out of Tennessee and Kentucky. You know, the guys who kill folks and peddle drugs and other nasty things around the southern states."

"So why in hell did you take it from him?"

"He made it so easy I couldn't resist. I stole from thieves all the time. Who they gonna report it to? Easiest money there is. But I didn't know this guy was connected until another convict in the joint with me put a shiv to my throat and tried to get me to tell him where the goods were."

Trez stood and looked at the garage that now seemed like a deathtrap. "So did you tell him?"

"Hell, no. I took the shiv away from him and shoved it in the soft part of his leg. I turned it a little till he convinced me he didn't know exactly where his orders came from."

Clark dropped his cigarette in the beer can. "He did tell me the bad boys from Kentucky would take out my wife and kids to find out where the goods are." He smiled slightly as he looked at both his nephews. "Good thing I never married."

Willy boiled inside. "Hell's bells, they were probably waiting for you the minute you stepped out of prison. They're probably out there on the street right now. You done killed us all."

"Calm down. That's why I was locked up a little longer. I told the warden what happened. He moved me to a max security prison and then kept my release date a secret. Besides, I got sense enough to lose a tail."

Trez flicked ashes on his floor. "Hell, can't we just give it all back?"

"You think that would stop 'em from killing us? Besides, I had to cut a deal with the feds to keep 'em from tacking on more time for stabbing the bastard who tried to kill me."

Willy's eyes hurt. "You made a deal with the feds? You mean they know about that loot, too? Damn, Clark, we may all wind up in jail."

"You keep moving this stuff around, we likely will. But the feds don't really know about the booty. They know who the guy who tried to kill me is connected to. They're after him. I promised to be bait."

Willy looked at Trez. "You got any hard stuff? I need a real drink." He turned toward Clark as Trez handed him a half-pint of Old Charter. "So, they follow you around all the time and now they know about us?"

"Not all the time. I generally know when they're tailing me. I got a phone number to call when I make contact with the bad guys. Or they contact me. The tough part is keeping them from finding out about the goods."

Willy's voice was up two octaves. "The tough part is not getting us all killed."

Trez took the bottle from Willy and swallowed a slug. "One thing for sure. I ain't storing it here. Why not sell it and be done with it?"

Clark shook his head. "You ain't been listening. The minute we put even one piece of this stuff on the street, the law and the Dixie Mafia will be all over us."

Trez stood and held up both hands in a gesture of futility. "Can't sell it, can't store it, can't give it back. Why not burn it?"

"Because it may be the only reason they're letting you stay alive. Once they find out where it is or that it's been destroyed, they got no more use for any of us." He paused and looked out the window again. "And they can't let this insult go unpunished. Otherwise, other folks might get the idea they can screw the Dixie boys and get away with it."

Trez begged Willy and Clark to spend the night, finally declaring he would set fire to the garage the minute they left, that he could not spend a minute alone knowing death waited as close as his garage. Clark and Willy brushed him off and left, but Trez followed.

Clark killed the Impala in Willy's front yard and Trez parked bumper-to-bumper, as if keeping his car close would keep him safe. Mexicans slowly passed by the Riviera, ran their hands across the fenders as if caressing it until Trez waved his hands and shooed them away. Shivering from the wet seat, he opened the back door of the Impala and sat behind his brother and uncle, wondering what secrets they had revealed during the drive home.

Clark paid little mind to Trez's chattering teeth as he turned to face Willy. "You sure you got nothing else you want to tell me?"

Willy shook his head a little too vigorously.

Clark looked over the wheel. "Gave you plenty of chances to come clean, but you done stooped to stealing from family. After all I done for you boys."

Trez leaned forward. "What's he talking about, Willy?" Willy looked out the side window.

Clark's tone was conciliatory, forgiving. "Look, the jewelry is different than the artwork. I stole it fair and square from another thief that ain't connected. That's my nest egg."

Willy was frightened and the fear made him furious at himself and at his uncle. "What about *my* nest egg? I took plenty of chances. You got me into a world of hurt by asking me to check on that hot stuff. You didn't mention nothing about no jewelry and I don't know nothing about it."

"Have it your way, but even though it ain't as hot as the artwork, there's still a pretty pissed-off thief out there who wants it back. You want to wake up some night and find him in your bedroom?"

"If I tell you where the jewelry is, you'll leave Trez and me high and dry to face these cold-blooded killers. You find a way to get us out of this, I'll give the jewelry back."

"What makes you think I won't just beat it out of you?"

"You need to take a better look. I ain't the kid used to follow you around on heists anymore. I took care of myself in jail. I don't set still for no beatings anymore. I'll kill you first."

Clark smiled. "You remember the night my friend Spiva took a bullet?"

Spiva was the only man Willy had ever seen shot, much less die. "I remember. Scared the hell out of me then, but again, I ain't that little kid anymore."

"Well, before Spiva took the warehouse job as night watchman, he was a security guy over in the ritzy section of Dallas. Installed burglar alarms and security systems for the bigwigs. He's the one helped me steal the jewelry. Had a pact going with the thief. Spiva swore he was in cahoots with the King of Diamonds."

Even Trez remembered the King of Diamonds, the athletic thief who plundered the richest of the rich in the most exclusive sections of Dallas, Highland Park and University Park. "That's the guy who robbed a load of diamonds from Ben Tom's buddy, ain't it? Jimmy Ling, wasn't it?"

Willy's mood changed a little. "Ben Tom always thought you was the King of Diamonds. You always wore those shoes that made a waffle print. He said you were athletic enough to do those leaps to the second story of houses like they claim he did."

Clark seemed not to hear. "He got his start stealing diamonds out of the Statler-Hilton by switching lockboxes out of their vault right under the security guy's nose."

Willy's bad mood returned. "So you think he was the one knocked off Spiva and now he's coming after you?"

Clark smiled. "Won't be coming after me. He'll be coming after the one with his jewelry."

"And why would he think I had it?"

"Who knows? He might have known one of the pawn shop guys you visited or the fence where you finally pawned a piece of art. How about this? Maybe he saw your dumb ass building a fire that would attract people for miles around and wondered what you were burning and what you kept?"

Willy's face grew dark with a look of fierce determination. "I'm hauling ass. We're moving out of this hellhole tomorrow."

Trez clapped a hand on his brother's shoulder. "Seems like the only thing to do. I aim to go with you."

Clark laughed out loud. "And just where are you boys going?"

Willy pulled the door lever. "Ben Tom's all hid out on the Red River. We'll follow him."

Clark turned to Trez. "You can't go anywhere. Sooner or later, that piece you let go with your washing machine will tie you to the Dixie Mafia. You'll bring this hell down on Ben Tom."

"So you suggest we stay here and get killed? I ain't spending one more day with that stuff in my garage."

Clark dropped his head. "We'll spend the night here with Willy, then if you boys will help, I know a good place where we can hide it tomorrow."

Trez shook his head. "Don't take this wrong, brother, but I ain't sleeping anywhere near that woman of yours. She'd slit my throat at the drop of a hat."

Clark lit a cigarette. "You can sleep in the back seat out here, then."

"What about them Mexicans?"

"You see any Mexicans?"

Trez and Willy both turned to look. No sign of wetbacks. Willy stepped out and searched the dark yard. "Where'd they go? Always had to run 'em off with my shotgun before."

Clark stepped out and stretched, leaving a waffle print in the mud. "Don't see how you boys got as old as you have without me taking care of you. I know that coyote. Won't be no more Mexicans coming over here till I say so."

18

WILLY ARGUED WITH COLLEEN MOST OF THE NIGHT ABOUT HIS brother and uncle staying in their yard overnight. The fight was still going on as he stepped out in the yard the next morning. He hurled one last threat and demanded she go back inside as Clark emerged from behind Willy's shop building. *How did he know where I hid the jewelry?*

Boiling with rage and fear, Willy walked toward him. "What are you doing snooping around here? You never let us snoop around your place; I expect the same courtesy from you."

Clark's expression showed mild curiosity toward Willy's rage. "Wasn't snooping. Just taking a leak. You sound like a man with something to hide."

"I sound like a man trying to protect his family from the hell you caused. Now, let's get this stuff hidden. You said you knew where to go with it."

"We'll need to take your pickup."

"What for? The less connection I have to this mess, the better I like it. Don't want nobody taking my plate number down. As I recall, that's what landed you in prison. Why can't we use your car?"

Clark pulled several tattered quilts from the trunk of his car and put them behind the seat of Willy's truck. "Because my car won't haul enough feed. We're going to a feed store in Seagoville."

Trez walked up, scratching his head and combing his thick hair with his fingers. "We going to see Mother?"

They pulled away from the feed store with several sacks of corn, hog feed, and bran and headed back toward Dallas. Trez looked back in the direction of his mother's house. "Thought we were going to see Mother."

Clark was impatient now, ready to get on with the business at hand. "Just hold your horses."

Clark had told them what they were going to do with the sacks of feed. Willy looked back at the sacks. "Why didn't you just get bran? Or just corn?"

"Cause we need sacks threaded with twine we can open and close. We got all they had."

At Trez's house, they made enough room to back the pickup into the garage and close the door. Willy crawled out the window. There was no room to maneuver on either side, but Clark stood inside the bed while Trez and Willy handed him the artwork one piece at a time. Clark poured a little corn or bran out of each feed sack into the pickup bed, wrapped each bronze with a portion of quilt, stuffed it to the middle of the sack, and poured as much feed as possible back into the sack. One piece of art to one feed sack.

Trez bit his nails between each maneuver and walked out the side door to see if anyone was watching after they finished with each piece. When the whole process took less than an hour, he felt a sense of calm replace his anxiety. It was an ingenious idea. The pieces were cushioned against damage and hidden where it seemed nobody would ever think of looking. Then he remembered they were in his garage.

"Don't even think about leaving these sacks here."

Clark stood and rubbed a sore back. "We're taking them out to Buck and Irene's farm."

Willy's eyes widened. "No, we ain't. You willing to put our mama, your own sister in danger?"

Trez agreed. "And that don't even take into account you're putting hot stuff right under Buck's nose. He'll try to hock it sure as hell."

"That's why we got this particular mix of corn, bran and regular hog feed. It matches what he has in an old feed crib he hasn't used in years. The feed was there when he bought the place. It's all bad and he can't just throw it on the ground because it's liable to kill whatever eats it."

Clark paused to grin at his nephews. "Buck's too lazy to carry it off, so we'll take the bad feed that's in there now and replace it with these sacks."

With the booty now attached to Buck instead of their mother, Trez and Willy exchanged winks. Even this part of the plan was smart. The

110

treasure would be a long way from both of them, yet recoverable in case of a real financial emergency. The prospect Buck might be killed by the Dixie Mafia was also not all that unpleasant. A thought came to Willy. *What about Mother?*

"She knows exactly what I'm doing. She just doesn't know what's in the sacks. The less she knows, the safer she'll be."

Irene stayed inside the house while they worked in the barn. They removed all the old feed sacks, except for one layer. They stacked the sacks containing the stolen loot on top of the bottom layer, then another layer of old feed on top. The old feed sacks full of spoiled feed were dropped into Willy's pickup.

Back at the house, Irene hugged her sons hello and goodbye, then turned to her brother. "Remember what you promised me—that these boys won't be connected to any of your shenanigans."

Clark hugged her goodbye. "I promise."

They built an illegal bonfire in Willy's yard and burned the bad feed and sacks. The smell of corn burning and rank and soured meal was not as unpleasant as Willy had imagined when Clark started the fire without asking. Colleen hurled the vilest expletives in her limited vocabulary from the porch. For once, Willy agreed with his wife.

"What the hell you thinking, Clark? Neighbors could call the law down on us. How we gonna explain where we come by this feed? Should've dumped it on the way home."

"And you don't think a dozen feed sacks and feed scattered all over the road or in the bar ditch wouldn't arouse curiosity? Besides your dumbass neighbors build illegal fires every night."

Clark used a long stick to make sure a sack burned completely. "Anybody asks, we just tell 'em that old feed has been in your barn since you bought the place. Time to get rid of it. Plead ignorance about setting fires."

"We coulda burned it somewhere else."

"On somebody's else's land? You think that won't get the law's attention if we're seen? If brains were pneumonia, you couldn't catch a cold."

Trez stood back in the shadows, a wave of depression washing over him. It had been a rough two days. "You about done with me? I need to get some shut-eye. Besides, that damn smoke is ruining my seat covers."

Staring at the fire caused Willy's eyelids to get heavy. He felt a sense of calm wash over him for the first time in years. It seemed as if the fire was burning away all of his troubles. He felt flush as he thought of the jewelry stowed safely under the floor of his shop. Even the artwork in Buck's barn gave him a sense of security. He left his uncle stirring the last of the embers to be sure every last piece of tow sack was gone.

He bathed for the first time in three days and was relieved when he stepped into the bedroom in his briefs. Colleen was mercifully asleep. The prospect of a full night's sleep for the first time in days made him almost happy. He looked out at the fire. The embers cooled. His uncle was gone.

Life seemed to return to normal the next few weeks. He did not hear from Clark or Trez and figured no news is good news. He went back to haunting construction sites to find day work. To avoid his increasingly hostile wife and children, he spent most of his evenings sitting outside his shop guarding his treasure. In rainy or cold weather, he sat inside the shop, his chair firmly over the boards that covered the jewels.

Not having to deal with Mexicans in his yard was almost exhilarating. Clark had shown no gratitude for Willy's sacrifices, but at least he had stopped the flow of Mexicans in his yard. They had become the bane of his existence. As time passed, his fear of the Dixie Mafia and the unknown burglar who originally stole the jewels faded. Under the influence of a few beers, he and Trez determined Clark had made up the connection of Spiva to the King of Diamonds. Though they had read and heard about this so-called king, nobody had ever actually seen him. Either he didn't exist or the King of Diamonds was Clark himself. Ben Tom had said as much. And Clark was nowhere to be found. Maybe he had paid the ultimate price and they were home free. But neither believed that. They still had the jewels and art.

Construction jobs for Willy declined as rapidly as the expenses of raising two kids and a wife increased. Colleen had begun self-medicating with whatever Willy could pick up on the streets to keep her barely functional and control her violent outbursts. Willy began to consider fencing some of the jewelry. Just as he was ready to pry up the boards out of desperation, he found a job that would hold him for at least three months.

Full time employment filled him with resolve to turn his life around. He even began refusing invitations from fellow workers to join them for a few rounds after work and headed straight home to face the music. And the music was shrill and loud. Colleen had stopped keeping house altogether and Willy had to see the kids made it to school in the mornings. Still, the thought of the waiting treasure in his shop helped him to hold to his sanity. Contrary to his old habits, he showed up for work every day, allowed the skills passed on to him from Ben Tom and Purcell to be finally noticed. It looked as if the temporary job could turn into something permanent.

Then the loan shark showed up.

19

WILLY DECLINED ANOTHER INVITATION FOR A ROUND OF TGIF beers as he and his fellow workers walked through the gate in the chain link fence that enclosed the construction site. He whistled as he walked toward the almost new Chevy pickup he had bought last week. He put his lunch pail in the pickup bed and was reaching for his keys when he saw the loan shark. The shark was no taller than Willy, just bigger around. He fancied himself a cowboy and always wore a big hat even Willy recognized as ill-fitting and ill-suited to an urban crook. The shark walked between two much larger enforcers.

Willy tried to open the door before they reached him, but he was too late. The shark's pitted, swarthy face and black eyes were angry. Willy had never been told his name, only an address where he could be found when one was desperate for money. "Been trying to locate you boys to pay a little down on my debt. Did you move?"

Each of the escorts would tip the scales at over two hundred and neither was fat. They kept quiet while the shark answered. "We move all the time, but we're not hard to find." He ran a hand over the chrome rail on the pickup bed. "See you got yourself some new wheels."

Willy saw no need for further pretense. "I ain't forgot I owe you money. I'm just getting my feet back on the ground with this steady job. I can send you a little every week until we get it paid."

His pleading tone was met with silence. Not even a grin from the three. Willy unlaced and pulled off one brogan, withdrew the hundred he kept there and handed it over. "I can do one of those every two weeks."

The shark took the hundred and passed it back to a big enforcer as if it were dirty. "A hundred every two weeks won't cut it. We'll all be old and gray before you get it paid off at that rate. Besides, we all know your word ain't no good. We been patient. Time to pay up."

"What's it come to now, with the juice?"

"Two thousand, and that's a gift."

Willy felt his insides drop precariously. "I think I can raise a thousand, maybe twelve hundred if you give me over the weekend."

"You'll raise two thousand or we'll take it out some other way." He turned and nodded toward the larger of his two companions. The man grabbed Willy's wrist and took his keys out of his hand, then broke his little finger.

Willy screamed and walked in a circle until he could find his voice. "How the hell do you expect me to pay you if I can't work?"

"You'll figure it out. We'll be back on Monday." The man who had broken his finger started Willy's truck and drove away. The shark and the other escort walked away in the darkness. Willy dropped to his knees as tears came unbidden to his eyes. He was at least twenty miles from home, but only two from the Meatloaf Bar where he knew his friends were celebrating the end of the week. He removed his handkerchief, wrapped it around his pinky and his ring finger, tied a knot with his teeth, and began walking.

Most of his co-workers appeared too drunk to drive by the time he arrived at the bar. Willy announced to everyone within earshot that his truck and his money had been stolen. He quickly downed four beers to kill the pain. Two hours passed before he finally persuaded the co-worker who lived closest to his home to give him a ride. Willy waited at the passenger door while the driver threw up his guts. He walked to the driver's side and politely asked for the keys. "Why don't you let me drive?"

The man spit a few times and looked up. "Hell, no. You as drunk as I am. 'Sides, you ain't got but one good hand." He fumbled for his keys. "Bartender took my keys again. I'll be back in a minute." As he left to go back inside, Willy felt a tap on his shoulder.

He turned to see a kind, friendly face. The man was handsome and about Willy's age. Everything about the man seemed average. Average height, average build. He was dressed in one of the uniforms of the construction trade, the old-fashioned overalls of a journeyman carpenter,

116

complete with a pair of pliers hanging from one overall loop and a claw hammer with an extra long handle from another.

His smile showed the only thing unusual about him, a perfect row of white teeth. "If my friend Weldon the bartender runs true to form, he ain't gonna let your friend have his keys."

Willy was wary after his encounter with the loan shark and his henchmen. "How's he gonna get home?"

"Your friend is Weldon's brother-in-law. His sister would have his hide if he let him drive home that drunk. He usually sleeps it off in the back room."

It was the last straw for Willy. His expression showed the desperation boiling inside him.

The man started to walk away, then turned. "You got your own wheels I could take you to?"

"Nope. I was counting on my buddy for a ride. Wonder if the bartender would let me have his keys to get home?"

The man twirled a key ring and keys on his index finger. "Where you headed?"

Willy told him.

"That's a little out of my way, but I'd be happy to drop you off."

Willy began to relax as the man recounted stories involving the trials and tribulations of the construction trade on the way home. He thought he might have found a new friend, one who was not a thug, but clean-cut and sober. The man's grammar was good, his conversation so intelligent it sometimes went over Willy's head, especially when he started talking politics and the national economy. If not for his clothes, the man could have been a college professor. But when the man mentioned Clark Mallory's name, Willy felt trapped inside a moving vehicle and his little finger still throbbed. "How do you know Clark Mallory?"

The man kept his eyes on the road. "Well, when you mentioned your last name was Lawless, I figured you to be one of Purcell's sons. Purcell and I go way back, and he introduced me to his brother-in-law quite a few years ago. Where is old Clark these days? Haven't seen him in years."

Willy tried to get his mind off his throbbing finger long enough to think of an answer. He had not expected this. "Haven't seen him in quite a while, myself." When there was no response, Willy decided to test the waters a little more. "You knew he did a little stint in Seagoville, didn't you?"

117

The man turned and smiled. "I heard about that. Purcell always said he would steal the quarters off a dead man's eyes. A man with as much talent as Clark could have been a lawyer or banker. Too bad."

"That's what my mama always said."

"Still, even with all that bad business, he was always pleasant to be around. Always an interesting conversation to be had."

As they approached Willy's drive, it dawned on him he had only given the man general directions when they left the bar. *How does he know where I live?*

The man stopped at the path that led to Willy's shack. "This is your place, right?"

Willy pulled the door handle and found it locked. "Yep. You can let me out here."

"Really like those big oaks." He turned to face Willy, his face only slightly showing by the light from the half moon reaching through the oaks. "Listen, Willy. I really need to get in touch with Clark. I loaned him something valuable to me and I'd like to get it back."

Willy pulled the handle again. "A man that loans my uncle something don't expect to get it back."

Willy felt the car turn cold. The man's demeanor changed. "I do. You tell him Hoyle Broom dropped by and he needs to get in touch."

"Like I said before, I ain't seen him in months. Don't even know where he lives or his telephone number. Nobody sees Clark less he wants to be seen."

Hoyle killed the engine and stepped out. When Willy heard his door unlock, he stepped out and headed toward the house at a brisk pace. Hoyle caught up and stopped in front of him. "Look, Willy. The folks I work for are less patient than me. If we don't find Clark, they're gonna take out their frustration on you. We don't want that to happen, do we?"

Hoyle reached out a callused hand with manicured nails and gave Willy a slight, but firm, slap on the cheek. The bitch slap reminded him of Junior, the man who had hit him with the phone receiver in jail.

Hoyle looked toward Willy's shack. "You don't want to ever lie to me or my friends, Willy. I can help you, but not if you lie to me. Now, you get hold of Clark and find out where my property is."

"Say I can do that. How do I get in touch with you?"

"The restaurant next to the Meatloaf. Leave me a message there."

Willy watched the black LTD drive off.

He called in sick the next day, complaining of a broken finger, and spent the day and half the next one trying to get Colleen's old Pontiac to start. When he finally did, he went directly to Trez's house. Trez had taken the day to nurse a hangover. Willy turned down a morning beer and got right to the point. "We have to find Clark. This thing is blowing up in our faces." Willy related his conversation with Hoyle the previous night, blamed him for the broken finger. He didn't want to mix loan shark problems with his other problems.

Trez stared at him a long time before speaking. "Wonder if they know where I live? You could come over here until it blows over."

"You got room for four?"

"Was just talking about you."

"You want me to leave my wife and kids alone over there? Besides, this man found me outside a bar. He knows a lot about me and I expect he knows as much about you. Even knows Dad."

Trez stood. "Let's go look for Clark."

In the driveway, Trez stopped when he saw the Pontiac. "Why are you driving that piece of crap?"

"Pickup got stole."

Trez snapped his fingers. "I thought that looked like your new ride down at that chop shop on Singleton. Bet it was. Come on, they may not have cut it up yet."

The truck was hidden a block away from the real chop shop in a small garage at a private residence. Trez had a friend who worked in the shop and knew about the garage where they held cars until they were ready to be cut up. They were inside the garage in a matter of minutes; Willy found his extra key in the tool box and drove his truck slowly out of the neighborhood, feeling alive again.

They returned the Pontiac and spent the rest of the day traveling to Clark's old haunts, including the house they had lived in on Gould Street in Pleasant Grove. The house was vacant and falling in. They tried all his old watering holes and felt obligated to have a beer in every bar just to get the conversation moving. When they finally stopped at Fat Boy's near Willy's house, they were drunk.

Trez raised his beer bottle and clinked it against his brother's. "I say we tell 'em about the feed sacks and be done with it. Stuff's too hot to do us any good, anyway."

"Clark said they would have no reason to keep us alive if they get their stuff back."

"I been thinking about that. Makes no sense. Looks to me like they aim to kill us if we don't turn it over or find Clark for them. Even if they don't kill us, they can make life damn miserable. You got a broken finger already. May be your neck next. What if they go after that crazy woman you're married to and try to beat it out of her?"

Willy's smile was involuntary. "Maybe we ought to let them do just that. Getting hold of that bitch would serve 'em right."

Trez laughed out loud. "So, what do we do?"

"Well, we put out the word we're looking for Clark. Maybe somebody will contact one of us in the next few days. We'll let him deal with the Dixie Mafia."

Willy stopped in his driveway and leaned his head against the headrest, screwing up his courage to face Colleen. He forgot to turn off the headlights. When he leaned forward to push the knob, he saw something moving under the porch and reached for the shotgun he kept in his gun rack. He almost shot it before he realized who the creature was.

Willy returned the shotgun to its rack and closed the pickup door. When he turned to head for the house, he found himself facing the revolver he kept in the nightstand by his bed. Colleen's eyes were wilder than usual. Her hand was on the trigger, not the trigger guard of the .38 revolver, and the hammer was cocked and ready to fire.

He batted her hand away and wrestled the gun from her. "Was that you under the porch?"

"It sure as hell was. Two men came by looking for you today. Scared the hell out of me."

"Who were they?"

"How the hell do I know? You think they're gonna introduce themselves to me pretty as you please? What did you do?"

"What did they say?"

"Said they was looking for you. One kept walking around talking about what a fire hazard our old shack is and what a shame it would be if all those big oaks caught on fire. They aim to burn us out. What did you do? You owe them money, or what?"

"First place, I don't know who they were. Second place, I didn't do nothing. Could be they're looking for Uncle Clark. He hangs around some really rough characters and they connect us to him."

"Well, you tell that damn uncle of yours to keep his trash off our property. Next time they come, I'll be ready. I'll send 'em both to hell."

"Just get back in the house. I'll take care of this tomorrow."

Willy leaned back against the pickup fender and watched her go inside. He was out of options. The two visitors were probably loan shark enforcers. He had missed the appointment again. First things first; he would deal with them and then deal with Hoyle and the rest of the Dixie Mafia. Hoyle seemed more patient and reasonable. He might have to part with at least some of the jewels to satisfy them both.

As he started toward his shop, he saw them—waffle prints in the dirt moistened by yesterday's rain. He bent to examine them. He only had time for an intake of breath before a black figure dropped from an oak limb and landed with barely a sound inches behind him. He felt a hand on his shoulder.

Willy's breath caught in his throat as he started to rise from his crouch. The hand on his shoulder pressed down as a voice came from the dark figure that seemed to have silently glided from the biggest oak tree in Willy's yard. "Stay where you are and don't turn around." The voice sounded guttural, unnatural, one its owner had disguised.

"You have something belongs to me. As soon as I collect it, I'll be on my way."

Willy controlled the urge to turn and face the man, imagining a gun or a knife awaited him if he did. "Don't know what you're talking about."

"I think you do. I spent several years waiting for Clark to get out of prison. He led me right here. Now, let's go get my property."

Willy felt something cold against his neck he imagined to be a gun barrel. Maybe a blackjack, which could be almost as lethal this close. "Can't get nothing if you keep me on my knees."

The voice changed timbre, sounding higher and almost effeminate. "Arise."

Willy stood. "Now what?"

Again, a change in timbre and tone. "I have no time for foolishness."

"Tell me what you're lookin' for and maybe I can help you, but I doubt it."

"Your uncle took something belongs to me. The firebug he hired to burn that trailer house told me he gave it to you for safekeeping."

"The stuff he asked me to look out for burned in that fire, I reckon. I heard after the fire he had some valuable shit in there. Didn't know nothing about it before then."

"Firebug says different. He saw you burn the box that held my precious things and carry off what was inside." The man had a litany of voices.

Willy felt strangely calm. After all, what else could go wrong? He was ready to die, was starting to prefer it, in fact. "Look, fella, do what you gotta do. Clark's been out of the joint for months now. You think he wouldn't have already taken his stuff back from me if I ever had it?"

There was no answer for what seemed too long to Willy. He heard the sounds of men's voices across the street, took a chance and turned to look. Bubble lights were in the street in front of Willy's house and spotlights swept an area that included Willy's lot. But the focus seemed to be on the coyote's yard. It was full of men in uniform. Willy felt a touch on his neck and turned enough to see the blackjack as the man in black disappeared into the darkness. He felt a momentary sense of relief, but he now had the Dixie Mafia, a loan shark's muscle, and maybe the King of Diamonds lining up to do him harm.

122

20

WILLY DIDN'T SLEEP. THE COMMOTION WITH THE COYOTE AND the wailing of illegal Mexican men and women kept up until two big vans hauled them away in the wee hours. With his hands behind his head, he lay back on his pillow and contemplated his predicament and options. There seemed to be none.

He could not return to work, at least not in his pickup. The loan shark would steal it again and punish him for taking it back. Even the chop shop owner might be after him. He also could not leave his wife and children alone now that all his nemeses knew where he lived. If he hocked or fenced the jewelry to pay off the loan shark, he would have nothing to get the King of Diamonds off his back.

The loan shark musclemen had taken his truck, broken his finger, threatened his wife, and promised to burn down his house. The King seemed like a choirboy by comparison. As for Hoyle Broom, Willy found himself liking the man in spite of himself. There was no proof he was a hired killer in the Dixie Mafia.

In the many calculations and self-talk with himself about the jewelry, he had come to the conclusion all of it could be worth as much as fifty thousand. Clark had referred to it as his retirement plan. Surely one piece would be worth the two grand he owed the loan shark. The acrobatic man in black might forgive him one piece. Might not even notice it was missing.

Figuring the broken finger earned him at least one more day off work, he pulled his pickup behind the shop, took a hammer and crowbar from his toolbox and dropped them on the wood floor of the shop. He sat in the pickup, holding his .38 in one hand and a beer in the other, until dark.

He crept into the shed as if he were burglarizing his own shop and, as quietly as possible, pulled back the boards over his beloved treasure. The sounds that came from the shed a few minutes later shattered the silence and caused his dogs to retreat under the porch. A moaning, waling sound like a coyote makes in the dark of night was followed by repeated howls that resembled two tomcats issuing mutual territorial threats. The boots, the velour sack and its contents were gone.

Willy beat his head against the floor until it bled. His mind racing, he slumped down and leaned against the shop wall to try to recover. It simply could not be gone. There was no sign of tampering with the nails or boards. He had checked them every day since hiding the jewelry. Only a varmint could have slivered under the board floor and taken them. Maybe a raccoon. But would he have taken boots and all?

He kept a box of matches and a Coleman lantern on a work bench. When the light from the lantern illuminated the room, he moaned with relief when he saw the toes of his old boots protruding from a tarp on the floor. They had not been there the day before. He reached inside one of the boot tops and came back with an envelope that bore his name. He tore it open and found a note:

> Give the hog feed to Broom if he agrees to take care of your loan shark. I took the trinkets. Needed them for a little vacation I am taking. I left you something better. Look deep into the hole. You need to hold onto it for a few years before doing anything with it. I will leave an easy trail to lead the King away from you to me. Don't screw up this time.

Willy held the light over the hole where the boots had been, reached down and brushed away loose dirt to reveal one of Clark's ragged quilts. He tugged on the quilt and felt the outline of something solid underneath. He carefully brushed back the fresh dirt until he could see the outline of a box before lifting it out. It seemed too light to hold anything.

He removed the quilt and the box it was protecting. He shook the dirt from the quilt and focused his lantern light on the box. It was about twelve by twenty-four inches. Willy's hands shook as he examined the painting on the top of the box. It looked like a Japanese flower garden. After several tries, he determined the box could be opened by sliding the top.

Inside he found a scroll that looked like ancient parchment, a few crisp paper cards that felt more like ultra-thin wood, and one folding book. A painting of people in various poses dressed in Japanese fashions graced each page. Some were erotica, almost caricatures of ancient people. It all looked worthless to Willy until he picked up the newspaper article someone had stuck in the tiny book.

The newspaper name was not shown. Neither was the date. And parts of the article had been marked through with black ink. But Willy could identify words like valuable, shunga, shin hanga, woodblock prints and something about famous architect Frank Lloyd Wright being a collector of such work. He pieced together enough other words to determine Wright had financial troubles and had used the prints as collateral for a loan. Some of his collection had been placed in a safe deposit box in a motel in Japan for safekeeping and a thief had cleverly exchanged a box full of worthless paper for the box of valuable prints.

The rest of the article was hard to follow with all the redactions. But the word that drew Willy's attention was burglary and the phrase "valued at close to a quarter-million dollars." There was something about a trail from the Metropolitan Museum of New York to the Dallas Museum of Art. The home of a wealthy patron of the arts in Highland Park was also mentioned.

Willy read the note again. It was obviously from Clark. *What did he mean by Broom taking care of the loan shark? Was he in a strong enough position to bargain? Was he saying these little Japanese paintings that looked like comic books were more valuable than his precious jewelry? And how was Clark going to lead away the King of Diamonds?*

Willy slept in a drunken stupor on the shop floor. His eyes popped open with another burning question to match his pounding headache. *How do I find Broom before the loan shark comes for my pickup and for my hide?* He penciled out a message to Broom saying he might help him find his goods if he could help him out with a fellow who loaned him money. He put it in an envelope and left it at the restaurant.

Willy reluctantly drove the Pontiac to work, leaving his pickup behind the shop. The construction foreman was furious for the work missed, but needed Willy's skills badly enough to let him return. Considering the state of his head, he put in a good day's work. His nerves were still shot when he walked through the gate at quitting time.

Just as he feared, the loan shark was in the parking lot, sitting on the hood of the Pontiac in a new pair of boots and a big belt buckle. Willy scanned the area for the two thugs who usually accompanied him, but they were not to be found. He drew courage from that. "You come alone?"

He slid off the hood and pulled back his coat to reveal a gun belt complete with holster. Willy saw that the holster contained a Colt .45 with bone grips. "My boys got more important business than your skinny ass. Seems hard times is making all you deadbeats try to skip out on loans. We're spread pretty thin, but I aim to take you off the list today."

Willy decided to chance it. "I got the money. You need to follow me over to this little bar where the fellas from work hang out. One of them is loaning me enough to cover the two grand I owe you."

"Two grand? You keep forgetting the juice. It's up to twenty-five hundred now. You get in the car with me and leave that junker here."

Willy turned and stared boldly at the man who had been making his life miserable for longer than he cared to think about. He sized him up, noted the proximity of the gun, and determined he could take him, gun and all. If it came to that, he would. The leech had sucked his last drop of blood from Willy. If neither Broom nor Clark was at the Meatloaf, he would do whatever was necessary.

No sign of Hoyle Broom in the bar's parking lot or inside the bar itself. The loan shark was getting irritated when they didn't find him in the restaurant, either. No sign of the LTD he had driven Willy home in, either.

As Willy was about to reach for the gun, he felt a hand on his shoulder. Hoyle's deep voice was welcome. "This the guy you owe money to, Willy?"

The shark was not amused. "Sure as hell is. You the man gonna cover his debt? You don't look much like a banker." Hoyle was still dressed as a construction worker.

"The wife and I are hard workers and savers. We occasionally help out a friend when we can. They always pay us back with a reasonable rate of interest. It's more than we can make in a savings account."

"I could give a shit less about your personal finances. Just hand over the two grand plus five and I'll be out of your hair."

Hoyle pointed toward the alley and spoke politely. "It's in a box in the

126

trunk of my car. That's probably why you didn't see me when you walked up. I was staying close to it. Come on over."

Hoyle opened the trunk. The bottom was covered with a white sheet and four pillows. "It's under that pillow on the left. Let me move it and you can have your money." Hoyle removed the pillow, revealing a shoe box underneath.

The shark opened the box and saw twenties and hundreds. Hoyle pointed to the stash. "Would you like to count it?"

"Damn right I want to count it. What's with all the pillows, anyway?" The shark bumped his cowboy hat when he stuck his head almost into the trunk, removed the bills and started peeling them back into the box in rapid order.

Hoyle chuckled softly. "I spend a lot of time in my car or in bad motels. I like my creature comforts."

The shark was past a thousand in counted bills when Hoyle pulled the .45 from his belt, stuck a pillow against his head and fired twice. He handed the Colt to Willy, picked up the shark's legs and dropped him into the trunk. The movement was so swift the loan shark lay dead in the trunk before Willy could utter a sound.

Broom picked up his hat and threw it in the trunk. "Pitch the gun in the trunk and get in." Hoyle stuffed the cash into his pocket, closed the lid and they drove away.

They were several miles away from the Meatloaf bar before the full impact of what had just happened smacked Willy hard. His hands began to shake. He wanted out of the car, but Hoyle had it moving along at the speed limit. "My car is back there at the construction site. If you'll take me back there, I'll get out of your way."

Hoyle looked away from the road long enough to smile at Willy. "That wouldn't be polite, would it? I kept my part of the bargain, now you need to keep yours. I got word from Clark that you could take me to my property. Your note said the same. Then there's the matter of getting rid of that body back there."

Willy thought about it for a minute, went over Clark's note in his head. Didn't figure he had a choice. "We'll need something bigger than your trunk to haul it. Course, your trunk is already full. Maybe a pickup or a van or something."

"Why?"

"You'll see when we get there."

Hoyle reached down to the hump in the floorboard and came back with a phone. Willy had never seen a car phone before. Hoyle dialed a number and made arrangements to pick up a van. They pulled into a used car lot just out of the Dallas city limits. A white plumber's van was parked outside the locked gate—Ace Plumbing professionally painted in black letters on both sides. Hoyle pointed to it. "Keys are in it. Get in it and I'll follow you."

Willy's brain was partially functional again. "Listen, Hoyle, where we're going is where my mother and stepfather live. We go up there this time of night, he's likely to shoot both of us."

"Hell, it's barely dark. Can't you just explain we're picking up something belongs to you? Is the stuff in their house?"

"No, it's hidden in some feed sacks in his barn about two-hundred yards from the house. He don't know it's there and is likely to be mad as hell when he finds out."

"Any way we can get in there and load it up without them even seeing us?"

"It's possible, I guess, but you don't know Buck Blanton. My guess is he's killed more than one man."

"I'll try to stay on his good side. If he catches us, maybe I can buy him off."

Willy stopped a mile or so from the house and stepped out of the van as Hoyle pulled alongside. The wind had gotten up and Willy had to put his head almost in the window for Hoyle to hear. "Let's leave your car here. Maybe we can sneak in with just the van."

"Good idea." Hoyle stepped out with a flashlight in his hand.

Willy cut the lights on the van and eased past the house and parked behind the barn. So far, so good. His confidence began to build. They might just get away with it. Willy opened the feed room door and Hoyle shined his light on the feed sacks. "You mean the art is inside those sacks?"

Willy nodded. "All wrapped in blankets. Clark said the feed was better than packing material, just heavier."

"Sounds just like him. An ingenious idea. Is there something in all the sacks? Looks like too many."

Willy felt a little twinge of pride. "I know which ones."

Hoyle pulled a knife from his pocket and moved to cut one open.

"Guess I wadn't thinking. We won't need that van if you aim to take each piece out."

Hoyle mashed on several sacks Willy pointed to until he was satisfied something besides feed was inside. "On second thought, let's load 'em up like they are. The sacks are a good way to transport these babies all the way to where they're going."

When half the sacks had been loaded into the van, Hoyle stopped and faced Willy in the dark. "You do realize that these sacks had better have the bronzes inside. We do know where to find you."

"They're in there all right. I'll just be glad to get rid of 'em."

Willy pushed the last sack into the van. When he closed one door, he saw Buck's boots.

21

BUCK SMILED A GAP-TOOTHED SMILE, BOTH HANDS BEHIND HIS overalls bib. Willy knew the hands held his sawed-off shotgun. "Why, hello, Buck. We was just trying to get away without bothering you."

Buck looked inside the van at his sacks of feed. "You stooped to stealing hog feed now, boy?"

Willy tried to hold his voice steady. "Mama said you had a bunch of spoiled feed out here you couldn't throw out because it might be poison for your cows and hogs. Thought I could use it as fertilize for the garden me and Colleen are thinking about putting in."

Buck pulled the shotgun. "Garden, my ass. Better to stop lying now before I have to show your mama just how low you sunk before I scattered your brains all over the barn. What are you up to?"

Buck felt the slight nudge against the back of his neck as Hoyle put a cold barrel there. "Sorry we disturbed you. Buck, is it? We'll be out of your way in just a minute more."

Buck made a move to turn, but felt the push against his neck again. From previous experience, he recognized the feel of the barrel of a large caliber gun. "You don't know who you're foolin' with, mister." He looked at Willy. "Who the hell you brought onto my property, Willy? I'll take this out in hide."

Hoyle's voice was smooth. "No need for anybody to get upset. Like I say, we'll be out of your way in a matter of minutes. How much you want for the feed?"

"Since we both know them sacks got more than feed in 'em, I figure you owe me ten thousand for storing stolen goods and putting myself and my wife in danger."

"Well, we both don't know what's in the sacks, Buck, but I do." Hoyle pushed the two grand in bait money he had used to trap the loan shark against Buck's ear. "This ought to more than cover it."

Buck took the money with one hand, stuck it into a bib pocket and snapped it shut. He looked at Willy. "You and me still got a score to settle."

Hoyle tapped him on the head with the .45. "Now, now. We don't want to hear any more talk of hurting Willy here. I need him to stay healthy. Understood?"

When Buck did not answer, Hoyle tapped him a little harder. Buck nodded.

Hoyle tapped him hard enough to hurt. "I need to hear you say you understand."

"All right, dammit. I understand."

Hoyle pushed him toward the feed room. "Now you hand me that little short shotgun and get inside there until we can drive off. Should be easy enough for a man of your talents to get out. But don't let me see you in the yard until we're gone. Understood?"

He shoved Buck inside the feed room and Willy closed the hasp and attached a snap to the loop. "He'll be out of there by the time we get to the highway."

Hoyle nodded. "Just as long as he don't get out before then. You hear that, Buck?"

Willy broke the shotgun and tossed away both shells, put the bowed gun in front of a van tire. He felt and heard the satisfying crack as he drove over it.

Willy felt good, almost giddy, at the thought of Buck locked in his own feed room, his pride-and-joy shotgun broken. The feeling left abruptly when he saw Hoyle's LTD leaning a little sideways on the shoulder. He had almost forgotten there was a dead body in the trunk. He turned to his passenger as he rolled to a stop beside the car. "Guess I'll see you where I parked the Pontiac."

Hoyle never turned to look at him. "You can get the Pontiac any time. First thing is to get rid of the body and the gun. You go on to your house. I'll meet you there."

"My house? What are we gonna do there? Look, I can't be..." Willy never got to finish the sentence. Hoyle started the car and left.

Willy stopped at the entrance to his driveway and waited. The LTD drove up and into the driveway minutes after. Hoyle got out of the passenger side and walked to Willy's window. "What are you doing parked out here?"

"Figured it would save backing up when you leave."

"As I recall, you got a deep well on the west end of this lot. You drive on down there and park so I can pull in behind you and not be seen from the house. Your well is a good place for your loan shark buddy."

"You aim to leave a dead body on my property?"

"Not on your property. In your well."

Hoyle stopped beside the well and took a closer look at the complex cover Willy had designed to secure the old well opening. "Damn. May be easier to get into Fort Knox."

Willy took pride in the complicated design. No kid was going to get killed in a well on his property. "I can get it disassembled in a few minutes with a screw gun."

"Then go get one."

"Have to run an extension cord from the house and my wife and kids are asleep in there."

"Can't you sneak in there without waking her?" Hoyle's eyes grew cold. "Make sure she don't come out of the house."

"What about the noise from the screw gun?"

Hoyle looked at the surrounding houses. "Expect you hear saws and power tools all times of the day and night around here. Am I right?"

"Expect so, but just the same, they ain't usually disposing of a dead body."

"I'll crank the van and the car. It'll cover the noise a little. Just get on with it. We don't have all night."

When he stepped on the porch, Willy saw Colleen's eyes shining like a cat's from the under the porch. He was trapped. Nothing to do now but go ahead with the plan. He checked to see if Hoyle was looking, stared at her, and shook his head with a finger to his lips. He hoped his nutty wife would not reveal herself. The look she gave him was accusing and furious, but she kept her silence.

With the right tools, Willy had the cover off in less than a quarter hour. Hoyle shined a flashlight down the well. The opening was barely large enough for a body. "It's one of them old-timey wells just big enough for a tall, skinny bucket to go down. Let's see if he'll fit."

Hoyle put a hand under each armpit and lifted the man's trunk out of the car while Willy lifted his legs. "You want him standing on his feet or head?"

Willy couldn't see what difference it could possibly make to a dead man, but the thought of him on his head, possibly submerged in water, was somehow disturbing. "Feet first." He put his feet into the hole and moved back to help with his trunk. The body stuck when it got to his chest.

Hoyle stepped back. "Damn, this little bastard is heavy and wider than he looks. Only way he's going in that hole is if we lift his arms. You hold them up and I'll push him through this top pipe. Should be wider after about six feet."

Willy lifted both arms and held the man's hands as Hoyle put a foot on one shoulder, then the other. The intimacy of holding hands with a man, particularly a dead one, made Willy nauseous. He lost it just as the man finally slid through. He heard a muted splash of water as the body reached the bottom.

He wiped his mouth with a shirt sleeve and looked down in the dark hole. "What am I gonna do when he starts to smell?"

"That hole is probably at least sixty feet deep. You just screw those boards back down; the smell will never come up."

"What about varmints? They bound to scratch and sniff around here for weeks."

"Get you a bag of lime and drop it down the hole if it'll make you feel better. Just do it all no later than tomorrow night. Remove all signs, then stay away from there permanently."

"What about hauling in some gravel or dirt from somewhere to fill it up?"

"You want to call attention to the well when a dirt and gravel truck backs up to it? Just do the lime, put the lid on, and cover your tracks. A month from now, you'll forget it's even there."

Willy knew he would never forget a body buried in his backyard.

Hoyle seemed to be getting nervous. "Get the screw gun and extension cord away from the well right now and put it in your truck. Then get in the van and follow me."

Hoyle drove the car and Willy followed him in the van to the same used car lot where they had picked up the van. Willy watched Hoyle take a small bottle out of the car pocket. He stepped out of the car, popped the trunk, and took out the loan shark's .45, his hat, and two bloody pillows. He poured the contents of the small bottle he had taken from the glove box over the gun and wiped it down with the clean part of one pillowcase. He put it all in the floorboard of the van as he sat in the passenger seat.

Willy looked down at the gun. "That bleach you poured over the gun?"

"Rubbing alcohol. Meant to do that back at your place and drop the gun down the well. We'll take care of it when we get back."

"Can I keep the gun? May need it if this guy's goons come after me." Willy had admired the gun the first time he saw it. It looked like something Matt Dillon might have carried.

"You want to keep a murder weapon?"

"Only got an old .38 revolver for the wife. No handgun for myself."

Hoyle shook his head, then seemed to consider it. "I was thinking we could drop the pillows down the well, but they might get stuck and keep the lime from going all the way down. Best to burn them right after I leave. Don't wait till morning. Understood?"

"I'll burn 'em soon as I get back. What about the gun?"

Hoyle seemed deep in thought and did not answer. He directed Willy to stop a quarter mile from his house and told him to get out. As Hoyle came around to take the wheel, he met Willy face to face in the front of the van and put the .45 under his chin. "End of the line for you and me."

Willy's voice quaked. "You aim to kill me? Why?"

"You're a liability now we got what I came for. Seen too much."

"I did everything you told me."

Hoyle released the pressure, but kept the gun under Willy's chin. "We generally don't leave any unfinished business behind, but you might be more messy dead than alive. Think that crazy woman you live with got a look at my face. I'd have to kill her, too."

He put the gun back in his waistband. "I'm gonna let you live, Willy, providing you keep that woman under control. And I might need you to do something for me later. You won't see me again unless I need you or you screw up."

Willy exhaled as Hoyle opened the door to the van, emptied the gun and handed it to Willy. "Can I keep the gun?"

"Too risky. Drop it in the well. I guarantee the goons won't be coming for you. They been paid off and warned off."

Willy stood in the yard holding the bloody pillows, the cowboy hat, and the gun as the van pulled away. It was the first time he had been alone since the nightmare night had begun. He put the gun inside his belt, the hat on his head, and hugged the pillows to his chest as he walked back toward the house. He talked aloud to himself as he removed folded newspaper from the sweatband to make the hat fit, trying to get his head around all the events.

The loan shark would never bother him again, but his goons might, despite what Hoyle said. But the Dixie Mafia in the person of Hoyle Broom seemed satisfied. Willy felt he had acquitted himself well with Hoyle, maybe even made a friend he could call on for something import-ant later. He did regret the loss of the bronzes. Having them stored in that feed room at Buck's had given him a sense of security, something to fall back on, to fence in case of emergency.

Now, he had a dead body in his yard. Okay, it was in a well, but the well was in his yard. The goons might have seen Hoyle shoot their boss. They were almost certain to have known Willy was the person he was coming to visit when he disappeared. Willy tried to reconstruct the scene in the alley by the Meatloaf. Who could have seen or heard the shooting? Sure, the shot was muffled by a pillow, but if someone was close enough...

22

WILLY DECIDED TO ACCEPT HOYLE'S WORD THE GOONS HAD been taken care of. That still left the matter of the King of Diamonds. Now, he had no jewelry to give him in exchange for his life. Clark had taken it. Of course, Clark said he would get the king off his trail. How could he do that?

Then, there was the matter of the strange art Clark had left in place of the jewels. Stolen, of course, and maybe more dangerous to keep than the bronzes had been. Did it belong to the King of Diamonds, the Dixie Mafia, or who? Clark's note had said he had to wait a few years to dispose of it. How many is a few and who would buy it? He had liked the fact he could walk around with the jewelry snug against his belly. What do you do with stiff, dirty, ugly paintings? Who would want the things, anyway?

He talked himself into feeling better as he walked by the house. After all, he had not shot the loan shark. Anyone watching would know it was as much a surprise to him as it was to the shark. He had not stolen the jewelry, only rescued it and moved it to a better place. Same for the bronzes, which should be on the way to Tennessee or wherever the current headquarters of the Dixie Mafia was located.

He did regret Hoyle had given two thousand in cash to Buck. That money was technically his. Well, it was the loan shark's, but it should have reverted to Willy when the loan shark no longer needed it. After handling all the stolen bronzes, stolen jewelry and coming close to two grand in cash, he got nothing for his efforts.

It was pitch dark, cool and still. A good night for building a little fire. Willy was still talking to himself, watching his feet as they delivered him to the well. A small shout escaped when he looked up into a gun barrel. Colleen stood astraddle the well, pointing her .38 at Willy's left eyeball.

"I seen what you did."

Willy was not in the mood. He had after all, become a big-time gangster. He had handled a large quantity of stolen goods, worked with a criminal organization, and disposed of a loan shark in one evening. He slapped the gun away from his face and took it away from her. He pulled the Colt .45 and stuck it in her face. "You point that damn gun at me ever again, I aim to kill you."

Defiance filled her eyes. "We all as good as dead, anyway. Got a dead man not thirty yards from our front door. What did you get yourself into?"

"Nothing that concerns you. Go in the house and keep quiet."

"Nothing? What about them bloody pillows you're hanging onto like they was a baby or something? And you look like a halfwit in that hat."

"Got into a little scuffle with those goons came by here and threatened you. They won't be bothering you again."

She was skeptical, but considered the possibility he might be telling her the truth—that he had defended her honor and safety again. Last time, it had sent him to jail for a year.

Willy pulled back the hammer of the gun and felt the satisfying click as the cylinder rotated. "I said for you to go in the house. I got things to do. I'll be in there in a minute."

Behind the shop, Willy sprinkled the pillow cases with a little gasoline, covered them with pine needles and acorns and the paper from the hat, and set them afire. He sat in his usual chair right outside the shop door and watched them burn. He twirled the gun, practiced a fast draw out of his waistband, wished for a holster. He forgot the hat was still on his head.

Willy drove his pickup to work the next morning, feeling it was now or never with the goons. The truck was still there when he got off. He offered a six pack of beer to a co-worker to follow him home in his Pontiac. Willy returned the man to the construction site and picked up two sacks of lime on the way back. Minutes after full dark, he poured it down the well and replaced the cover. With the .45 in his waistband, he felt almost safe for the first time in months.

He bought a quick draw holster for his Colt .45 on Friday. After work each day, he went to his shop and strapped on the gun and holster, put on his hat, carried the same folding chair and sat equidistant between his art treasure and the well that contained a loan shark's dead body. It was the only time he felt safe, away from prying eyes.

On the fourth day of Willy's ritual, Trez's curiosity finally got the best of him and he risked incurring Colleen's wrath by stopping by to find out what was going on. Irene had told him the feed sacks were gone and Buck's gun was ruined. He especially wanted details on Buck's shotgun.

Willy told him only that Clark sent a man with a letter authorizing him to collect the bronzes. Nothing more. Certainly nothing about the Japanese artwork, the jewels, or the dead body. He couldn't resist bragging a little about the way he and the fellow from the Dixie Mafia had stood up to Buck and taken his shotgun from him.

Trez, like Willy, had hoped to somehow cash in on the bronzes, but he was happier knowing they were gone and there seemed to be no connection to him. "You think Clark recovered that one piece left in the old washing machine I sold?"

Willy seemed annoyed by the question. It opened up a can of worms he had effectively sealed. "How else would he have known about it if it wasn't him or one of his buddies got it in the first place? He never as much as took his eyes off the loot, even had somebody watch it every day while he was in prison. Trust me; Clark's got that piece."

About the time Trez headed home satisfied he was not going to be killed to get at the loot, a Kentucky farmer plowed a few yards inside the Tennessee state line. He paused when he saw a white van with Ace Plumbing on the side being pulled over by two cars with magnetized bubble lights, but no identification. Four other cars, including a black van, soon joined the spectacle on the side of the little-traveled highway.

The next morning, the farmer read about an incident in the Mayfield paper. It seems the Department of Agriculture stopped the van on suspicion of transporting agricultural products into the state without declaring such products at the border. Several sacks of dangerous feed and seeds containing possible harmful pests and insecticides were confiscated. The farmer breathed a little easier that his crops were made safer.

The following morning, a black Chevy Suburban stopped in the shaded driveway of a regal century-old mansion in the University Park neighborhood of Dallas. The old home had been meticulously maintained. The stately oaks in the large lot had been trimmed and encircled with fresh out-of-season flowers. A middle-aged couple, both a little taller than average, followed two sun-glassed men from the home. The man carried a small briefcase and the woman a purse. The two sunglasses each carried a small piece of luggage they deposited in the rear of the Suburban.

The man's thick, dark hair was flecked with gray. He was dressed all in black with black basketball sneakers. The woman had fawn-colored coiffed hair and carried a little extra weight, but her expensive clothes hid it well. Her walk, her expression, her makeup, even the texture of her skin bespoke a life of wealth and privilege. They entered the rear side door of the Suburban and sat on upholstered benches facing each other. The woman reached across to take his hand as the Suburban pulled away.

At lunchtime, another visitor arrived at the same home, crossed the lawn in shoes that left a waffle print. He used a key to enter. In less than half an hour, he exited the same way he entered, but this time he carried a large, expensive suitcase. He walked down the sidewalk at a brisk pace, whistling a merry tune for the duration of the twelve block trip to his own stately home. Less than an hour later, University Park Police knocked politely on his door. A plain clothes detective presented a search warrant. A half hour later, the occupant of the house is led away in cuffs. A uniformed cop wearing rubber gloves carries the expensive suitcase.

The next day, a parcel arrives at the Riverby Post Office addressed to PO Drawer 7. Inside a padded envelope is a small maroon, velour bag secured with a draw string.

A week later, a letter arrives for Irene Blanton. She recognizes the handwriting as her brother Clark's. The letter seems disjointed at first, almost childish, like a child's fairytale without a plot. The sentences don't seem to form any coherent whole—until she remembers the instructions Clark left her when he went to prison. A code of sorts, so he could send her messages without being discovered by prison authorities.

He had never used the code before, so it took her almost an hour to find the instructions and another half day to translate what he had written into the message he meant to convey. She got in her car and headed to Riverby, to Ben Tom, the only person in the world she dared share the story with.

23

IRENE FOUND HER ELDEST SON AND HER EX-HUSBAND IN DOWN-
town Mesa, where they were restoring the old bank building. She had expected
to share Clark's message with only Ben Tom, but she felt an urgent need to
share her burden and Purcell knew something was on her mind. The weather
was nice, so Ben Tom dusted off three old bank lobby chairs that sat under
the awning outside the bank. Irene was noticeably nervous as she addressed
Purcell first. "I see you finally made it back to your old stomping grounds."

She turned to Ben Tom. "He tried to drag me back here many times
over the years."

Ben Tom looked at both parents. "What are you talking about?" He
turned to Purcell. "You been here before?"

Purcell laughed as he smiled at Irene. "Grew up not much more than
a stone's throw from where we're sitting right now."

"How come I never heard about this?"

"I ran away when I was fourteen under bad terms. Didn't see any need
to bother my kids with problems between me and my old man. We never
made up. I couldn't move back here till he died."

Ben Tom thought about this new information for a few beats of his
heart, realizing it could be the strong pull that brought him back here, the
unusual connection he had always felt for the community.

But Irene did not want to talk about Mesa, did not want to stray from
her message. "You can't ever repeat what I'm about to tell you."

Ben Tom and Purcell glanced at each other, nodded their assent to
Irene's terms.

"Your Uncle Clark has left the country with his wife and we may never see him again."

Ben Tom leaned in. "Wife? Left the country? Clark ain't even married."

Purcell smiled. "What are you talking about, Mama?" Irene blinked at the term of affection he had used when they were married.

Irene asked for a glass of water. Purcell popped to his feet, returned with a snuff glass full of cold water from his water jug. He handed it to the woman he still loved gently and more completely than anyone before or since. She looked up when her hand touched his and said with loving and playful eyes, "Thanks, you old rascal."

Ben Tom knew his parents were still in love, but could not live together. "Okay, now fill us in."

"Clark has been married for about two years. He got married while he was in prison to an heiress who lives in a highfalutin neighborhood in Dallas. One of the Park Cities."

Purcell stood. "Now why would a rich lady marry a known thief who's in prison for doing the only thing he knows how to do? Hell, Irene, you forget he stole your own sons' guns and sold 'em right out from under 'em?"

She shook her head as if chasing away a mosquito. "I don't know the whole story, but she caught him burglarizing her house one night many years ago, when they were both young. She had been stood up at the altar by some rich boy. Clark said she was the most beautiful and refined woman he had ever seen. And you know that brother of mine can turn on the charm."

Purcell's expression showed his doubt. "Your brother ain't exactly known for the truth, either. You mean to tell me this gal just fell down next to a sack of her own jewelry and fell in love with the thief who was stealing it?"

Irene looked to Ben Tom for support. "I don't know for sure what happened, but he said he returned the stolen stuff and threw himself on her mercy. They spent the night talking and somehow sparks ignited between them. The good kind, you know." She turned toward Purcell. "I know it seemed incredible to me too when I heard it, but he called and told me before they got married."

Ben Tom could not believe it. "But you know for a fact they did get married?"

"There's no doubt about it. He swore me to secrecy, then invited me over to her mansion and we had a meal and coffee. I had to sneak off to keep Buck from finding out."

Purcell scoffed. "You couldn't take that sumbitch to a cockfight, much less a fine home."

Irene knew that was true. "You weren't exactly a choirboy when I married you. Kathleen, Clark's wife, is a beautiful, refined, kind lady. She showed me every courtesy."

Purcell harrumphed. "Women love a challenge. She probably thought she could change a man who's been a thief since he was in first grade."

Ben Tom touched Purcell's shoulder to silence him. "So now this new wife and Clark are gone?"

She showed him the letter and he read it. "Can't make heads or tails out of this. Reads like some kind of messed up kids' fairy tale."

Irene took it back, handling it like it was a treasure. "I couldn't either, until I found this code he gave me when he went into prison. Said he might need to get me a message others couldn't read."

She pulled a second letter from her purse and handed it to Ben Tom. "This is what it really says."

Ben Tom's eyes grew wider with each word, each sentence. He whistled as he handed it over his shoulder to Purcell.

Purcell read it while Ben Tom pondered all the questions the letter left unanswered. "So he spilled the beans on the Dixie Mafia and on the King of Diamonds. Doesn't say where they're going or who's taking them."

Purcell handed the interpreted letter back to Irene. "Witness protection. Has to be. I have a friend who did pretty much the same thing. Disappeared with his wife and two kids. New name, new location. Still in the good old USA, but never heard from again."

Irene shook her head. "Can't believe Kathleen would go off and leave that mansion of hers and all her friends. Course, I understand if her folks ever found out about Clark, they would take the mansion, anyway. She must really love him."

Ben Tom ran his fingers through his thick hair. "Guess it was either that or watch him get killed. He told Willy and Trez the folks he was dealing with would definitely put your lights out."

Irene was tearful. "Don't you see, though? He did it to protect Willy and Trez, too. Even you, Ben Tom. He got these bad guys all arrested and their stolen property was returned to the rightful owners."

Purcell knew his brother-in-law well. "May have worked out that way,

145

but you can bet he was covering his own ass as well. He could have been a kept man, lived out his days in a big mansion. But he knew his days were numbered. Made the wrong people mad."

24

MESA, THE GHOST TOWN, WAS SHORT ON A LOT OF THINGS AND was fresh out of water hoses. So Purcell was torn between staying and trying to put out the fire that threatened all the buildings or driving to Riverby to alert the fire department. He decided on the former. He went at the wall between the building in flames and its neighbor with vengeance and a crowbar, removing fuel from the fire's path, trying to guide it away from the other buildings.

The former feed store was almost gone when Ben Tom arrived minutes ahead of the fire department. He had seen the fire from several miles away, turned around to make a call. He ran to his father. "What the hell happened?"

"How the hell should I know? These old buildings are all fire traps."

The firemen shook their heads, not bothering with the old feed store that was engulfed, concentrating their attention and limited water on the surrounding buildings. Two hours passed before they felt it was safe to return to Riverby.

Ben Tom watched the smoldering ruins as mental images of the precious artifacts turned into ashes burned into his brain. "You slept in here last night, didn't you? Fell asleep with a cigarette in your hand?"

"Now what makes you think that? I got a fair enough bed over in that trailer you drug up."

"What makes me think that? It might be the mattress in the floor that didn't quite burn. There's a big burn hole in the middle of it. Looks like it's been slept on."

"Hell, son, it's been in a fire. What did you expect?"

"Got a little whiskey in you and decided to take a little nap, didn't you?"

"Don't matter what happens, you always blame whiskey or cigarettes. Besides, I don't see what you're worried about. That old building needed tearing down, anyway."

"What about all the stuff I had in it?"

Purcell "Wasn't any of it worth a plug nickel, and you know it." He looked at the trailer behind Ben Tom's truck. "What's that behind your truck?"

"What's it look like?"

"Looks like some type of livestock trailer and that looks like a horse inside."

"Your eyes don't deceive you."

"What the hell are you up to now? You don't know one end of a horse from the other."

"I aim to learn. I was taking this gray I just bought out to Joe Henry Leathers' ranch to get some advice."

"He that long, tall drink of water wears them boots all the way up to his ass?"

"He runs the Two Hearts Ranch and practices law in downtown Riverby. Knows more about horses than anybody in this part of the country, maybe the whole state. "

"Well, that's three things you ain't got in common." Purcell said this as he shuffled away, shoulders slumped. Ben Tom knew his father had a guilty conscience, but would never admit, even to himself, that the fire was his fault. He looked old, and Ben Tom decided to follow him.

He found his father inside the building behind the one that had burned. The former dry goods store building was full of smoke and smelled acrid, but it was also full, floor to ceiling, with boxes of shoes.

Purcell turned on him angrily. "What the hell you following me for? Mind your own damn business." Ben Tom opened a few boxes, found some new and some used pairs. He looked at his father, shook his head and walked out.

He worried more about Purcell as he headed for the Two Hearts Ranch. And he worried about his brothers. He couldn't shake the feeling he had abandoned them, though they were grown men and should be capable of supporting themselves. Ben Tom never imagined he would go so long without contact, but the pure, innocent, country air had made him reluctant to breathe urban air again. At night, he dreamed and knew with almost certainty both brothers were in some sort of trouble. And he no longer wanted to rub shoulders with trouble.

At the Two Hearts Ranch, he led the gray mare down the ramp of the expensive horse trailer he could not afford and proudly showed her to Joe Henry. The tall lawyer's half smile was hesitant, skeptical. "Looks familiar. Where did you say you got her?"

"Fellow named Pennebaker over in Bonham. He's big into cutting horses. You probably heard of him. Got a national reputation."

Joe Henry nodded. "Bob Pennebaker. I know him. He tell you he was into cutting horses or somebody else tell you that?"

"He did. Said this gray was a champion."

Joe Henry stared at his boots. "And what is it you want me to help with?"

Ben Tom was caught off guard by the question. "Well, I was hoping you might give her a try and see if I got my money's worth. Maybe cut a few cows on her."

"Well, I don't have any cutting stock caught up at the moment; don't really own any for that purpose. But we can try her out in the corral if you want to."

Ben Tom could not wait to see this wonderful animal work. The stories Pennebaker had told were magnificent. He led her into the corral. Joe Henry walked over and looked into the mare's eye. "You got a saddle and bridle?"

"Sure do. Bob said the saddle and bridle went with the horse." He returned with both and a too-thin blanket in a matter of minutes.

Joe Henry put two fingers in the gullet and threw the saddle across his shoulder. "Now, I don't aim to demean a man's purchases, but this saddle and bridle are not cutting equipment. Wrong horn, wrong stirrups. Saddle's not even double-rigged. Looks like a woman's pleasure saddle."

Ben Tom looked disconsolate and felt dumb. He did not know what double-rigged meant. "It was one of the prettiest ones he had."

Joe Henry laid the blanket and saddle on the gray and looked into her eye again. "Tell you what, Ben Tom, let's put this mare in the round pen instead of the corral. See what she's gonna do. You an experienced rider?"

Ben Tom recalled the times he and his brothers had ridden an old swaybacked horse around his uncle's farm without benefit of saddle or bridle. "Since I was a little kid."

"Cause if you ain't, I don't recommend mounting this gray. I think I recognize her."

Five minutes later, Ben Tom's head bounced off the dirt. Flat on his back in the round pen, he writhed in pain. The gray stood against the rails, staring at her most recent casualty.

Joe Henry leaned over Ben Tom and offered a hand up. "You hurt bad?"

Ben Tom lied, grunting with pain as he managed to gingerly stand. "Nah. I'll be okay. What happened?"

"Hate to tell you this, but I think I know this old horse. I thought she looked familiar when I first saw her, but couldn't believe it was her again, back from the dead, until I saw her break in two when she threw you."

"Back from the dead?"

"Word got around the last fellow she threw and stomped on shot her."

"Is she as bad as that look on your face says she is?"

"Horse traders all over this part of the country have sold and resold this old outlaw. Pennebaker has sold her plenty. People take her back and he gives them part of their money back or charges them to train her and they never come back to pick her up."

Ben Tom's face flushed with the pain and with shame for having his ignorance about horses taken advantage of. He could not believe he had been thrown so easily. He didn't even remember it. He had always been good at anything physical. He could do anything with his hands, with any part of his body for that matter. How could he not ride an unruly horse?

"What would you do if you was me?"

"Take her back or shoot her. Horse been treated this bad this long and dumped as many people as she has ain't gonna ever get better."

Shooting her was out of the question. Ben Tom tried to straighten, but could not.

Joe Henry took the bridle off the horse and replaced it with a halter. "Come on, I'll go with you to take her back. Haven't seen Bob in quite a few years. Be interesting to hear what he has to say."

Bob's rented barn and covered arena was twenty miles east of the Two Hearts Ranch. Joe Henry was surprised when he saw the covered arena on a lot beside the state highway that looked like a converted truck stop. Ben Tom's pickup was still rolling when Joe Henry stepped out and walked back to the trailer.

Ben Tom's face contorted in pain as he stepped out and joined him. "Think I ought to go ahead and unload her, or wait till I see if he'll take her back?"

"You go find Bob. I'll unload her. Unless I miss my guess, you'll find him in some sort of office around here."

Ben Tom knew where it was. Minutes later, Bob scowled as he followed Ben Tom toward the covered arena where the gray was tied. "Did you warm her up or get right on her? This horse always required a little warming up. You got to untrack her."

"We lunged her in a round pen till she broke a sweat before I got on. No more than got my foot in the right stirrup before she broke right in two and dropped me flat on my back."

Bob stopped before they reached the gray. "I'm real sorry about that. Tell you what I'll do. I stand behind the animals I sell. You leave her with me for sixty days, just two months, and I'll put a handle on her will be the envy of any cowboy in the country."

Ben Tom's back started to feel better. "You'd do that?"

"Sure. No charge, either. You only pay for feed and upkeep and her stall charge at four bucks a day. That barely covers my cost."

Ben Tom was still thinking about the dirt cheap training he was about to receive when Joe Henry stepped into view. Bob's face fell. "Joe Henry Leathers. Long time, no see. What brings you out to visit? Need a good horse?"

Joe Henry nodded toward Ben Tom. "Came with him."

Bob Pennebaker let that soak in for five seconds. He focused his most sincere smile on Ben Tom. "Tell you what. This old mare may be getting a little sore in her old age. Sorta like old folks get rheumatism. Could be she may never get back to where she was."

He pulled a wad of bills from the front pocket of his Wranglers, peeled off ten hundreds, and put them in Ben Tom's shirt pocket. "I'll give you your money back and then if I get her completely straightened out, you can buy her back. No obligation."

Joe Henry stepped closer. "Thought you gave fifteen hundred for her."

Ben Tom was flustered. "I did, but..."

Bob interrupted him. "I usually do a restocking charge, but any friend of Joe Henry's." He peeled off five more hundreds and handed them to Ben Tom.

"Don't want you to be out any money 'cause of me."

Joe Henry nudged him toward the truck before he could give part of the money back.

25

BEN TOM NEVER FULLY RECOVERED FROM THE HORSE WRECK, but he continued to work as if there were no pain. He learned to live with it, and he continued to buy horses. Horse jockeys (traders) and trainers learned his name, sought him out.

When it was time for the Riverby Christmas parade, Ben Tom owned six horses, but none would do for a parade. A handsome local horse trainer with some notoriety and a gift for gab heard he was looking and gave him a call. Ben Tom drove away from JJ's little ranch with a beautiful red roan in his trailer.

JJ had impressed Ben Tom by making the roan gelding lie down, sitting on his stomach, then straddling the saddle as the horse stood. JJ claimed the horse had at least ten grand in training, but JJ needed cash for medical bills and would let him go for a paltry seventy-five hundred.

When Ben Tom unloaded the horse for the parade a month later, everyone whistled softly. The roan not only had a beautiful color, but near perfect conformation. Unfortunately, it did not like the local high school band and threw Ben Tom at the first beat of the drum. He was mortified as he struggled to his feet on the downtown square and led the horse away.

Next morning, he took the roan back. JJ seemed elated to have the roan again. Said he had been crippled without him at a recent ranch roundup. Ben Tom waited for his money to be refunded, but JJ asked for a week's training fees in advance so he could get the roan back into shape.

An undersized palomino in a stall caught Ben Tom's eye. It looked like a yearling, not big enough to carry most grown men, but JJ said it was nearly two and ready to begin training. Said the horse was a late bloomer, that late growth was bred into him.

The horse was not ready for actual riding, but JJ saddled him and lunged him in a round pen. The little horse knew when to stop and reversed directions when JJ simply pointed. When JJ shouted "tongue," the horse would lick his lips. Ben Tom saw the perfect horse for Penny. They could ride together along the banks of the Red. He purchased the little yellow horse for fifteen hundred and left him there for his training to be completed.

As they unloaded the roan, JJ saw Ben Tom's almost new saddle in the tack room of his trailer, admired it and asked to borrow it, asserted it might have been the saddle that made the roan buck. He vowed to fix that.

Ben Tom had arrived with a roan who had a propensity to buck. He left behind both horses, a saddle and bridle, and almost two grand (an extra five hundred for a month's training on both horses). When he returned a month later, Purcell went along for the ride. JJ was not there, but Ben Tom's saddle sat outside the barn on a stand. It had been rained on repeatedly and had aged a few years in only a month.

Purcell shook his head. "No excuse for leaving a man's saddle out in the weather. Like poking a man in the eye with a sharp stick."

But JJ had told the truth about the palomino's expected growth spurt. It looked to have gained two hundred pounds. When JJ finally arrived, he led the palomino out and loped him in the round pen. Purcell knew little about horses, but thought the horse looked awkward and certainly not polished, but Ben Tom fell in love with the little colt. JJ pronounced him ready to take home. Ben Tom looked around for the roan. "What about the roan?"

JJ took Ben Tom by the arm and guided him away from the barn and Purcell. "Listen, Ben Tom, I been using that roan doing my daywork jobs. You know I hire out myself and my horse to ranches around here working cattle. I got several people wanting to buy him. You know how he catches everybody's eye."

The praise made Ben Tom tingle with pride. "So, if you been using him, I guess you got the buck out of him?"

154

"Never even offered to kick up his feet since you brought him back. Think it might have been your saddle after all. I left it out so the weather might shape it to his back."

"Where is he?"

"Well, see, that's the thing. I left him over at the Bar T. The owner himself wants to try him out."

"Yeah, but he ain't for sale. I figured to take him back today."

JJ kicked the dirt with a worn boot. "See, Ben Tom, here's the honest truth. I need that horse. Can't quite earn a living without him. Remember I told you I was hurting when I let you have a twenty-thousand-dollar horse for seventy-five hundred."

Ben Tom nodded. "So, what are you saying?"

"Let me buy him back from you. I'll pay you all your money back."

Ben Tom did not want to let the roan go. It was by far the most beautiful animal he had ever owned, with the possible exception of the pure-bred golden lab he bought as a pup for six hundred. "I just don't know. You say you can't make a living without him?"

"That's right. I'm hurtin', man. Got the wife and little girl to support. Medical bills. My little girl has this condition, you know. How about I throw in an extra five hundred for that old sorry saddle of yours? That'll make it eight grand in all."

Ben Tom thought about the bills coming due and his usual shortage of cash. "Hate not having a horse, but I guess if a man has to support his family." He held out his hand for the cash.

JJ ignored the hand. "Oh, you won't be without a horse, that yellow gelding is right as rain. You got another saddle? I got one in the barn I can let go for seven fifty. Been using it on the yellow horse. It's made to order for him."

Ben Tom had a collection of saddles, old and new, but when he saw the one made to order for the yellow horse, it seemed to cry out Penny's name. "Just take the five hundred out of the eight grand you owe me."

JJ spit on one palm, rubbed his hands together and put one forward to shake on the deal. Ben Tom returned with the palomino and an IOU scribbled on notebook paper.

26

FIVE YEARS AFTER PARTING WITH HIS BEAUTIFUL RED ROAN, Ben Tom Lawless had bought and sold more than thirty horses, still owned eight, and had more than twenty automobiles, six of which could be driven. He had more than a dozen buildings filled with antiques, six rent houses, two commercial buildings, and still owned most of downtown Riverby and all of downtown Mesa. Purcell had filled most of Mesa's buildings with his own junk.

Ben Tom saw JJ, the new owner of his red roan, once during that time, but JJ waved and moved quickly away. Ben Tom did not chase him, assuming he was embarrassed because he could not pay him. He figured he would pay when he could. Maybe the money had gone for medical bills for his daughter and Ben Tom was pleased to help with that.

Ben Tom's current supplier of horses and most things equine was named Betty. She seemed hesitant to give her last name. Ben Tom figured it had something to do with a deadbeat husband, illegitimate kids, or a father she was ashamed of. Betty had bought some antique Coca-Cola signs from Ben Tom with a promise to pay in thirty days. Said she had a buyer for them. Six months later, Betty showed up at Ben Tom's mini-ranch, five miles outside of Riverby and six miles away from his home. She unloaded two mares and a colt.

An hour later, she drove away with an empty trailer, two thousand of Ben Tom's money and her debt on the signs paid in full. Ben Tom had purchased the two registered quarter horse mares and the foal. The buck-skin mare was twenty-six and the palomino mare was twenty-eight. Both were in foal. The colt was a mousey-brown ugly duckling, the result of a renegade unregistered stud breaking into Betty's pasture.

But Ben Tom felt like he had struck pay dirt because he had talked Betty into two free breedings from her stud she claimed to be a world champion. Betty called the next day saying she had failed to tell him the buckskin mare could no longer chew nor digest regular horse feed and had to be fed a special mixture. Ben Tom went to the feed store with the list she recited and left with a month's supply that cost almost two hundred bucks. When Purcell saw the mares, he shook his head. "Don't you see she pawned these off on you so they would die here instead of on her place? That she couldn't afford to feed the buckskin?"

Ben Tom was still pleased. "They sure look good for as old as they are, don't they?"

"I hear it costs about a hundred and a half to bury a horse these days. And that colt looks about three generations deep into inbred. He's downright deformed."

"Yeah, but they're bred back. I'll get myself two registered colts out of the mares and two more breedings after they deliver these."

Six months later, Ben Tom was doctoring the palomino for hoof thrush when Irene drove up. She appeared distraught when she stepped out of the car. Ben Tom left the palomino tied to a cable hung from a tree limb and asked his mother to sit with him under one of his giant post oaks. She was filling him in on Buck's trouble with the law and his recent stroke when a pickup they both recognized parked behind Irene's old Ford Falcon. Willy stepped out.

The mongrel colt they named Mouse picked that moment to attack the palomino with hooves and bared teeth. Ben Tom rushed to rescue the mare. The waving motion of his arms as he tried to scare Mouse away disturbed the tied mare more and she bolted against the cable. Willy and Irene ran to help, but their shouts sent the old mare into a panic mode. She stepped over the cable and wrapped it around one ankle. Irene, who had about an hour's experience with horses, reached down to free her. The horse knocked her down. When Ben Tom heard her cry out in pain, he leaned down to help her up just as a bone cracked in the mare's pastern.

Ben Tom gave directions and told Willy to take Irene to the emergency room while he went for the vet. The veterinarian advised putting the old mare out of her misery, but Ben Tom would have none of it. She had a live colt inside her, and besides, he could not hold with killing a defenseless animal. And it was his fault she broke her leg, not hers. The vet put a cast on her leg and left.

Irene returned with her arm in a sling taped to her stomach. She had dislocated her shoulder. Ben Tom brought glasses of tea as they sat back under the tree to watch the old mare struggle with her new cast. He looked at his brother for the first time. It was hard for Willy to disguise his pleasure when Irene told him about Buck's trouble with the law and about his stroke. But he seemed anxious for the talk to leave Buck, horses and the beautiful weather. He clearly had something to say.

Ben Tom kept the conversation with Willy light, asked about Colleen and the kids as he studied his younger brother. Willy's face was now deeply lined and seemed to be an unnatural color. He sucked nervously on one cigarette after another. He finally turned to Irene. "Mom, don't you need to lie down?"

Ben Tom was shocked at how Willy's voice had changed. His voice was coarse and whiskey-smoked, his throat full of gravel. When Irene went over to lie down on a hammock suspended from an oak limb, Willy got serious. "I got problems with Colleen and the kids. She's been messing around with the coyote lives across from me. Threatening to leave me. Kids are turning out to be little thieves and criminals. I need to get a place where I can watch after 'em."

Ben Tom looked toward the hammock. "You sure about Colleen foolin' around? She's a lot of things, but I never figured her for that."

"You think I did? Course I'm sure."

"What do you want me to do?"

"I need to get them out of the city. I know where there's a house if you can help me move it."

"Move it where?"

"Here. We need to get away from the city like you did. Things will get better if I can get her away from that trash she's foolin' around with."

"I know you, Willy, and I'll help you, but you have to tell me the truth. Your story makes no sense."

Willy stood and walked away a few feet, glanced at his mother to be sure she could not hear. "Everything I told you is true. But that ain't all. Things are hot for me in Dallas. That damned Clark left me in a world of shit and I can't find him."

Ben Tom was surprised, though it made perfect sense, that Willy did not know Clark had left, probably under witness protection. "Thought you turned over the stolen goods to the Dixie Mafia. They still after you?"

Willy holds up two close fingers. "Hell, brother, me and Dixie boys are just like that. But Clark was mixed up with the King of Diamonds and he thinks I'm holding some jewels Clark stole from him. Threatened to kill me."

Ben Tom laughed. "You need to read the papers once in a while. That old boy's been locked up for a while. I hear he died in prison."

Willy nodded as if this new information was of little consequence. "You know anything about Jap art?"

"Not a thing."

"When Clark took the jewels, he left behind these Japanese paintings that look like cartoons painted on thick paper."

"So?"

Willy took a long drag off a cigarette, coughed. "I been doing a little fencing." He held up an open palm as if warding off an attack. "Just enough to get by till construction comes back. Anyway, when I tried to sell one of these pieces to another fence, he went ape shit and threw me out. Says the stuff is hotter than a two-dollar whore. There's even a reward offered by the museum that owned it. They got private dicks out looking."

Ben Tom leaned forward. Clark had not mentioned this in his letter to Irene. It was like his uncle to leave behind an ace-in-the-hole and let someone else take the heat for it. "I got an old bank safe in Mesa where I can store the art till we decide what to do. Will that ease your mind?"

There was a slight break in Willy's voice. "It's in my truck. Need to get rid of it before it burns a hole in me."

"Then you can stay where you are if I take the art?"

"That ain't all my problems. You remember the loan shark who kept hassling me? He's in my well."

The revelation startled Ben Tom. "You killed a loan shark?"

"Hell, no, but my Dixie Mafia friend did, then made me drop him in my well. I got to get away from there. How about taking a look at this house I found?"

Ben Tom's mind dropped into his protective mode, then into a fixit mode.

At sunup, he hooked his four-wheel-drive Dodge dualie to a heavy equipment hauler trailer he had just traded for and followed Willy back to Dallas. Willy stopped at a construction site less than a mile from his house where a construction headquarters office building had a for sale sign on it. Willy grew animated as he described the little building to a skeptical Ben Tom. "It's got a little kitchen and bath, a waiting room that will serve as a living room, and three offices that can be used as bedrooms. They're even throwing in a bed the foremen nap on. Hell, it's better than the shack we live in now."

"How much you pay for it?"

"They want five thousand."

"Guess that means you haven't bought it. You got five thousand?"

"No. I figured I would borrow it from you with the house as collateral. We'll pay enough rent to make payments."

Ben Tom knew his own checking account was overdrawn and Willy was flat broke and out of work. "Where you aim to put it?"

"Figured on some of your land or one of your lots. Maybe out on your farm. Hell, Pop tells me you own most of the real estate in that part of the country."

"Five thousand is a lot of money."

"Hell, where else can you buy a three bedroom house for five grand?"

Ben Tom conceded the point, but was less interested in the price than in the challenge of moving it and making it suitable for a family to live in. He asked to use the construction company phone. Banker Mark Conley agreed to approve the hot check if Ben Tom came in to sign the paperwork for a loan the next day.

It took them the rest of the morning to unhook plumbing, get a permit, construct a makeshift ramp, and ratchet the house onto the trailer using Ben Tom's boomer chains. It was just the type of big job that got Ben Tom's blood flowing. There was no chance the house was going to move, but he wasn't so sure about turning over, trailer, pickup and all. It was the construction foreman who pointed out the worn trailer tires.

It worried Ben Tom, but he figured a blown tire was also something he could handle. Another challenge to test his mettle. He turned to Willy.

"You better follow me. We'll be going slow and I don't want some big truck running up my ass."

"I got to run over and pick up Colleen and the kids."

"Now?"

"You best go with me. May have some trouble rounding 'em up."

Ben Tom noticed Willy's house and yard had a rundown, abandoned look, but the thing that grabbed his attention when Willy parked in front of his house was the bar across the front door. It had been padlocked from the outside. "You got Colleen and the kids locked in there?"

"Windows are nailed shut from the outside, too." Willy noticed Ben Tom's look of incredulity. "I told you she was foolin' around with that coyote, but it was really the wetbacks she was messin' with."

When Willy opened the padlock and lifted the bar across the door, Colleen came at him with bloodshot eyes. She went for his eyes with long, dirty fingernails that looked like claws. But Willy had been there before. He was ready and grabbed both wrists before he lost an eye. He wrestled her to the ground and put a knee in her back. He looked up at Ben Tom "May have to tie her up."

"You need to get your knee out of her back before you break something." He got down on both knees and spoke to Colleen. "We got you a nice new house to live in and a nice spot to put it on out in the country. You willing to get in the truck and behave yourself till we get there?"

Willy's two teenagers barreled out of the house, stepped over their mother, glanced at Ben Tom, then sprinted out into the yard. Waylon got behind one big oak and Ruth Ann another. They peered around the giant trunks. The girl's hair was dyed several colors, but purple was prominent. The boy had hair that reached almost to his waist. Both had feral looks in their eyes.

Eight hours and eight tires later, they completed the two-hour trip back to Riverby. Ben Tom spent his last twenty on a used tire only two miles from their destination. Willy stayed with Colleen and the kids while Ben Tom drove Willy's pickup back to the nearest town. It took two hours to find a tire that would work. When he returned, Colleen and both kids were inside the house on the trailer.

It was four the next morning when they finally unloaded the house next to an old abandoned farm house Ben Tom had bought furnished when the couple who lived there died. Ben Tom jacked the portable house up and put it on concrete blocks. He went home to update Penny and returned with more tools. By late afternoon, he had hooked the new house to the old house's cistern and water pump and a line above the ground led to the septic tank. Texas Power and Light turned on the power, and Willy figured out how to connect the propane tank. They moved beds out of the old farmhouse and spent their second night in the new house.

Willy drove thirty miles to the nearest wet town and returned with a case of beer. He popped the first one and surveyed his new abode. "Ain't this nice."

Ben Tom studied the above ground plumbing and makeshift wiring. "Why the hell didn't we just move you into the old farmhouse?"

"Colleen had her eye on this new one. Never had a painted house before. She wouldn't stay in that old shack thirty minutes. Besides, you know you got money made on this little construction office if you ever want to sell."

He downed the last of his sixth beer. "Course, we're at home now and I'll probably try to buy you out one of these days soon if you don't try to make a killing on it."

27

BEN TOM WORRIED A LITTLE ABOUT HAVING WILLY CLOSE AGAIN, about what his friends in Riverby would think of his brother and his family. But the unidentified, strange voice that spoke to him from within, the presence who thirsted for people to take care of, seemed temporarily placated. He now had his father and one brother as dependent on him as his own wife and children. All he needed was his mother and Trez and his mother-hen complex would be sated.

As he drove to Mesa the next morning, he looked forward to telling Purcell another son had moved to Riverby. Ben Tom enjoyed his daily visits with his father. Their roles had somewhat reversed, but their relationship was better than it had ever been. When they worked on a project, Ben Tom issued orders as if his father was his slave, but he always smiled inwardly. Purcell complained incessantly about everything Ben Tom did, but even a stranger could sense a feeling of glowing pride in his son's skills and his generosity and kindness toward people and animals.

Ben Tom found his father sitting in the yard of his trailer house. A fifth of Wild Turkey was snuggled between his legs, and a pile of cigarette butts lay at his feet. He didn't make his usual attempt to conceal them from Ben Tom.

"Looks like you're bound and determined to kill yourself with whiskey and cigarettes."

"Won't be any skin off your nose, I reckon."

"Guess you heard your middle son has moved down here with us."

Purcell took a drag. "Now where would I hear that? He finally leave that crazy bitch?"

165

"Nope, she's the reason he moved. Said he wanted to get her away from bad influences in the city."

Purcell's eyes narrowed. "Where they living?"

"I put them over at the old Taylor farm place."

"That old house needs some work, but Willy's capable of getting it set up, I guess."

"Not living in the old farmhouse. I bought a nice little construction office and we got it set up over there."

"Where did you get a construction office?"

"Close to where Willy lived."

Purcell struggled to stand. "I ain't even gonna ask how you got it down here."

Ben Tom noticed his father's clothes hung on him like they belonged to a bigger man. He had noticed some weight loss before, but had attributed it to hard work in hot weather and poor eating habits. Purcell's face seemed filled with pain as he walked toward his front door. When he stumbled, Ben Tom put a hand under his elbow.

Purcell jerked his arm back. "I don't need no help."

"You sick, or is that whiskey talking?"

"Nothing wrong with me." He pointed a finger at Ben Tom. "This thing with Willy and Colleen and those hellions of his will come to no good. You made yourself a reputation down here. One of 'em will kill it."

Purcell's prediction came true less than a month later. Frustrated when Waylon refused to cut his long hair after the kids at his new school made fun of him, Willy weaved his son's long locks into pigtails, tied ribbons in them, and made him go to school wearing his sister's skirt over his jeans. Willy had no phone, so the principal called Penny. When she went to the school to pick up Waylon, Ruth Ann slipped into the back seat.

Penny turned to face her. "Honey, you can't come home. We're just taking Waylon to get a change of clothes."

The kids had unmercifully teased Ruth Ann about her purple hair, so she screamed at the top of her lungs to go home. Penny relented and drove away. She knocked on the door of the construction office and faced a sullen Colleen, who took out her anger on Penny.

By the time Willy got home from working with Purcell on one of the buildings in Mesa, Colleen and the kids were gone. A neighbor told Ben

Tom he had picked them up on the side of the highway hitchhiking. He took them to the bus station where Colleen bought tickets for Dallas.

At Mesa the morning after she left, Willy vowed to his father and brother not to chase after them. When he did not show up for work the next day, Ben Tom went to Mesa looking for him. Willy's truck was not there and Purcell's was parked in front of his trailer house. He knocked on the door but got no answer. When he didn't find Purcell in any of the Mesa buildings, he tried peeking in the windows of his house, but his father had hung some burlap material over them.

It was too early for him to have passed out from drinking. Worried, Ben Tom jimmied the front door. The shock of what he saw inside almost made him fall back from the front steps. Purcell had never invited him into the trailer before, had in fact, always closed the door in his face the few times he had tried to follow him inside.

The little trailer was full, floor to ceiling, with used clothing, used appliances, car parts, shoeboxes, even some small farm implements. Even the kitchen stove was inaccessible. There was no place to sit in the living room. A trail led to the bathroom and a back bedroom. He found Purcell in the floor, a few feet away from his bed.

28

WILLY SHOWED UP FOR HIS FATHER'S MEMORIAL SERVICE WITH-
out Colleen or his children. He left as soon as it was over without explain-
ing where he had been or if he would return. But no explanation was
necessary. Ben Tom knew he had gone back home. He thought of the work
that would be necessary on the construction office to make it suitable for
rent to the general public. A project he would have assigned to Purcell.

As he spread Purcell's ashes over the small patch of land where he
kept his horses, the sharp stab of grief was his first realization of how much
he had grown to depend on his father, how much he would miss his more
or less constant companion.

Ben Tom suffered his first real bouts with depression during the next
few months. Traces of gray appeared in his hair; the back pain he had
learned to suppress came back with a vengeance. Purcell had been the
object of Ben Tom's practical jokes, had kept him laughing almost all day,
every day. Now, he laughed no more. He had always thought of himself
as invincible. Now, his mortality, in the persona of a hunchback, followed
him all day.

When the crippled palomino mare gave birth to a stillborn colt, Ben
Tom heard his father's voice saying I told you so. The vet begged him to
put the old mare with a broken leg out of her misery while she was sedated,
but Ben Tom refused. He used his tractor front end loader and a shovel to
dig a grave for the colt and built a small fire beside where the mare rested.
He spread an old saddle blanket on the ground and sat by the fire. When
she stirred with pain, he lifted her head and slid his legs under so that

one cheek rested on his lap. She seemed to take comfort as he patted and stroked her face. He slept beside her, letting her breath warm his face.

The mare nickered at daylight, struggled to stand on the partially healed leg that would never be straight again. When she finally stood on all fours, a car pulled into the farm driveway and startled her. Ben Tom was also startled when Trez stepped out of the car. He seemed as crippled as the old mare as he hobbled toward them using a cane. Ben Tom had not seen his brother in almost two years until their father's memorial service. Trez had shown up late and left early that day—left without as much as a word to Ben Tom.

As he watched Trez walk, he thought of the many times his little brother had flirted with death and disability. He had always been accident prone. There was the motorcycle wreck where he broke several bones and took a layer of hide off one side of his body. And the car wreck where he was passed out in the back seat of a car driven by a drunken friend. The friend died. Then there was the time he was high and thought he could fly off the side of a mountain. Trez likely survived because he was so relaxed. And there had been numerous on-the-job accidents, mostly caused by working under the influence of alcohol or drugs.

As he drew closer, Ben Tom noticed Trez's thick, wavy hair was long and matted even worse than it had been at Purcell's service. As the hair caught the light of the rising sun, it appeared as if Trez had loaded it up with too much gel and hair spray, then sprinkled it with a fine layer of dust to keep his coif sturdy. It looked like a clown's wig. Trez's usual charming grin revealed two missing teeth and the rest darkened by drug use. The usual cigarette hung from a corner of his mouth. Ben Tom's brother no longer looked four years younger than him, but twenty years older.

Trez laughed loudly. "Where can a man get a beer this time of day in these backwoods?"

Under the oak tree with iced tea, Trez told his sad story. He had been more off than on work for two years. He blamed it on injuries, but Ben Tom knew it was mostly drugs and alcohol. The last injury, a fall from stilts, had maybe cracked a couple of ribs and his hip, he said. He intended to apply for workmen's compensation and disability. But his immediate problem was that his free and clear house was going to be taken for back taxes. His utilities had already been cut off. He needed a place to stay for a few days.

Trez grinned. "Willy told me about that little construction office he bought and drug down here."

"He bought?"

"I figured you financed it. I know Willy ain't got a pot to piss in or a window to throw it out of. Never has had, never will, as long as he's married to that crazy woman."

"I rented that little house a week ago. Every piece of rent property I got is full of antiques or rented, and I need the rental income."

"How about I sleep on a cot at your house for a few days? Just till I get on my feet."

Ben Tom knew that was out of the question. Penny might allow it for one night, but no longer. She would not abide Trez's smoking or drinking. He knew every piece of property he owned, real and personal in great detail. He closed his eyes and mentally scanned each location for empty space. Nothing.

When he opened his eyes, his gaze came to rest on the fish trailer that sat in the corner of the pasture under some bois d'arcs and locusts. He had recently bought it for more storage. One heck of a buy. It had been part of a tractor-trailer rig used to haul fish and of course, had been refrigerated when it was used. He could probably convert the cooling unit to air conditioning, bring in a portable stove and an outhouse.

Trez was not impressed with what he saw. Ribbed steel two inches above floor level ran the length of the trailer a foot apart, making it difficult, if not impossible to walk. "There ain't no windows."

"Not a problem. I'll cut some."

"I can't walk on that floor."

"I got lotsa plywood. Let me feed this mare and we'll get started."

By late afternoon, Ben Tom had the trailer floor covered in plywood and a half bed he had taken from one of his buildings sat on it. A folding lawn chair sat between an old bedside table and a fifties-era coffee table with a glass top. The mattress was decked out with sheets, blankets and pillows. An antique armoire from Ben Tom's collection stood at the back of the trailer, near the folding cargo door.

Trez raised his shoulders as if he hurt. "Let's take a break."

"Break from what? I ain't seen you lift a hand."

"I'm tired from watching you work. You know I would help if I was able."

Under the oaks with iced tea, Trez seemed troubled. "This is temporary, you know, till I can get my utilities turned back on."

"And what about back taxes?"

"Figured you might see your way clear to a loan. That way, I can get out of your hair and move back home."

Cleaning up Trez's financial disaster consumed three months of Ben Tom's time. When it became clear Trez would never raise the money, he sold Trez's house by White Rock Lake, paid his back taxes and delinquent utility bills, deposited two thousand left over in a savings account in Trez's name.

The savings account ate at Trez. He wanted to spend that money. The more he thought about it, the more he figured he had more than that coming out of a nice house with no mortgage. "How come you nearly gave away my house?"

They sat under a tree in front of the fish trailer. Ben Tom smiled. "You signed the paperwork. You knew the price. You forget you let the place go for years? The roof leaked; the floors were rotting; you never fixed the porch. Then there's five years of back taxes and several months of utilities. Want me to go on?"

"What the hell am I supposed to live on? Hell, you won't even allow me money for cigarettes and beer."

The questions and demands grew in frequency and intensity, especially when Trez needed money for beer. "I'm tired of being babysat out here with you. I don't want to live in no fish trailer anymore. I want my own place. I got my own money."

Josiah Welch, a local evangelical preacher, approached Ben Tom in downtown Riverby the next day. "People say you're the biggest real estate speculator around here."

Ben Tom tried to shake off the praise, but could not. "And you are?"

"Pastor Josiah Welch of the Rivers Crossing Church."

"That Pentecostal or what? My family was Pentecostal."

"We are not affiliated with any national church organization. We prefer to seek the truth without the constraint."

"Sounds good."

"Know anybody who might be interested in a nice piece of land with a mobile home on it?"

The preacher seemed to be an answered prayer. "Where might that land be?"

"No more than three miles from where we stand."

"How much?"

"I fear my little church is in desperate straits, sir. We also have a family in dire straits. For a buyer willing to act quickly, we will let it go for the unheard of price of only eight-thousand dollars. The trailer alone is worth ten."

Ben Tom strolled over the two acres and examined the trailer house. Everything the preacher said seemed to be true. But . . . he had been bitten before. "I didn't just fall off a watermelon truck, Reverend Welch. What's wrong with it?"

"Check it out for yourself. The plumbing works, the septic system is in good order, even the window unit cools perfectly."

When Ben Tom finished verifying everything the preacher had said, he determined the man was the answer to a prayer. He used Trez's equity money, matched it with six grand of borrowed money and took possession of the land and the trailer. Twenty-four hours after the land title was transferred, Ben Tom took Trez out to look at his new home.

But the trailer was gone. A neighbor told Ben Tom a truck had pulled it away under the cover of darkness, ripping away rather than disconnecting plumbing and electrical, as if they were in a big hurry. Ben Tom called the sheriff.

Two weeks later, the County Sheriff located the trailer on a used mobile home lot. Paperwork was attached to the door and sides. Ben Tom ripped off one seizure notice and saw Mark Conley's name in fine print.

Mark leaned away from his desk, affected his normal hands-behind-the-head posture. "We did loan the preacher the money, but we always sell off mobile home notes to a firm that finances them as a specialty. They're not too forgiving when they repossess. Wish you had told me you were going to buy that trailer with the money I loaned you. Thought the loan was for a piece of land."

"It was. Didn't see any need to even mention the trailer, since I got it for next to nothing. The land was worth more than what I paid for it and the trailer."

"Now you know why."

"How do I go about getting the trailer back?"

"Suppose the preacher didn't tell you he was way behind on the payments."

"I only checked to make sure the land was free and clear. You'd have thought a person, especially a preacher, would have mentioned that."

Mark shook his head as he peeled back one sheet of paper and looked underneath it as if he expected to encounter a scorpion. "He owed nearly six grand on the mobile home. Said he had a big high-paying job in Oklahoma when he borrowed the money. Traveled all over the country. Some kind of computer consultant."

"If he had such a good job, why did he get behind?"

Mark was apologetic, knew he had been duped just like Ben Tom. "He had tax returns and a W-2 that showed more than six figures. Should have known better."

"What do I do now?"

"Assuming he hasn't already left the country, maybe you could catch him at his church Sunday morning. Get your money back."

29

PANGS OF GUILT STUNG BEN TOM AS HE WAITED IN THE YARD at Rivers Crossing Church to waylay a preacher. The tiny church looked more like a one-room schoolhouse than a church. He slouched in his seat and waited for the congregation to leave. When Josiah Welch did not emerge, Ben Tom entered the tiny chapel and called his name.

Josiah soon walked through a door behind the pulpit. He was buttoning his shirt and his hair was wet. "Well, Mr. Lawless. You're a little late for church."

Ben Tom surmised the preacher lived in the church, but did not feel comfortable discussing financial matters, especially unpleasant ones, in the presence of the Lord. "Would you mind stepping outside? I need you to take a little ride with me."

When they stopped in front of the land Ben Tom had purchased, Josiah Welch jumped out of the car and beat a path to the site of the torn electrical, propane, and plumbing connections. "Why, what happened? Did you decide to move the trailer?"

"Seems that trailer you sold me was repossessed. You failed to mention you owed money on it."

"I could have sworn I told you I might be behind a payment or two. A needy family in our church has been taking up all of my excess funds, but I never imagined the bank would foreclose."

"Bank didn't. They sold your loan off to some trailer house lender."

"How can I make it up to you? I did, you may recall, ask nothing for the mobile home. I just assumed you would take up the payments."

Ben Tom conceded the point. "I bought that trailer for my brother to have a place to live. Not only is it gone, but now I find out there were delinquent taxes due on it and unpaid water, propane, and electric bills due. They're threatening to cut off all my utilities."

"What would it take to restore my good name with you?"

"You could give me all my money back."

Josiah looked up to the sky. "Alas, if only I could. As a man of the cloth, I give all of my assets to the poor. The only thing I have in the world is the little church building we just left. But I will sign over its title to you right away."

The idea of owning a church appealed to Ben Tom on some level. Two weeks later, he owned one. Josiah agreed to pay him rent based on weekly collections in the offering plate. The next Sunday, Ben Tom and Penny and their children sat in a pew near the back. He did not want to appear mercenary, as if he attended only to collect his rent. In fact, that was not the reason they attended. He wanted his wife and children to know he now owned a church building. "Of course, it's God's church, I'm only a caretaker," he told them. He also wanted the experience of attending services in a building he owned, hoping God would smile down on him. It felt good and Ben Tom was moved by Josiah's sermon on tithing. After the congregation left, Josiah turned over half the collections, still in the plate, as per their agreement. Ben Tom dropped a ten spot in the plate and left it all with the preacher. The process repeated itself for several weeks.

Ben Tom cajoled Mark Conley into loaning him enough money to retrieve the trailer house. He reconnected all the utilities, repaired the damage the trailer had incurred being moved. But Trez found it wanting. "I don't like it way out here. Plumb on the other side of town from where I live now. My dog is likely to get run over out on that road." He pointed west. "And did you see that trashy place down there? Think I'll stay where I am."

"You'd rather live in a fish trailer than in this nice mobile home?"

Trez looked at the lawn that needed mowing. Ben Tom kept the lawn around his fish trailer mowed. "I don't see a TV antenna. Got my television programs all set up in the fish trailer. My alarm goes off at four o'clock every Tuesday and Thursday so I can watch old episodes of *Seahunt* with Lloyd Bridges and *Highway Patrol* with Broderick Crawford."

Ben Tom knew it wasn't the television. Trez had just settled into a comfort zone. He had always been a nester, content as long as his basic needs were met. And those needs were met as long as Ben Tom gave him a weekly allowance for beer and cigarettes. Trez felt he earned his allowance by feeding three horses and two dogs and watering a few potted plants. How would he do that if he moved eight miles away?

The decision suited Ben Tom; he already had a renter for the trailer in mind. They settled into an uneasy truce until Trez demanded his money back for the trailer he refused to live in. And he had no means of transportation. Ben Tom bought him a used Dodge pickup. A month later, Ben Tom left the ramps down on his heavy equipment trailer overnight. Willy arrived drunk in his pickup, drove up the ramps, and passed out in the seat. The next morning, he forgot where he was, stepped out of the truck and fell off the trailer, reinjuring his ribs and hip. The pain made him irritable, made him want more money for more beer to ease the pain.

Ben Tom did not have more money to give. "You're turning into an alcoholic."

"Told you I was an alcoholic when I came out here. Why don't you take me to AA meetings?"

When Penny bought him a Bible for Christmas, Trez turned it over and over in his hand, shaking his head, before he finally said thank you. When Penny left, he complained bitterly to Ben Tom. "This is The Good News Version."

"So?"

"It ain't a King James version."

Trez could complain as much as he wanted about Ben Tom, but he was not allowed to complain about Penny. They argued for more than half an hour about his ingratitude. Ben Tom finally asked, "If you can tell me the difference, I'll buy you the version you like."

Trez threw the Bible back at his brother. "Okay, I never read either one. Satisfied?"

When Ben Tom and Penny arrived for Christmas Eve services at Josiah's church, nobody, including Josiah, came. Ben Tom checked the pastor's living quarters. All of his possessions were gone.

30

THE PHONE CALL FROM COLLEEN WOKE BEN TOM IN THE
middle of the night. Her voice was an odd combination of terror, anger
and slurred speech. "You need to come up here and get your brother. They
got him in the loony bin."

It was mid-morning when Ben Tom finished filling out the paperwork,
paying fines and pleading his case to get Willy out of Timberlawn Psychi-
atric Facility. Willy had almost killed a Mexican who had made advances
to his daughter. Colleen had called the police. Willy had resisted. In the
Dallas County Jail, he had stabbed a fellow inmate with a pencil. The
inmate had broken three of his ribs and damaged his spleen beyond repair.
A week later, the hospital that removed his spleen sent him to Timberlawn
because of his erratic behavior. Colleen was fine with Willy being in jail or
in a hospital, but not in Timberlawn, not a mental hospital.

Paperwork finally approved, Ben Tom helped Willy into his new
Dodge dualie and drove him home. A foreclosure sign was in the yard and
a seizure notice for back taxes was tacked to the front door. Willy's pickup
was up on blocks with the hood up. Colleen was under the porch.

"I see your wife is still nuts."

"It's that Butamol she takes for asthma."

"Looks more like crystal meth to me. Either that or she needs to be
taking something to calm her down and is not taking it. Thought you got
her on some prescriptions."

Colleen's claws scratched at Ben Tom's window. She seemed to have
flown from under the porch like a witch on a broom. He rolled down the

window and she looked at him with red, slanted, dead eyes. She stared at Ben Tom but spoke to Willy. "See your rich brother has finally decided to pay us a visit. Well, I'll tell you this. He ain't welcome here. Him in his new truck and nice clothes."

Willy stared straight ahead, as if looking into her eyes would put him under her spell. "Least he got me out of that nut hospital. More than you can say."

Colleen waved her hand to include the coyote's house, their shack, the well and Willy's shop. "Your do-good brother left us behind in this shithole to deal with all the problems while he moved out to the sticks."

Ben Tom could think of nothing other than his beautiful, gentle, soft-spoken Penny and his two handsome well-behaved children. He wanted nothing more than to be home with them at that moment. He turned to his brother. "Get some clothes. You're going home with me till you get well."

Willy did not move a muscle. Ben Tom opened the door. "Okay, I'll go get you some clothes."

Ben Tom had only been in the house a couple of times before. The stench was overwhelming as he entered. He was shocked at what he saw. Visqueen had been tacked to the living room ceiling and it drooped. When he touched it with a finger, water sloshed and some spilled out. The electricity was off, the commodes stopped up, and no water came from the kitchen faucet. He felt Colleen's dark presence behind him. He turned to face her. "Where are the kids?"

Willy came in the door in time to answer. Colleen left like she could not bear to be in the same room as Willy. "Waylon is in prison for burglary. Ruth Ann run off with a Mexican. She's carrying his bastard child."

"Why have you let the place go like this? At least you could fix the roof. Woulda been easier than hanging Visqueen."

"Been trying to stay out of sight. You forget what I told you was in my well? People see me on the roof liable to come by and pluck me off like shooting fish in a barrel. Besides, I spend a good deal of my time watching that Jap art and looking out for the King of Diamonds. I told you he came by and threatened me."

"And I told you he was in jail or probably dead. Are you working any?"

"Transmission's out on my truck. I hocked my work trailer and they sold it out from under me. They still got my tools, though. Maybe you could loan me enough to get 'em out."

Ben Tom felt helpless for the first time in his life. But only momentarily. He helped Willy stuff some clothes in a garbage bag. "You were right when you said you wanted to get your family out of this hellhole. Should have stayed where you were down there."

Willy nodded toward the front porch, where Colleen spent most of her time. "She ain't ever going back out to the country."

"I'll be back tomorrow with my tools. See what I can fix."

Ben Tom felt wealth-guilt as he stepped into his '95 Red Dodge and drove away with Willy asleep beside him.

He took Willy back when he was well enough and spent the next thirty days driving back and forth from Riverby to Willy's house. He repaired the roof, paid off his back taxes, retrieved his tools from various pawn shops, got utilities turned back on, and repaired his pickup—all with borrowed money. He even took Colleen to a doctor who prescribed pills for what he said was probably a manic-depressive or schizophrenic disorder. The pills calmed her down, brought her out from under the porch, placed her in a chair where she sat in a stupor all day until the pills' effects wore off.

Ben Tom had spent all his nights for a month working on Riverby properties, but without Purcell to look after things, he felt his situation slipping out of control. It had been years since he had done any work of substance on his historical home on the banks of the Red River. He had never completed the inside, and nothing had been done outside. It was in a serious state of disrepair, and Penny was losing patience.

Ben Tom explained he needed to get back and resume work on the house, hoping Willy might offer to come along and help as his way of paying him back. But Willy did not offer. As they stood on the porch and Ben Tom prepared to leave, Willy had a coughing spasm and could not catch his breath. He spat off the porch and Ben Tom saw blood.

"Noticed you been coughing a lot lately."

"Reckon I'm coughing up my lungs. Docs that took out my spleen told me I had cancer in both lungs. Said it had spread to my liver and bones."

Ben Tom leaned on a porch post for support. "Why did you never mention this?"

"What good would it do?"

"What do you aim to do?"

"No idea. Colleen is so sick in the head she can't take care of herself, much less me. Kids too sorry to come back. When the pain gets too bad, I'll end it with that .45 I showed you."

"That's a sin that will send you straight to hell."

"You got a better idea?"

"Yeah, I do."

Two hours later, they stopped in front of Ben Tom's vacant church. An hour after that, Willy was comfortably installed in Josiah Welch's living quarters. Two hours more, the refrigerator was full, and the bed was made. Willy reclined in the chair Ben Tom had scavenged from one of his buildings. Ben Tom handed his brother a beer and took a Coke for himself. "Where better to get well than a church. We'll call this a wellness house."

For the next several days, Ben Tom stopped by morning, noon, and night to bring groceries and supplies to his brother. He carried him back and forth to Parkland Hospital in Dallas twice a week for chemo, made sure he took all his meds.

They sat on the porch and reminisced about old times and their hardscrabble upbringing. The illness softened Willy. He said he had always wanted a Jeep, so Ben Tom made a trip to Dallas and bought him a nice used one with borrowed money. Willy was so sick he could barely drive it from the church to Riverby and back.

During one of their nightly discussions on the church porch, a car pulled into the church parking lot and two women, a blonde and a redhead, walked boldly toward them. The redhead spoke first. "Sorry to intrude, but we sensed a negative aura coming from this church when we drove by. Is there anything we can do to help?"

Willy looked at Ben Tom, who spoke first. "A negative aura, you say. You girls preachers or something?" They did not look like the evangelists Ben Tom had encountered before. They were both pretty, wore light makeup and were stylishly dressed.

"We're evangelists. We conduct healing ceremonies." She pointed at Willy. "I sense you are very ill. Forgive me if I am wrong."

Willy looked past them and up to the moon. "You ain't wrong."

"We want to help. There are no guarantees, but if you're interested, we could try."

Ben Tom looked at Willy, who shrugged. "What do you do in one of these healing ceremonies?"

The redhead answered. "We lay our hands on the sick person, say a few words you won't understand, offer up prayers." She stepped up on the porch and gestured toward Willy. "May we approach?"

Willy nodded. She waved her hands slowly over his head, put one hand on his head and pressed down hard. She put the other hand on his heart. "I sense heat and despair. Do you feel your life has been wasted?"

Tears welled up in Willy's eyes. "It ain't amounted to much."

Both women's eyes glistened as the blonde spoke. "The negative aura came not only from your illness, but my hands tell me you have not been saved. Is that correct?"

The brothers both nodded. The blonde pushed Ben Tom to a corner of the porch. "We can save your brother. Maybe not from cancer, but we can give him new life in the Kingdom of God. But he must be born again."

"The preacher who ran this church left. And I know Willy won't go into a big church."

"We can baptize him right here, if he agrees to accept Jesus Christ as his Lord and Savior."

The next Sunday morning, Ben Tom pulled his heavy equipment trailer into the Rivers Crossing church parking lot. A big horse trough filled with water and covered with a sheet of plywood was held on the trailer with come-a-longs. Ben Tom used six wood pallets to make three steps onto the trailer. The evangelicals stepped up and stood by the trough.

Even with the steps, Willy was too weak and had to be carried up. Ben Tom held his brother in his arms while the two women alternately laid their hands on his head and heart, chanted and prayed in a language neither Ben Tom nor Willy understood. At their signal, Ben Tom eased his brother into the water-filled trough. The women stood on opposite sides of the trough and held Willy's head in a cradle made with their joined fingers.

The redhead spoke first. "Do you freely confess you are a sinner?" Willy nodded.

"Do you trust in Christ as your savior and repent of your sins?"

Willy's affirmative answer was filled with emotion. "Yes."

"In accordance with our Lord's teachings and by His command, I baptize you my Christian brother in the name of the Father, the Son and the Holy Spirit." The blonde put her hand gently on Willy's forehead and pushed his head under the water. He arose crying.

After the baptism, the two women came every day to care for Willy, finally telling Ben Tom they were trained hospice nurses and that Willy needed hospice care. Ben Tom offered to pay them, but they declined. Willy died peacefully in his sleep a month after being baptized.

31

WILLY'S SON WAYLON WAS FREE ON PROBATION AND ATTENDED his father's funeral along with Colleen and Ruth Ann. Colleen wanted the funeral to be held in Pleasant Grove, but Ben Tom paid the final expenses and vetoed that. Josiah Welch appeared during visitation at the funeral home to offer his condolences. Ben Tom hired him to officiate at the funeral.

Waylon, as retribution for Ben Tom not acceding to his mother's wishes, took a few of Ben Tom's tools back with him. Two months passed before Colleen called. "I ain't got a way to get back and forth to the doctor."

Ben Tom was surprised. "What's wrong with Willy's pickup? I put a new transmission in it."

"Some yahoos came and took that truck before Willy's body was cold. I figured you hocked it to get money for the transmission."

"What about the money from the sale of his tools and that old rent house he had? Over nine thousand as I recall."

"I got some left, but I was behind on a few things. Willy left me in a terrible mess, and I can't live on the crumbs you dole out. You want me to be left without any money atall?"

Ben Tom borrowed money to buy a three-year-old sedan, had it inspected and insured, then delivered it to Colleen. He left her with four hundred in cash and the car. On the third day of each month, Colleen called and asked for another four hundred.

A year after Willy's death, Waylon called Ben Tom, but not about the tools he had hocked. "Came home last night and Mama had Daddy's .45 stuck up to her temple. She had already slashed one wrist. Bleeding like a stuck hog."

"Is she dead?"

"I saved her. Took the gun away, put a tourniquet on her arm and hauled her ass to the hospital. I need two hundred bucks."

"Two hundred? What for?"

"After I got her in the hospital, I was pretty upset and had a wreck on the way home."

Ben Tom shook his head. "Suppose you were driving your mother's car."

"What else would I be driving? Anyway, I ran into this crazy bastard—it was his fault. I need the two hundred to get her car out of the pound."

"How did her car get into the pound? Can you drive it?"

"I went down there and looked at it this morning. Pretty bunged up, but I think it will still move."

"So why is it in the pound?"

"Look, Uncle Ben, I had to get away from that car. The guy who ran into me chased me and waved down a cop. I pulled over, bailed out, and took off running. When I went back, the car was impounded."

"So you were drunk."

"I stopped and had a few beers to calm myself down. You try catching your mama with a gun to her head and bleeding from a slit wrist. See how it makes you feel. You'll be downing a few beers yourself."

"First things first. How is Colleen? When can she come home?"

"As long as they believe my story that the cut was an accident, she can come home tomorrow. That's why I need the two hundred, so I can go get her."

"I'll come up and get your mama. She in Baylor?"

"That's where I took her. You don't need to come up here, just wire me the two hundred and I'll take care of it."

"Sounds like the car may not be worth two hundred after the wreck. I need to look. I may decide to leave it there."

"The car ain't worth much, but she had her stash money in the console. You know, that money from you selling all of Daddy's stuff. Hell, one of them attendants at the pound probably already found it."

"Why would her money be in the console of the car?" Ben Tom put two and two together. Waylon had stashed his mother in a hospital, went home to get her money and was escaping in her car when he had the wreck.

"You know Mama is crazy. Said it was the safest place for it. If you'll wire me the two hundred, I'll get the car and see if I can find the gun, too."

"The gun? Willy's .45? Where is it?"

"You know I'm on probation. I can't be caught with a gun. When the guy I hit started chasing me, I had to throw it out the window. Somebody else finds that gun, they'll find Mama's fingerprints all over it and they'll lock her up in Timberlawn for trying to off herself. She may never get out."

Ben Tom rubbed his forehead, tried to ease the headache this conversation brought on. "Whoa. Back up. Why did you take the gun with you in the first place?"

"Panicked, I guess. At first, I thought I might need proof she tried to commit suicide. Then I realized they could keep her locked up if they found out she tried that."

Now it came together. Waylon had left his mother, returned home, taken her money and the .45 and left in her car for parts unknown. Now the gun was on the side of the road and the stash was probably gone.

Ben Tom stood outside the gates of the auto pound, recalling the time his assembled-by-hand '55 Ford Victoria had been inside the chain link fence—how Willy had tried to scale the fence. Now, he was back at the same location driving a new one-ton dualie flatbed truck with a car hauler behind it. He wondered how one claims a vehicle involved in a hit-and-run-and-who-knew-what-else without chancing an arrest.

He had decided not to chance it when someone tapped his shoulder. Waylon smiled as he turned. "I figured I would find you here."

"And how did you get here?"

"I got one or two friends left. Women still like me."

Ben Tom believed that. Waylon was a handsome man and could be charming to women. "Maybe you could get one of your lady friends to loan you two hundred to get this car out of hock."

"Hell, they would in a New York minute, but none of my friends got that kind of money. Don't know why you're worried about the two hundred. Must be more than four thousand in the console. I'll pay you right back."

Ben Tom started to ask how Waylon knew how much money there

was, but he already knew the answer. "It's not the money as much as the chance of getting arrested for something you did last night. How about I give you the money and you go get it?"

"You know I can't do that. I'm on probation. There might be a beer can or such in there. Any sign of alcohol would land me right back in jail."

"Then I think we just have to leave it in there." As Ben Tom turned to walk toward his truck, he saw an arm hanging out the window of a custom black '58 Chevy pickup. The arm belonged to a dark-skinned man with deep lines and prominent bones in his face. The man watched them intently.

Ben Tom walked closer. "Damned if it ain't Deacon Slater. How long has it been?"

Deacon stepped out and shook Ben Tom's hand. "Too long."

Ben Tom looked his old friend over. He had aged, the face was craggier, but not by much. He figured he had to be in his seventies. "I ain't believing this. This is where I first met you when I was just a boy. You hang out here waiting for folks to come along you can help?"

"You're not too far from wrong. I heard about the wreck. It's all over the neighborhood where you used to live. Willy's son and wife being involved and all. Thought I might catch you here."

"Nice of you to come all the way down here just to see me. Wish Willy was here."

"I heard about Willy. Too bad."

"Well, seems like I'm stuck in time. I got the same problem I had back when we first met."

"No money to get it out?"

"I got the money, but I don't know if the car is worth it." He pointed at Waylon. "Waylon there is Willy's son. Nice kid, but ain't got a lick of sense. I think the car might be mixed up in some sort of hit-and-run. I'm afraid to claim it."

"I know the guys in there. Want me to find out?"

Ben Tom paid the tow charge of two hundred plus twenty for storage and another fifty to have the car towed by a union-and-city-authorized tow service to the front gate. He inflated one flat tire on the front using the air tank he always carried on the flat bed of his truck. Waylon watched impatiently. When the car was ready, he got behind the wheel.

Ben Tom twirled the key ring on his finger. "You ain't driving this thing. The frame is bent, wheels are out of line, and it's leaking oil."

"What the hell do you expect me to drive?"

"I'll take you home. I aim to winch the car up on the trailer and haul it to my farm. I'll check it out. If it's safe, I'll bring it back to your mother."

"And how am I gonna go get Mama out of that hospital? They said she could go home today."

"Really? When I called, they told me they were keeping her for at least a week. I'll have the car back by then."

Waylon opened the console and reached inside. Ben Tom reached across and grabbed his hand. "Best leave that be. I'll make sure your mama gets her money back."

Waylon stepped out of the car, made an obscene gesture toward his uncle, and stalked toward a car parked on a nearby street.

Ben Tom called after him. "Hold up, Waylon." Ben Tom approached, put a hand in the small of Waylon's back and pulled the pistol out of his waistband before Waylon could stop him.

"See you found Willy's gun. Good. I'll hold onto it until we get this sorted out."

"You can't just take Daddy's property. That gun belongs to me."

"Remember? You can't be caught with a gun. Just looking to keep you out of trouble."

Ben Tom turned away and walked toward Deacon. "Told you he was trouble. That's probably his girlfriend over in that car."

Deacon smiled. "I can see a lot of Willy in him. But I'm glad he's gone. I got something I want to show you."

32

DEACON PULLED A POST OFFICE DRAWER KEY WITH THE NUMBER seven on it from his pocket. "I been paying the rent on this box for a long time. Clark left me the money to pay it. Said I could give it to you when I thought the time was right, or when the money to pay the box rent ran out. Well, the money ran out last month. Hope the time is right."

"What's in the box?"

"Well, we both know Clark. Whatever it is, it's probably stolen."

Ben Tom laughed nervously. "Just what I need. Stolen goods."

"Speaking of stolen goods, Clark told me he left Willy with some rare Japanese prints. Said they might have been part of Frank Lloyd Wright's collection."

"Yeah, I know about those. They got too hot for Willy to handle, so I found a place to hide 'em. I'm waiting for a way to return them without going to jail."

"This may be your lucky day. Since Clark told me about the prints, I kept my ear to the ground. You know I come across a lot of unsavory characters in my neighborhood. I hear there's a twenty-grand reward offered by a Japanese museum."

"I'm afraid to admit I have the prints. And I don't know where Clark stands for sure. The prints might send him back to prison if he's still on the lam. Course, Willy won't have to worry anymore, but they could come after his wife for possessing stolen goods or some such thing. Or me."

"Let me look into it and see what I can find out. Maybe you can collect anonymously or something like that."

"I wouldn't feel right taking a reward for something that my uncle stole. But I sure would like to get rid of the Jap art."

"Write down your number and I'll call you if I find out anything."

Ben Tom reached into the console of his truck and produced a business card. Deacon read it and smiled. "Blacksmith, Wood, Iron, and Leather Artist, huh?"

"A man has his dreams. One day soon, I'll have time to make that card come true."

"I expect you will. By the way, where's the cross you wore around your neck?"

Ben Tom had to think a few minutes. He knew where everything he owned was, but he could not remember where he had hidden the cross. "In a safe place." He shook Deacon's hand warmly. "Come to see me when you can. Don't just call."

Colleen's car was hardly worthy of salvage, so Ben Tom pushed it off the trailer beside Trez's fish trailer. Trez whistled when he saw the damage. "Told you not to buy a car for that crazy bitch. Look what it got you."

Ben Tom stood back and looked at what had been a clean car. "I'll try to sell it for salvage after I'm sure it wasn't involved in any felonies."

He handed Trez Willy's .45. "You recognize that?"

"Sure do. Willy loved this gun. He carried it around every minute he was at home. Wore a holster like he was some kinda old-time gunslinger. Scared to death he'd need it any time. I always admired it."

"Do you know where he got it?"

"I think it belonged to his loan shark."

"Well, Waylon got ahold of it and I think it might have been used in a killing or a holdup. Can't tell. You keep it under your mattress until we know for sure."

"I may need it for protection. Got any shells?"

"Look in the cylinder, dummy. You're holding a loaded weapon."

Trez laughed and took the gun inside.

Tee Jessup and Joe Henry Leathers advised him to use the money he had found in the console to buy another car, but Ben Tom borrowed more money and bought Colleen another car almost like the one Waylon had wrecked. He insured and inspected it, hauled it to her house and left it in the yard. He picked her up at the hospital and drove her home.

She did not speak to him at the hospital or on the way home. She glanced at the car when she stepped out of Ben Tom's truck. When he handed her almost four thousand in cash he had removed from the car's console and the keys to the car, she wrapped her long fingers around both and said nothing.

Halfway to the house, she stopped and turned. "You know Waylon hocked that chop saw he took from you. Said he would pay you back." The admission seemed to give her satisfaction. She went inside the house and locked the door.

Ben Tom's hand was unsteady as he tried the post office box key. The dark velvet Crown Royal sack with gold drawstring looked as if it had been subjected to a lot of use and abuse. One side was darker than the other as if the light side had been exposed to the sun or the dark side had been rubbed against someone's oily skin. He pulled the opening and looked inside.

Necklaces, bracelets, rings all nestled in a bed of loose diamonds and diamond chips. Willy had lovingly described them many times, cursed his uncle for taking them away. He had spent the last years of his life fearing the King of Diamonds would come for them and kill him because he no longer had them.

Ben Tom failed to see his wooden cross until he started to put the sack back inside the drawer. When had Clark taken his cross and why? He put the cross back around his neck, returned the sack to the box and turned the key inside the lock. He presented the paperwork Deacon had given him to a postal clerk and arranged for rental invoices to be mailed to him.

Joe Henry Leathers listened intently as Ben Tom explained the infamous contents of PO drawer seven in Riverby, Texas. Ben Tom prefaced every sentence with, "Don't say nothin'."

When he finally told the whole story, a long period of silence followed. Ben Tom leaned forward. "Ain't you got anything to say? I thought lawyers were mouthpieces."

"Do I have permission to talk? You told me at least a dozen times not to say anything."

"You know what I mean. I meant this is all secret."

Joe Henry poured them each a cup of coffee. "So what do you aim to do with the jewels?"

"I'd like to find out who originally owned them and return them. Can you handle that without getting me thrown in jail?"

"I'll have to see the jewels. Get a picture. Then I might take a trip to the Dallas County Courthouse and see if I can find any theft records that match what you have."

Ben Tom smiled. "That would be great."

"What if I can't locate the owners? What if they're already dead? You ever consider selling them to somebody? Seems like you could use the money."

Ben Tom stiffened. "What makes you say that? Where did you get the idea I needed money?"

"Relax. You know the bank is my client. So are most of the directors. Mark Conley is my client. This is a small town and that's a small bank. Don't get your dander up. Not many secrets here."

Ben Tom stood as if to leave. "Even if I did need the money, I damn sure ain't taking any money for something that was stole. I got the money to pay you to find out where I can return the loot and I can sure pay you to do it without revealing my name. You willing to do it? You are a lawyer, ain't you?"

Joe Henry smiled. "Take it easy. I'll see what I can do."

33

SEVERAL MONTHS PASSED BEFORE JOE HENRY LOCATED THE people who had a right by inheritance to the stolen jewels. They were heirlooms, and the family was thrilled they had been recovered. In the Dallas County district attorney's office, they signed agreements not to press charges against Ben Tom or any member of his family. Joe Henry represented Ben Tom, who firmly declined to attend.

He also declined the ten-thousand-dollar reward the family generously offered, told the family to donate the money to a charity focused on children and to send him a framed receipt. Said it would give him pleasure to hang it on his wall.

He kept Colleen's car insured and registered and mailed her a subsistence check each month, even after he managed to get her qualified for a government disability check. He never returned Willy's gun for fear Colleen might try to use it on herself again. Trez had grown almost as fond of the gun as Willy had been and begged for it, so Ben Tom said he could keep it permanently. Ben Tom had moved a lot of his possessions out to the property where the fish trailer was parked, so Trez had become his security guard. He also fed the two mares until they died.

The burden of Willy's funeral expenses, supporting his widow, regular handouts to her children, and Trez's increasing medical expenses began to show on Ben Tom. He needed to make some money fast. He went further into debt to buy some properties he thought would flip quickly for big profits, but he set the price too high and they did not sell. He tried out several pyramid schemes including a miracle cleaning product, a miracle food supplement, and a laundry ball that negated the need for detergent. None worked. Then he invented a pet feeder that could be used inside or out and kept pet food safely away from ants and other pests. The product made sense. He made his own prototypes.

Dressed in full cowboy regalia he considered a combination of Tee Jessup and Joe Henry Leather's tastes in cowboy attire, he rented a booth to display his invention at a new products show at the World Trade Center in Dallas on September 11, 2001. When terrorists flew their planes into the WTC in New York, officials worried all trade centers in America were at risk. In the middle of the show, Ben Tom and others were given less than two hours to gather up their products and belongings and evacuate the building.

Ben Tom's product prototypes were light and easy to manage. He loaded them in the wooden boxes he had designed for them, secured the lids, put them on his dolly, and wheeled them toward the exit. He thought a terrorist attack on the Dallas center was unlikely, but the world was turned upside down that day and one couldn't be too careful.

As he passed an artists' show on the way out, someone tugged on his arm. He turned and faced a bald fellow who spoke English well, but with a strong accent Ben Tom did not recognize.

"Are you a real Texas cowboy?"

It was the highest compliment Ben Tom could receive, but he could not accept it at face value. "Just a wannabe, I guess, but I do ride a little. Name's Ben Tom Lawless."

"Peter Umlauf. I'm in a bit of a dilemma. My sculptures arrived by freight from the airport and now they are pressuring me to depart. I can't just leave them here because they offer no secure storage. I'm unsure what to do."

Ben Tom felt the familiar surge of warmth that always arrived when he was asked for help. "What can I do to help?"

"I noticed you in the parking lot. You have a rather large truck. Do you suppose I could pay you to transport my sculptures to a motel or other facility where I might find secure storage?"

Ben Tom looked at the packing crates, thought of the brand new set of tie downs waiting in one of his toolboxes. "Sure. Let me unload my stuff onto my truck bed and I'll come back for your boxes." He pointed at four crates. "Is this all of 'em?"

"Yes. You're sure you don't mind? I'll be happy to pay for your services. I am, as I said, in quite a dilemma. I can't let these crates out of my sight."

Thirty minutes later, Ben Tom ratcheted down the last tie-down strap across the last crate. "Mind if I ask where you're from and where you want to go with these crates?"

"I'm from South Africa and I am embarrassed to admit I have no idea where to go. I checked out of my motel because of poor service and an unclean room. The Trade Center promised secure facilities for my sculptures. I assumed I could locate another motel rather easily."

Ben Tom was familiar with most of the respectable motels and hotels in the vicinity and he and his new friend Peter visited them all. No vacancies. The attack in New York and evacuation of various buildings had filled them to capacity and even their secure storage facilities overflowed. Peter inspected one or two, but could not bear to leave his sculptures in a room filled with items as mundane as luggage. After two hours of conversation and searching, Ben Tom was thoroughly impressed with his new friend. He had never met anyone from South Africa, much less a world-renowned sculptor, and Peter's melodious and accented English sounded like music to Ben Tom.

"Tell you what. How about coming home with me? I can provide a warm bed and put these crates in the same room where you sleep."

Peter was incredulous. "You would invite a complete stranger into your home? This would not be safe in South Africa."

"It is in Texas."

"Do you have a ranch with buffalo or cattle and horses?"

"I have a few horses, but not a real ranch. I have a friend that does, though. Another one has a roping arena."

Peter considered the invitation for several minutes. "I would love to meet more real Texas cowboys and see a Texas ranch, but I'm afraid I need to get home. This attack will keep the world upset for days, if not weeks. Air travel might be restricted now and will only grow worse."

At the airport, they found the restrictions were so bad Peter could not get clearance to fly home. They told him it might take as long as two or three days, even a week. So he went to Riverby with Ben Tom, who showed him around town like he was a trophy. Penny promised to keep an eye on his art while Ben Tom took his new friend to Joe Henry's ranch and Tee Jessup's roping arena. Peter was fascinated with team roping and calf roping. He stayed two days before even checking into shipping his artwork and himself back home.

He feared shipping his sculptures much more than flying home himself. He had enough influence in South Africa to request and receive special consideration and extra precaution in shipping his work to America, but worried such influence disappeared after nine-eleven. Airlines and freight companies confirmed his fears. As a foreign national, he would be treated like a likely terrorist and his crates would be considered possible bombs.

When he found the crates would have to be opened and their contents inspected, he was distraught and showed it. Ben Tom did not know how to reassure him, but Peter came up with his own solution. He left his artwork in Ben Tom's care and left on the first flight that would clear him.

Joe Henry and Tee were almost as fascinated with the South African sculptor as Ben Tom was. After securing their sworn secrecy, he showed them the crates he had stored in Mesa's bank vault and the vault door he had reinstalled.

Tee put a hand on the top crate. "What's inside?"

"Don't say nothing, but valuable artwork. This guy is famous in South Africa."

Joe Henry tugged on his earlobe. "Maybe. But why would he leave something so valuable here?"

"I told you. He didn't want to have to open it and they're opening everything after the terrorist attacks."

Tee nodded. "Artists can be weird. How long does he want you to keep it?"

"Didn't say, but I expect he'll send for it anytime. Said to look for a call from a freight company."

Joe Henry dragged up a dusty cane bottom chair. "What if the crates are full of bombs, or drugs?"

34

PETER UMLAUF'S CRATES HAD GATHERED ALMOST A DECADE of dust before Mark Conley visited the old bank in Mesa. Mark banged on the glass windows cloudy with dust until Ben Tom appeared and opened the door. Ben Tom was more stooped than his years, his face more lined than it should have been. The years after Willy's death had been filled with a constant stream of demands on his time and resources. He provided care and financial support for the family Willy left behind and for Trez, who continued to live in the fish trailer. It also seemed Ben Tom was like a beacon in the desert for every needy person in East Texas.

They came from all over, scalawags, con artists, bums, and good people down on their luck. Even stray and abandoned pets, especially horses, found their way to his door. Four decades of being an easy mark or being overly kind and generous, depending on how you looked at it, had earned Ben Tom a following of people who were in need. He never turned any of them away, even the ones known to use his money for alcohol, drugs, or to fund a gambling addiction. Ben Tom always figured this time would be different.

The roller coaster ride in the markets for antiques and real estate had only exacerbated his precarious situation. The regal home on the Red, no longer fit for human habitation, had been abandoned. A stately old commercial building in downtown Riverby had been renovated, filled with antiques, and made suitable as Ben Tom and Penny's residence and primary place of business.

It suited them to live behind their storefront antique store, so Penny could wait on customers while Ben Tom searched for more antiques. He also sold used cars, trailers, tractors, and other farm equipment on the road that ran by his farm. Trez helped out with these transactions.

But Mark Conley hardly noticed Ben Tom's wearied face and posture. Ben Tom, however, did notice Mark's. The bank president pulled up a dusty chair and almost fell into it. He jerked his tie away from his collar and wadded it in one hand as he looked up and gave Ben Tom a smile filled with pain.

"Need a favor, old buddy."

Ben Tom's face showed his concern. Mark's words were slurred and he reeked of alcohol. "Anything you need, friend. You've always helped me out plenty."

"Hate to have to ask you this, but I'm in a bad way. I need ten grand by Friday."

It was Monday, and Ben Tom was confused. *Why would a banker need ten grand by Friday?* "I ain't sure what you mean."

"Sounds strange, I know, coming from a banker. But I let myself get overextended at the bank. I need to cover up my mistakes before the directors find out. Could lose my job if I don't."

Ben Tom tried to make light of the uncomfortable situation while he thought how he might help. "Ain't you got this backwards? You're the one that loans me money, not the other way around."

Mark did not smile. "It ain't no laughing matter. My family, my house and ranch, my whole future is on the line. If I don't put that money back by Friday, I could even go to jail."

Put the money back? Jail? This sounded ominous and explained the liquor-breath. "You know my bank balance ain't seen ten thousand for more than a few hours in years. It goes out as fast as I put it in."

"You're the only one I can turn to, the only one who will keep my secret."

Ben Tom thought of the stranger who had offered him ten thousand for his '55 Ford over the weekend. He had laughed at him, but had taken his card. He fished around in his too-thick billfold for it. By noon on Wednesday, the Ford was parked in front of his antique shop and the buyer peeled off hundreds into Ben Tom's open palm in full view of everyone on the town square. Ben Tom's breath caught in his throat as the man drove away his most prized possession. He hoped Penny wasn't watching. They had begun dating in that car.

He went inside and stuffed the bills into a large envelope, sealed it, and wrote Mark Conley on the front. He felt better as he strode toward the bank. But Mark was not in the bank. When he asked to see him, a teller took him aside and whispered he might find Mark at Wheeler Parker's; that he wouldn't be in the bank for several days at least.

Wheeler Parker was a known bootlegger who lived on the banks of the Red, a few miles northeast of Ben Tom's house. His shack by the river, The Wheelhouse, was a known hangout for men who preferred the company of other men and whiskey to that of their families. Ben Tom had accompanied Joe Henry there once when Joe Henry had gone to retrieve a client close to jumping bail and forfeiting the bond Joe Henry had helped him to obtain.

The joint seemed harmless enough. Just a place where lonely, down-on-their-luck, and usually older men could buy liquor cheap and drink in peace and quiet. But it was not a bar where one would expect to find the pristinely dressed and well-mannered Mark Conley. Ben Tom was confused as he walked to the two adjoining buildings on the corner of the Riverby square.

Joe Henry Leathers, attorney-at-law, occupied the corner building and Tee Jessup, CPA, occupied the old building next door. Joe Henry owned them both. The lawyer was in court, and the CPA was with a client, so Ben Tom took up residence in Tee's waiting room. He sat quietly, listening to the sounds of Verda Lemon's police scanner in her Four Forces Beauty Salon that connected to Tee's office. No matter how long he pondered, he could not come up with an answer, but he figured Tee would know what to do about Mark Conley.

Tee followed his client out of his office to the street, holding up a finger that told Ben Tom he would return. On the street, Tee asked his client to wait and returned to his reception area. He saw the distressed look on his old friend's face. "What's up?"

"Need some advice."

"Sure. Can it wait till morning? I got a sort of emergency with this guy out there. Probably won't be back till after bedtime."

Always accommodating, Ben Tom nodded. "Sure. Guess it can wait. Joe Henry can't talk to me either. Till when?"

"How about I meet you at the old Mesa bank building at sunup? I'll bring the shyster next door and we'll have some of your good coffee like the old days." Tee dearly loved to sit on the wooden sidewalk in the old ghost town with his two best friends.

Ben Tom waved. "Sunup, then."

The coffee was hot inside the old bank vault when Tee and Joe Henry arrived the next morning. Joe Henry pulled back the tarp that hid the crates left behind more than a decade ago by Peter Umlauf. "I still can't believe this guy left his artwork here all these years without ever contacting you. I'll bet he's dead. You ought to crack these open and see about getting them to his next of kin, maybe collect a reward."

Tee laughed. "You're just curious to see what's inside."

"And you ain't, I suppose."

"Have to admit I am." He looked over at Ben Tom. "Let's get a crowbar and see what's in there." They all laughed. It was a long standing joke between the three friends that Ben Tom would not touch the crates entrusted to him. He would guard them with his life—all of his life.

Ben Tom waved them both out of the vault and onto the porch. They passed the usual compliments and complaints on the weather and generalities before Joe Henry got down to business. "You hear about Mark Conley?"

Tee waved off the comment. "Before we get into that, we need to find out what Ben Tom came to see us about yesterday."

The ominous timbre of Joe Henry's deep voice had made the hair on the back of Ben Tom's neck stand up. "Mark Conley is who I came to see you about. What about him?"

"Showed up at a directors' meeting with alcohol on his breath, slurring his speech. They fired him on the spot."

Ben Tom's voice was a loud whisper. "They fired him?"

"That's a mostly Baptist group over there. Won't stand for drinking on the job."

Tee shook his head. "I heard they were just looking for an excuse. I been hearing about and seeing a lot of questionable loans when my clients come in."

Ben Tom was incredulous. "But he just built that big house. Told me he had almost five hundred head of cattle and just bought another hundred."

Joe Henry and Tee exchanged knowing looks. Tee walked beside the old bank window to the edge of the board sidewalk and looked out on the deserted street. The scene always took him back in time, relaxed him, like he was in a time warp a hundred years earlier. "I think it was the loans on the house, cattle, tractors that really took him down. The loans he made to himself, not so much to other customers."

Ben Tom stood and leaned against a porch post. He needed it to hold him up. "I was going in to see him this week to renew a few notes."

Tee stared at his boots. "Better get ready. I expect the examiners will be in there in a matter of hours, not days. When something like this goes down, they usually do a full-blown audit."

"Don't say nothin'." Ben Tom filled them in on his visit with Mark.

Joe Henry gave Tee an ominous look. "That more or less confirms what I heard. They think Mark may not just have made one too many loans to himself, but he may have moved funds from a customer's account to his own to cover overdrafts. This could be criminal."

Tee leaned forward. "He really asked you for ten grand?"

"Yep."

"Good thing you found out what was going on. You might have given it to him. He'd more than likely have it drunk up by the end of the month."

Ben Tom lost interest in the conversation after that. His guests sensed he had become morose and stood to leave. Ben Tom offered more coffee in go cups, but they declined. They had been gone for two minutes when Tee returned and stuck his head back in the vault where Ben Tom was cleaning up. "You're not thinking of giving him the money, are you?"

Ben Tom shrugged. "Where am I gonna get that kinda dough?"

◆•••◆

Ben Tom stepped into the Wheelhouse Bar at just after three that afternoon and let his eyes adjust. Mark Conley sat slumped in one chair, only partially conscious. He touched his shoulder and Mark looked up through red eyes, but did not speak. Ben Tom slid the envelope filled with money across the table, Mark covered it with his hand, looked up with a crooked grin, and mouthed, "Thank you." Ben Tom patted him on the back and left.

Tee was waiting when he returned to his farm. Ben Tom always went there when he needed repair, when he needed respite from the pressures of daily living. And Trez had a knack for making him laugh at his own troubles.

Tee stepped out of his dad's restored '57 Chevy pickup and walked toward him. They stared at each other for an uncomfortably long time as Tee tried to read his mind. "Don't lie to me now. You gave him the money, didn't you?"

35

BEN TOM SEEMED SMALLER AS HE SAT IN TEE'S OFFICE SIX months after he loaned his last cash to an alcoholic banker. Tee was peeved at his friend for doing it because he knew more about Mark Conley's situation than ethics would allow him to reveal. The bank president had been drinking too much for quite some time and was a full-blown alcoholic when Ben Tom turned over ten thousand in cash to him.

Now, the bank called in its chips, trying to survive, to fight off regulators who wanted it closed. Tee rapped on his desk because he did not feel he had Ben Tom's full attention. "I looked over all your notes. Most of them are short-term and most have come due since this disaster started." Tee paced beside his desk. "But you knew that, of course."

Ben Tom did not look up. "I never been late on a payment. Not once." Tee knew that was true. Ben Tom had always managed to pull a rabbit out of his hat just when Tee thought he was going down for the count. Tee had always called him a creative genius and had to admit Ben Tom was a shrewd buyer of antiques and artifacts. When he needed money, he usually located and bought one or more items and turned them before he grew too fond of them to let them go. The longer he held them, the more he raised the price. Pretty soon, nobody could afford them.

Of course, he had had a willing partner on financing in Mark Conley, who renewed all his short term notes without asking uncomfortable questions.

"Damned if I know how to criticize a man for being too generous, too caring, but that's my job, I guess. You're going to have to cut a few people

205

loose. Stop the bleeding. Start thinking about yourself and Penny. Focus on that."

Tee knew about his support for Willy's family and for Trez, but he did not know about the dozens of aunts and uncles, nieces, nephews and cousins, derelicts and deadbeats that thought of Ben Tom as super rich, a ready source when they got into tight spots. Ben Tom knew he would have to start with Willy's family. "Will it be enough if I slow the bleeding to a trickle instead of a flood?"

"Bleeding is bleeding. If you don't stop it, it will kill you sooner or later. You're also going to have to raise some cash fast. Sell some stuff you want to keep. Drop the price on some real estate and turn it. You can get out of this hole if you can get your debt under control. You have enough assets. You're not bankrupt."

"How long you figure I got?"

"Six months, probably less. And that's if you let the bank and the regulators in on your plan."

Colleen and Waylon did not take the news well when Ben Tom told them things might change. They always figured the money he doled out each month was rightfully theirs. Some figment of their distorted imaginations told them Willy had left an estate that would feed, clothe and shelter them forever. This in spite of the fact he had spent his life dead broke.

Ben Tom warned them things were tough, but he kept right on giving them money. In fact, doling it out during emergencies cost him more than the monthly stipend had because their lives were one emergency after another.

Trez also did not take it well. Ben Tom tried to stick to his guns. "Won't hurt you to do without beer and cigarettes till I can get back on my feet."

"Since when is it any of your business what I do with my money? I get damn little else in the way of creature comforts living out here all by myself in a damn fish trailer, looking after your shit. I already told you I'm an alcoholic. You can't just ask me to quit cold turkey."

"You been after me for a long time to take you to AA meetings. They won't cost anything. I can take you now."

Trez felt he earned his food, clothing, shelter, as well as beer and cigarettes by feeding horses and dogs as well as providing security for the small farm where he lived. He also had a vastly distorted version of his net worth after liquidating his single valuable possession, his house.

But his major concern was that he would not receive the new hip he thought would relieve his pain forever. This in spite of orthopedic surgeons trying to lower his hopes and expectations, advising he was not a candidate for replacement. They increased his pain meds to compensate for the bad news.

The pain meds worked better than beer for Trez, so well he overdosed a few times, putting himself into a drugged stupor. Ben Tom hid the pills after the second episode and began handing out a daily ration. This further frustrated Trez. When Ben Tom applied for and obtained government assistance for Trez's medical bills, Trez found a few docs who were more liberal with their scrip pads. Soon, he had pain meds Ben Tom did not know about. The drugs altered his brain chemistry, turned him from a happy, joke-telling, affable drunk into a man addicted to pain killers that sent him on a roller coaster ride from high mountains of euphoria to the deep, dark valleys of depression.

Ben Tom found him outside his fish trailer on a warm summer morning. He and his little brother had spent the entire day together the day before, and he had left Trez high on a mountain the previous night. The sight of his brother's cold body dropped him to his knees with surprise and dismay. Trez had plunged into a valley of despair during the night. Willy's .45 lay in the grass beside him.

Trez's death affected Ben Tom much more than Purcell's or Willy's. He had been with Trez at least once, usually twice every day for years. He had comforted him when he was down, laughed at his jokes when he was up; had taken him to doctors and hospitals; had seen to it that he had food, shelter, clothing, beer and cigarettes for more than a decade; filled out paperwork for the hip surgery that never came; argued with care providers and bureaucrats on his behalf.

Trez had fed his horses and dogs, watered his plants, told Ben Tom he loved him every day, apologized after most of his fits of complaining or visits to the deep valleys of despair. He filled a need in Ben Tom deeper than Trez's need for his older brother.

Ben Tom felt a sense of urgency to fill the hole left by Trez's death, but he was out of brothers. Irene lived alone and cared for a sister, so she could not fill the need-to-be-needed void in Ben Tom. And there was the matter of troubles with the bank.

In a few weeks, he recovered enough to sit down with Tee again and try to figure out a way to keep the bank from calling his loans and foreclosing on his real estate. Tee drummed his fingers on Ben Tom's file folder, trying to adopt the image of a stern CPA helping a client who was not a close friend. "You refuse to lower your real estate prices. You refuse to part with antiques. You even keep buying, adding to your already bloated inventory. Last time I counted, you had sixteen cars. You're out of time and out of cash."

"How much time do I have?" Ben Tom, for one of the few times in his life, felt helpless. He knew of no rabbits to pull from a hat. He had no alternative plan he could implement quickly.

"You asked me that six months ago and I told you six months, maybe less. Now, it's more like weeks. If the regulatory authorities take over, they won't show you any mercy. They won't know you from Adam."

"So what can I do?"

"The only thing I can think of to raise the kind of money you need quickly is an auction."

36

THE SATURDAY DAWNED CRISP AND SUNNY. TEE AND JOE HENRY arrived at sunup, barely glanced at their offices as they watched strangers mill around the downtown square at first light. Ben Tom's antiques were on tables and on the grass in two vacant lots and scattered all along the sidewalk. Two of his downtown buildings were also scheduled to be auctioned. It was an event the likes of which Riverby had never witnessed. Tee pulled his hat down and put on the denim jacket he had pulled from behind his pickup seat and carried on his arm during their first look at the antique and junk-filled tables. "Can't believe it's this cold. Glad I had this jacket in my pickup."

Tee examined the green wool sweater his friend wore. It was full of holes, decorated with evergreen and snowflakes, contrasting sharply with the lawyer's black ostrich boots and 50X beaver black hat. "See you're ready for Christmas."

"I don't like to keep my good garments behind my pickup seat. This is all I could find in there."

"Looks like it's been in the floorboard and picked up a little grease."

"We can't all be clotheshorses like you."

"What is it they say about the pot and the kettle?" Tee focused on the tables scattered across the lots. "Don't know about you, but it looks like he's still holding out on the good stuff. The buildings will have to go for a good price to raise the money he needs. This junk sure won't do it."

"Yeah, he's got some really good western pieces I hoped to bid on. Don't see any of them out here."

"I knew he would hold back, keep the things he loves most. Where you reckon he is?"

Joe Henry pointed. "There he comes across the square now. I don't like his posture. He looks pissed."

They intercepted Ben Tom in the middle of Texas Street. "When does it start?"

"Eight." Ben Tom, always affable, was clearly irritable.

Tee had never seen him like this. "You seem a little irritable. Something not going to suit you?"

"Nothing suits me. I been up all night, guarding all my stuff left out here in the open. People who suggest auctions don't give much thought to all the things that go into putting one on."

Tee had half expected this reaction. Ben Tom felt the auction had been wrongfully forced on him. Tee was an easy target, because he had suggested it. "It was either have your own auction or watch the bank repossess your stuff and have one of their own. This way, you get at least some semblance of control and you save your credit rating."

"My credit is first rate, top notch."

Joe Henry could see an argument coming. "Look at this way. This auction will raise enough money to get you out from under most of your debt. Give you lots of leeway for the future. If the bank had foreclosed, and the auditors would have forced them to, your credit would take years to repair."

Ben Tom still bristled. "I got news for you two. Look around. You see any antique buyers?"

The crowd's scruffiness was only interrupted by a few farmers who looked well-to-do. "These are farmers, junk dealers, curiosity seekers, and people looking to pick over my bones. The farmers are the only ones with money and I ain't got much in the way of farm equipment."

Tee looked at Joe Henry. He did not want to remind Ben Tom he had urged him to delay another week, to mail postcards to the antique dealers and buyers he knew. But once the auction decision had been made, Ben Tom's attitude was like a criminal sentenced to death who wanted to go directly to the chair.

When the auction started, each shake of the auctioneer's fist and the sound of "sold!" was like a hot branding iron on Ben Tom's heart. Watching him flinch with each sale worked on Tee and Joe Henry. Trying to stay ahead of the auctioneer and select some things they could buy to help out, they wandered away from Ben Tom to the next area to be auctioned.

They were back on the square buying hot dogs from a vendor at noon when they saw Penny trotting toward them. "Do you know where Ben Tom is?"

They both shrugged as Tee answered. "Thought he might be back inside having lunch with you."

She looked desperate. "I looked in every building downtown. Can you help me find him?" She touched Tee's arm, a rare gesture by the ultra-shy Penny. "You know about Wallace Briscoe, the retired doctor who's buying up cattle and horses and land around here as fast as he can?"

Joe Henry nodded. "I know him. Did a little title work for him."

Tee had a knowing expression on his face. "Did he make a firm offer on the buildings?" He had been present weeks before where Dr. Briscoe had made Ben Tom an offer on the old JC Penney building and another building that formerly housed Woolworth's five and ten.

"Yes. He said he would up his previous bid, but I don't know by how much. I spoke to the auctioneer and he said we had two hours to firm it up. Otherwise, they go on the auction block."

Joe Henry looked at Tee. "Is he making a fair offer?"

"His first one was a lowball, for sure, but who knows what might happen in the auction. I don't see any real estate speculators here. It could go for next to nothing. I urged Ben Tom to accept it. If he's increased it, I would take it for sure."

"You go to Mesa; I'll head to the farm. He'll be at one or the other."

Joe Henry found him sitting between two giant post oaks on the farm. Three antique metal chairs sat empty around a table made from an old Coca-Cola sign. Antique cowboy tin cups filled with coffee sat in front of each empty chair. An old gallon trail-ready coffee pot sat on some stones surrounding a glowing fire. It was usually a friendly, welcoming site, a place where Joe Henry had enjoyed many cups of coffee. But today seemed different. The look on Ben Tom's face was not the welcoming one he always found there. He removed his black hat and used it to gesture toward the empty chairs. "Expecting company?"

A long, uncomfortable silence followed. Ordinarily, Ben Tom would have been on his feet, offering a variety of things to eat or drink. His eyes were red. In the embarrassing silence, Joe Henry noticed the chairs he thought were empty each held something. A pocket knife in one, a cap in a second, a hat in the third.

Ben Tom finally spoke. "Having a little powwow with my dad and my brothers."

His voice was ragged, cracked. Joe Henry looked away rather than see the tears. Ben Tom stood, picked up the coffee pot, poured a fourth cup of coffee, and dragged up a fifth chair. "You probably think I've gone crazy, and I ain't so sure I haven't. Couldn't stand there a minute longer and watch my life unraveled by a bunch of bone pickers."

Joe Henry's eyes widened when Ben Tom placed the .45 in the middle of the table. Ben Tom smiled. "Don't worry. I ain't the type. Always do what The Man Upstairs tells me to. He wouldn't want me to take my own life. Just can't figure what to do with this thing. Should have put it in the auction, I guess. You want it?"

"It's a beautiful weapon, but I think not."

"Don't blame you. It had some history, even before Trez used it on himself."

"I don't mean to rush you, but Dr. Briscoe has upped his offer on the buildings and you ain't got long to make up your mind."

"He did, did he? I told Tee he would." He gestured toward the three empty chairs. "Pop took care of us as good as he could, but I looked out for my brothers when he and Mama couldn't do it anymore. After we were grown, I tried to take care of all of 'em. Pop too."

"I know you did."

"But trying wasn't good enough. Look at what's happened. Pop's gone, then Willy, then Trez. I'm the oldest. I should have gone first. I failed, I guess."

"Don't see how any man could have done more, done it better than you."

Ben Tom agreed to follow Joe Henry back into town. Tee sat in on the final negotiations and wangled five thousand more out of Dr. Briscoe. Ben Tom wanted twenty thousand more. As the deadline approached, Tee pleaded. "If it were me, I would not only sell those buildings, I'd sell almost all your real estate, your cars, your junk, and most of your antiques. A man should do what he is called to do, his highest calling, and yours is creating something beautiful and useful out of nothing."

They closed the deal on the buildings five minutes before the deadline and pulled them out of the auction. The auctioneer was not happy, but he stuck to the agreement made in advance.

Relieved their friend would have enough with the sale of two buildings to get the bank off his back, and with the things they had spotted to buy already gone at fire sale prices while they looked for Ben Tom, Joe Henry and Tee sat down on the square and watched the auction continue.

Tee spoke first. "He still won't have any cash left when this thing is over. The bank will take it all. Maybe a lawyer can explain why a man with a bigger heart than either one of us, a man who always does right by others when it is harmful to himself, is so down on his luck."

"Takes a bean counter to do that."

Tee nodded. "I watched most of it happen, but how do you criticize a man who is too generous, too kind hearted. You and I both know there is no better man in this whole county than Ben Tom Lawless."

"You should have seen him out on his farm holding council with his dead family members. It was a sight to see. Think he blames himself for what happened to them."

Tee shook his head. "He has a belief system, a strong one, but I don't pretend to understand it. He talks a lot about The Man Upstairs when he does something that seems dumb to me. Says that's what The Man wanted him to do."

"I could never understand why he hates cash so much and loves old things with a reverence I never witnessed before."

"I'm no psychologist, but I think it has something to do with his uncle and several other family members being thieves. They would steal stuff and quickly turn it into cash. He wants to do the opposite, turn cash into stuff. He figures every one of those pieces will someday bring joy to somebody. He doesn't figure cash on its own can do that."

"You fellers ever read Job in the Bible?" The good reverend Josiah Welch stood a few feet away, taking in every word.

Tee did not care much for Josiah Welch. He knew he had swindled Ben Tom and suspected he had done the same to others. Nothing worse than a man who uses religion to take advantage. He spoke without looking directly at the preacher. *"The Lord gave and the Lord hath taken away, blessed be the name of the Lord."*

Josiah's and Joe Henry's eyebrows raised. Josiah spoke first. "Very good."

Joe Henry shared Tee's feelings about the preacher. "You saying the Lord is going to take away even more?"

Their contempt was not lost on the preacher. "I know you fellers found out about my prior evil ways. Instead of me converting him, Ben Tom converted me from my evil ways by setting a good example of a Christian life, how a man ought to live. I have confessed my sins to God and to Ben Tom Lawless. They have both forgiven me. I hope you two can do likewise."

Startled, they both nodded. Joe Henry asked, "So what about Job?"

"Then came unto him all his brethren . . . they comforted him over all the evil that the Lord had brought upon him; every man also gave him a piece of money, and every one an earring of gold. So the Lord blessed the latter end of Job more than his beginning."

The preacher wagged his finger knowingly. "Paul tells us in Ephesians 2:10: *For we are God's handiwork, created in Christ Jesus to do good works, which God prepared in advance for us to do.* Mark his words. Ben Tom Lawless was created to do good works and he will continue to do so."

37

BEN TOM DISAPPEARED FROM THE STREETS OF RIVERBY THE
day after the auction. He entered his living quarters only from the back
alley after that terrible day. He was ashamed, afraid everyone in Riverby
assumed the bank had forced the auction. He felt the reputation he had
worked so hard to build was gone. And his financial troubles were far from
over.

The small sum left after paying his current notes at the bank was soon
gone, passed on to Willy's family as a hopeful final payment. He returned
to his generous ways, sometimes driving Tee Jessup to distraction as Tee
tried to chart a course for permanent financial security for his friend and
client. Ben Tom reverted to selling junk and used cars to pay his now
growing-again property taxes, insurance and maintenance costs.

But the auction and the deaths of his brothers and father had changed
Ben Tom. Always upbeat and positive, he now seemed morose, often
secluded himself for days at a time to grieve over his failures and losses.
The regal house on the river mocked him as it deteriorated daily. He had
let his lovely wife down, disappointed his children. He spent an inordinate
amount of time thinking about how the people who depended on him
would fare if he departed this life. Death seemed to stalk him.

Joe Henry and Tee still sought out their old friend, sat down with him
for coffee and bagels or a platter of Ben Tom's homemade biscuits, usually
at the old bank in Mesa, but sometimes on Ben Tom's small farm. His
back troubles were compounded with a variety of other ailments he tried
to conceal, but could not. His eyes revealed constant pain. His posture

revealed a broken spirit. But his voice still expressed unbridled optimism and the confidence of better days ahead.

——————

Two years after the auction, a small, lean man with unruly gray hair and matching mustache appeared on the Riverby square. His face was all sharp angles and protruding bones, with sunken cheeks and a cleft chin. The sharp lines along his cheeks were dotted with whiskers his razor had passed over. His hat was a cattleman's with a line of sweat along the band, well worn and worn well. He seemed comfortable in the hat and in his skin.

He stopped in front of the JC Penney building and addressed a short man sitting in a chair on the street. "Looking for the fellow who owns this building."

"You found him. Who might you be?"

"Name's Deacon Slater. I understood Ben Tom Lawless owned this building and most of the others on the square."

The rotund man drew himself to his full height and stuck out his chest. "Not any more. I'm Dr. Wallace Briscoe and I own most of the buildings Mr. Lawless used to own."

"You a medical doctor?" Deacon noted the potbelly and sallow complexion and wondered about a man who didn't follow his own medical advice.

"I am, sir. Partially retired. I mostly ranch now."

"Well then, maybe you might direct me to where I could find Ben Tom."

"You a bill collector?"

Deacon took offense, not so much for himself, but for his old friend. He wondered if Ben Tom was in trouble. "No, just an old friend."

The good doctor was leery of all strangers, but reluctantly directed Deacon to Joe Henry Leathers' office, figuring a lawyer could set him straight without getting anyone into trouble. Sitting in one of Joe Henry's impressive and massive horn chairs, Deacon told him, "I know Ben Tom from his days in Dallas. I have some news I think he will want to hear."

Joe Henry offered to take him to Mesa and the farm, Ben Tom's usual hangouts. "I appreciate the kind offer, but, no offense; I need to speak to him alone. If you could just direct me, I would appreciate it. I assure you I harbor nothing but good will and friendship for Ben Tom Lawless. He is a fine creature of God."

Deacon spotted Ben Tom's truck behind the old bank building in Mesa, but saw no sign of him. He started to worry a little as he rattled locked doors and knocked on windows cloudy with time and dust. Mesa was definitely a ghost town. Ben Tom might not own much in Riverby anymore, but from what Deacon saw through the dusty windows, he owned nearly all of downtown Mesa. At least he had filled the buildings with his collectibles.

The old Baptist Church sat in the middle of where the street ended. It was the only door he found open. When he walked inside, two women, a blonde and a redhead, dressed in matching light blue dresses greeted him. The blonde spoke in a soft, gentle voice. "May we help you?"

"Excuse my intrusion, ladies, but I was looking for an old friend of mine, name of Ben Tom Lawless."

The two ladies looked at each other, doubt and something akin to dismay in their eyes. The redhead turned to him. "I'm sorry, but Ben Tom values his privacy, and he asked us to keep his whereabouts secret except for family or emergency."

"Well, I won't lie and say that my visit qualifies as either. But I can assure you he will want to see me. We go back a long way."

"Perhaps you can tell us a little about your relationship."

"Well, we met in Dallas when Ben Tom was trying to get a car he had made from scrap parts out of the pound."

They kept their quizzical looks.

"Okay, I taught him a little about being a blacksmith. He's a creative genius that won't focus on his gifts. Spends his time doing things for others rather than himself."

The ladies laughed. "You certainly know him."

"You must be the two ladies who nursed his brother through his final days. I heard about that. What are you doing in this ghost town?"

The women started answering at the same time and laughed while the redhead continued. "We're still doing the same thing, spreading the Word and helping people embrace their Savior and cross to the other side with grace, dignity and peace."

"I know of no finer calling." Deacon held his palms up in a questioning gesture toward the rest of Mesa. "But in this place, this deserted town?"

"It's just a headquarters for us. We travel. Ben Tom provided us with this old church for our offices and financed our venture into a formal hospice organization. He still is very generous with us, too generous, I'm afraid."

The blonde stepped forward, seemed almost defensive. "We are not amateurs. We have the training to qualify. We're both registered nurses and have all the required licenses and permits. We will make it up to Ben Tom. And we never asked for any contributions. He just found a way to help."

"I don't doubt that. Sounds like my old friend."

They looked at each other and nodded. "Follow us."

They found Ben Tom in the back of Mesa's old livery stable. Years earlier, he had uncovered a few horseshoes, an old anvil, and finally, a forge while moving rotted lumber and other debris. He treated the site like an archaeology dig as he patiently uprooted and reassembled the blacksmith shop that had been there more than a century before. It was dark and dusty in the old shop and when the ladies and Deacon opened the big door, dust motes traveled through the sun's rays. Ben Tom sat in one corner of the old shed, rubbing a preservative into his wooden cross. He had not shaved for several days. He squinted, shaded his eyes from the light as he looked up with bloodshot eyes.

The sight of his old friend in what seemed to be a desperate situation and with such a forlorn expression shocked Deacon. He feared Ben Tom would not recognize him, was relieved when a smile broke out. Ben Tom stood, brushed off the seat of his pants, returned the cross to his neck, and embraced his old friend firmly. "Thought I might never see you again."

"I'm like a bad penny; I just keep turning up. How are you, old friend?" The nurses smiled and departed.

"Wonderful. Things have never been better and they're getting better every day." Ben Tom saw the doubt in Deacon's expression. "Seriously, everything is gonna be all right."

Deacon let his gaze roam the old blacksmith shop, the coals cold in the forge, the anvils and hammers. He felt right at home. "Looks about like my shop. You set this up?"

"Let's just say I uncovered it. You look like a man who could use something to drink."

Deacon felt his old friend seemed anxious to get him out of the blacksmith shop as he put a hand in the middle of his back, ushered him out the door and over to the bank building where he had set up a portable kitchen of sorts in the vault. In the vacant lot outside the bank's back door, the biscuits and sausages he had made that morning still sat in a Dutch oven over warm rocks.

He poured fresh honey on two plates beside the biscuits and set two glasses of iced tea beside the plates. They sat down in antique chairs at a table made out of an old Texaco sign. "So what brings you out of the dark city to the land of milk and honey?"

"I came to make a small contribution to the local hospice effort. I'm about old enough to need the services of those two lovely ladies."

"Suppose those fine women told you I helped them out. What I do amounts to nothing more than letting them use an old building nobody would rent anyway."

"Not the way they tell it, but it's a safe bet you're still giving away all you earn now and will ever earn in the future."

"Doesn't the Bible say a man makes a living by what he gets, but a life by what he gives?"

Deacon chuckled. "I'm not sure it's in the Bible, but it probably should be. In fact, I think Winston Churchill said that. Either way, I have good news on that front. Remember when I told you I would look into the Japanese art that Clark left behind?"

Ben Tom nodded, somewhat warily. Talk of the art always made him nervous.

"Well, I know a little mid-level art dealer in Fort Worth, and he knows another guy who knows another guy further up the chain. You know how it goes. He says he thinks he might be familiar with what you have and says he might have a buyer for it."

Ben Tom shook his head. "Can't afford to take a chance on selling stolen art."

"What if I bring him out here to look?"

"You trust this guy?"

"He comes well-recommended by a good Christian man I would trust with my life."

"I don't think I can show it to somebody I don't even know. Could be a trap."

Deacon decided to come at the subject from another angle. "How you been making out since you lost Trez?"

219

Ben Tom's face darkened, his voice cracked. "I keep asking why he did it. We were doing just fine. How about your family? You ever patch things up with the wife and kids?"

Deacon's eyes drifted as if going to another place and time. "Old wounds sometimes never heal, but it's as good as I can make it now. I'll spend the rest of my days trying to make it up to them." He slapped his shirt pocket for cigarettes that weren't there, a habit he had never broken. "I did some terrible things and expect to continue paying for that. I've made my peace with it."

Ben Tom took a sip of coffee, ignoring the cooling biscuit on his plate. "When Trez died, I thought of you. I never fully understood the frustration you must have felt until I found Trez that morning. I wanted to make amends, but there was just no way anymore. I can't make it up to Pop, Willy, or Trez. I let them all down and that's all there is to it."

He picked up Deacon's empty plate and placed it in the sink he had installed. "Now, I'm letting my wife and kids down. I know I told you things are good, but truth be told, I been going through a rough patch. I think my whole family is disappointed in me."

"I know you set the bar high, but how are you letting them down?"

"You seen the house out by the river yet?"

"No, I went straight downtown."

"Well, it ain't finished after all these years. I promised to finish it and just never have. Not even fit to live in. I guess I made a few mistakes with money. Seems like I've been short of time and cash my whole life. Auctioned off most of what I had to get out from under. Deacon, I feel like a damn failure."

"I've known you since you were a boy, and you're anything but a failure. A man who leaves the world a better place because he lived can never be a failure. I don't have enough fingers to count the folks you've helped. Why, what you're doing with those two evangelist nurses is success all by itself."

Deacon dug into the front pocket of his jeans and pulled out a wad of bills. "Open your hand." He peeled off fifty hundreds into Ben Tom's open palm.

Ben Tom stared at the five thousand in crisp hundreds in his palm. "What's this for?"

"Remember that piece you forgot when you moved out of my old shop? The one made out of pewter with brass into the flux around each piece? Made it look like gold. Has a bucolic farm scene, farmer and his wife, a mama cow and her calf?"

Ben Tom held up a palm to stop him. "Sure I remember it. Never forget something I made. I didn't forget it when I left, either. I left it behind for you as my way of saying thanks for all you did for me."

"You never said so. Always considered it yours. Either way, this art dealer paid me five grand for it. You want to get the piece back?"

Ben Tom studied the bills in his hand. It was badly needed. He needed it; Penny needed it. There were bills to pay, notes coming due within a few days. He shoved it back toward Deacon. "Can't take this. I gave that piece to you. The money's rightfully yours."

Deacon stood and slammed a fist down hard on the metal table. "Don't be a damn fool. That money is yours. You created the piece and you deserve to get paid for it. Don't even think of sending the money back with me cause I'll never take it."

He had never seen Deacon so upset. Ben Tom smiled. "Well, I guess I can't turn it down if you put it that way. I'll make you another one." He chuckled. "You know, there was less than fifty bucks worth of materials in the piece. I felt sorta bad leaving it as my only way of repaying you."

"The fella who gave me that money has a pretty good network of buyers and he's the one interested in the Jap art. He's in a bed-and-breakfast in Riverby now. Can I bring him out here?"

"Does he fence stolen goods or something like that?"

"Not a fence. He's legit. He knows a lot about stolen art and I suspect he may have fenced a few years back. I can't be sure, but there may have been a little jail time in his past. But he's a good Christian man today."

38

THE ART DEALER DIDN'T LOOK LIKE BEN TOM EXPECTED. NO shiny suit, no sunglasses, no Gucci shoes, not a thug. Paunchy, middle-aged and shy, he wore horn-rimmed glasses and looked more like a bartender who spent too much time indoors than an art dealer. The dealer's eyes bulged and he wheezed as he handled the thin scrolls that looked like ancient parchment, the crisp paper cards that felt more like ultra-thin wood, and the one folding book. A painting of people in various poses dressed in Japanese fashions graced each page. Some were erotica, almost caricatures of ancient people.

He sucked and blew his breath and mumbled more to himself than Ben Tom as he caressed the pieces. Ben Tom tried to interpret the self-talk and heard words like shunga, shin hanga, woodblock and Frank Lloyd Wright. Finally, the dealer looked up at Ben Tom. "Do you have any idea what you have here? There's at least a quarter million dollars worth of art here. An incredible find."

Ben Tom looked at Deacon, who wore a knowing smile. "Did Deacon tell you how I came by this stuff?"

"I have a good idea. I knew Clark Mallory, or at least I knew of him. I can assure you the Japanese government or the museum or the individual that lost this does not care how you came by it. They will pay a huge reward for the return of this art, no questions asked. If we can't locate the owner, I can sell it outright."

Ben Tom shook his head. "Can't accept money for something my uncle stole. Wouldn't be right."

"Is it right for you to keep it from the people who rightfully own it? Or from an admiring public who simply want to view this lost art form? It benefits nothing sitting out here in the dark."

"I don't aim to keep it. Never meant to keep it. I just need a way to get it back to the rightful owners without going to jail for stealing it."

"Would you trust me to see it gets back to the rightful owners?"

"If Deacon says you're all right, then you're all right with me. To tell the truth, it's been wearing on me for a lot of years. I'll be glad to be rid of it."

Deacon pointed several fingers at the art. "How much reward do you think?"

"Ten to twenty percent of the value. Twenty-five thousand, maybe as much as fifty."

Deacon touched Ben Tom's arm. "Couldn't your hospice ladies put that to good use? Don't you have a favorite charity or cause in Riverby?"

They struck a deal then. The art dealer would collect the reward and have checks made out to the Mesa Hospice, the Riverby Library, and Josiah Welch's Rivers Crossing Church.

But the art dealer had also noticed Peter Umlauf's name stenciled in black paint on four crates inside the vault. "Peter Umlauf is a well-known sculptor from South Africa. Is this more of your uncle's stolen goods?"

Ben Tom told him the story about the Dallas World Trade Center on nine-eleven. The art dealer could hardly contain his enthusiasm. "You know what's in the crates? He hasn't asked you to return them in all these years?"

"Nope. I figured he might have died. Can you get them back to his family?"

"I expect there's nothing really valuable inside or he would have sent for them at once. He was almost killed a few years ago in a light plane crash, but long after nine-eleven. Let's open the crates and see."

Ben Tom touched the crates. "Promised him I would look after them until he calls for them. No disrespect, but I don't want anybody opening them but him."

The art dealer laughed and turned to Deacon. "You said he was unusual and you were right." He turned back to Ben Tom. "Would you like for me to return them to him unopened? I feel sure I can find and contact him on the internet."

Ben Tom did not use a computer, had not thought of the internet. He looked at Deacon and then at the dealer. He felt a weight being lifted off his shoulders. "Let's put them in your van. Let me know what Mr. Umlauf says, will you?"

When he closed the door to his van, the art dealer turned to Ben Tom. "Suppose Deacon told you I bought that piece you did when you were a kid. I sent pictures of it to a few folks I know and found a buyer within a week. The sale is temporary, of course, until the buyer can closely examine it and have it appraised and checked for authenticity, but I know the sale will be finalized. Deacon said you would have to approve, too."

"Authenticity?"

"Just to be sure it's not a knockoff of work some famous artist did."

"Surprised anybody would be willing to pay for anything I made."

"The people who saw the piece say it shows rustic, original brilliance."

The description warmed Ben Tom's heart. "What does that mean?"

"It means, primarily, that it is a rare find. Of course, some of it is perception. Unknown artist, a piece created four decades earlier when the artist was a boy, undiscovered until recently, that sort of thing. I have to admit I'll turn a handsome profit when it's finally sold."

Ben Tom nodded. "Well, at least they like it."

"I particularly liked the way you used brass in your flux to make the piece look tinged in gold." The dealer drew in a deep breath as if he were afraid to ask the question he had wanted to ask since arriving in Mesa.

"I don't suppose you have any similar pieces around anywhere?"

Ben Tom seemed lost in thought for a few seconds. "Not right now. Why?"

"Because there is a very real chance I could sell as many pieces as you can make. Providing, of course, they are all of a similar quality and unique design."

Ben Tom seemed to drift away.

"Is there any chance you can recreate something you did forty years ago?"

"I never make the same thing twice. My mind won't work that way."

"I didn't mean the same, just with the same rustic brilliance. You have real talent, Mr. Lawless." He smiled for the first time. "And, I might add, a wonderful name for an artist. Lawless. Outlaw. Out of bounds. Not tied to tradition. Sounds great in an art show."

Ben Tom stared at the money in his palm when Deacon and the art dealer left. Inside the blacksmith shop, he dropped to his knees and sent up a prayer, thanking God for one more deliverance and asking why He always waited until the last minute to rescue him.

39

THE JAPANESE ART AND THE UMLAUF CRATES HAD BEEN GONE
for a few days when Colleen and Waylon walked across the street and tres-
passed in their old backyard. Ben Tom had helped them to sell their old house
and purchase the coyote's former house to live in. It was a slight improvement.
The coyote had moved on when crossing the border and finding illegal Mexicans for low paying jobs became commonplace and no longer as lucrative.

Ruth Ann visited her mother and brother occasionally, but seldom
stayed long. She and Colleen could not get along and Waylon had no use
for her third Mexican husband. The new owner of their old house and shop
had immediately flipped the property for a huge profit to a franchised service
station and convenience store. Construction workers dug holes for almost a
week to install fuel tanks on the back of the property facing the highway.
The whole area had been zoned commercial. Colleen still held the property
flip against Ben Tom, accusing him of being in cahoots with the buyer.

The house and Willy's shop had already been bulldozed, but a large
backhoe digging pits for fuel tanks was perilously close to the well where
Willy and Hoyle Broom of the Dixie Mafia had dumped the loan shark's
body.

Colleen shivered in the night air. "What are we gonna do if they find
his bones?"

Waylon waved his arms in frustration. "Done told you, Mama. We
don't know nothing about no body in no well. Worse comes to worse, we'll
tell 'em the truth. Can't throw Daddy in jail now. He's dead."

"Yes, but they might find a way to bring me in on it. And you with a record and all. And if this causes problems for those mobsters your daddy was foolin' around with, we could all find dead horses in our beds."

Two days later, Colleen breathed a sigh of relief as they pushed away Willy's rotting cover on the well and filled the hole with dirt. The following day, it became part of a paved parking lot.

—◆◆◆—

A month after the art dealer left with Umlauf's crates and the Japanese art, three checks for ten thousand each came in the mail; one for the Riverby Library, a second to the Mesa Hospice, and a third to Rivers Crossing Church. The library would remain open, the Mesa Hospice would now have a small clinic in the church, and Josiah Welch's church would last another year or two.

A week later, a small crate arrived from Peter Umlauf via the art dealer. Inside Ben Tom found a small sculpture of a South African spotted leopard poised on a tree limb. It was number 100 of 500 reproductions of the original, but instantly became one of Ben Tom's prized possessions. He framed the letter Peter wrote to him.

> Apologies, old friend, for not getting back to you sooner, but I knew my precious work could be in no safer hands than your own. I returned to my native country under a cloud of suspicion that erupted while I was in your country. This suspicion regarding my loyalty was further clouded by the events of nine-eleven. I was simply afraid to contact you, fearing my correspondence would be intercepted and misinterpreted by your government or mine. Also, personal property rights in South Africa were precarious in 2001 and have not much improved since. When some of my art was confiscated, I took solace that the artwork in your hands was protected.
>
> But do not think too badly for my beloved country. I did some work for Frederik Willem de Klerk, the last president before Apartheid ended, and a few zealots held that against me, even though I also did work later for Nelson Mandela. They put me on a watch list of sorts and there has been much harassment. Things are better now.
>
> This little leopard is only to remember me by. I can't possibly repay you. What you did for me is priceless. I will be in your debt forever.
>
> Peter Umlauf

Ben Tom hung the framed letter on the wall behind the leopard sculpture, focused a spotlight of sorts on both. He read the letter regularly to whomever would listen. A few days after receiving the sculpture, he leaned on a work table in his secret blacksmith shop, surveying the place where he loved to work, but always felt guilty about indulging his passion to create. He smiled as he stepped toward a darkened corner, pushed open a door that looked like a sheet of thick paneling, pulled a chain on a hanging light bulb.

The light was dim, but enough to illuminate the sculptures and works of art scattered in the secret room. They sat on giant antique oak and iron tables in what had been the stable. Like always, tiny glints of light off of brass, silver and gold leapt for joy at the sight of their creator. Ben Tom could clearly hear them speaking and singing to him. It always filled him with bliss.

He ran his hands over a post oak stump carved to look exactly like Kiowa Chief Santanta. His stern, regal countenance seemed to be holding council over the other works of art. Ben Tom wanted Tee to have that. Joe Henry would get the bois d'arc stump carved with a Texas Ranger Badge. Sculptures of pewter, brass, and iron, mostly complete, littered a huge oak table, enough pieces to last for three years of gifts for his beloved Penny. He knew exactly which anniversary, Mothers' Days, Valentine's Day and birthday each creation was made for. An iron table held metal and wrought-iron sculptures of horses and longhorn cattle he had made for his children and ones of dogs, cats, deer and exotic animals for his grandchildren. There were also bows made from bois d'arc and arrow shafts tipped with arrowheads he had found on the banks of the Red River.

Another table held the creations he had made out of a sense of fun, such as a complete set of poker chips made from yellow pieces or bois d'arc; wooden and metal book ends shaped like horses and cattle; wallets; belts stamped with his children's and friends' names; knives with bone handles; a huge sheriff's desk made from oak pegged with bois d'arc (no nails or screws allowed); custom branding irons; metal cutouts of Texas covered in leather with brands from the big ranches; walking canes; umbrellas; and Texas and US flags made from metal and leather.

He straddled the saddle he had made from scratch, ran his hand along the smooth, butter-colored leather he had used the make the custom chaps that lay across the cantle. The walls were decorated with bosals and hack-amores he had made from rawhide, knotted horse hair headstalls, custom bits and spurs. Stars cut from leather and iron littered the floor and walls. Ben Tom had a fondness for stars, took pride in being a native of the Lone Star State.

He had plans for almost every piece. He planned to train a horse to pull the buckboard he had designed and made, for example. There was a work of art for his mother and her sister, one each for Colleen, Waylon, and Ruth Ann, one for Josiah Welch and one each for the hospice ladies. He could keep for himself, of course, the '55 Ford that was three fourths complete. Being without the one he had originally made had left a void in his heart.

He chuckled as he made a mental note to see if anything remained that was not already meant for someone, if there were any pieces he could sell to the art dealer. Maybe. Then again, he still had three dilapidated buildings filled with a lifetime collection of antiques. Where other people saw junk, he saw salvation. Maybe he could sell a few pieces, enough to build himself a real studio and barn where he could refurbish antiques and practice building the things that filled his dreams and most of his waking moments. Maybe he could raise enough money to hire some help with refurbishing the great house by the river. But then again, he could not bear for any other artisan to touch his work.

He had always wanted to take Penny and hit the road, buying trea-sures. If he had a really nice place to bring them to, maybe he could rescue things lying unused and deteriorating in barns and homes all across the country, real treasures decaying like lost souls, calling him for rescue.

To Ben Tom's way of thinking, humans who made things transferred a part of their souls to those things, and it was his job to rescue those lost souls so they could help save other lost human souls. And God had given him the talent to rescue the pieces, to restore them to their original beauty, dignity and purpose, enabling them to bring years of pleasure to people who knew how to appreciate and use beautiful, old things. He had always felt it was his mission in life to save objects and to save people. But could he ever bear to part with the objects for money? Maybe he could give them away to the right people; people who would appreciate them, use them and take loving care of them.